A BILLION REASONS

NIKKY KAYE

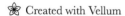 Created with Vellum

CONTENTS

MADDIE

Well, there goes my weekend of binge-watching Netflix in my pajamas.

"How long, exactly, is this retreat?" someone in the back of the boardroom asked.

Brian Gage, our illustrious CEO, said, "We leave for the mountains next Friday at noon, and return Sunday evening. Exercises begin with dinner on Friday, go all day Saturday, then we regroup Sunday morning to discuss the retreat and its results. You can leave anytime after that. Any questions?"

The head of Accounting raised his hand like a third-grader. "Is attendance mandatory?"

Oh no, he didn't. Over the long table, my gaze met with the almond-shaped eyes of the head of Human Resources. Susan and I rolled our eyes simultaneously. I shook my head in pity, already knowing enough about my new boss to know that *everything* about Brian Gage was mandatory.

He was the first to arrive and the last to leave. Actually, he was the second last, since as his new executive assistant I didn't dare go home before him. I kept trying to get the jump on him in the morning, but it was tough.

It was getting to the point where I might as well just sleep under my desk and try to sneak in a shower in the steel and glass en suite bathroom connected to his steel and glass office.

Right now, he seemed made of steel and glass himself as he stared at Mr. Accounting. The room was so quiet; you could hear his year-end bonus drop.

Standing to my left at the head of the table, Gage put his hands on his hips. His sudden movement was enough to make my fingers tighten around the pen with which I was dutifully taking notes. At least he hadn't elbowed me in the head. I rolled my chair to the side a few inches, not realizing how close he was.

Note to self: manda-fucking-tory.

After a long pause, he continued. "Spouses and significant others are not invited."

That wouldn't be a problem. The closest thing I had to a significant other took double-A batteries.

"At the retreat we will do some group and individual exercises in trust-building and effective communication," Gage said.

My eyes rolled again. Yeah, he could use some work on communication skills. I'd already noticed that in the few weeks that I'd been working there—not that I could say anything to him. I had a feeling that his previous assistant had left after recommending he remove the smartphone from his wealthy, tight, successful backside.

"Don't worry," Susan added from her end of the table. "There will be no building of towers out of office furniture."

Everyone chuckled, sort of. Then she met my gaze again.

"It's worse," she mouthed to me.

Great. This being my first "retreat," I had no idea what to expect. Usually retreat meant failure of some kind, or at least strategic withdrawal. Soldier retreated in battle, "exhausted" celebrities go to retreat clinics. Work retreats, I understood, were the worst of the worst—strategic withdrawal with a bunch of passive-aggressive blowhards, after which you all feel like exhausted failures. Yippee.

Why had I taken this job again? Oh right, it turned out my college degree in Rhetoric was rhetorical, after all.

I'd spent the past two years since graduating floating from one temporary job to another. The most useful skill I'd been able to apply was my ability to touch type one hundred and twenty-five words per minute. Thankfully, I'd developed some expertise in ghostwriting correspondence and internal communication, but it wasn't my calling.

I was still waiting for something to call me—or at least text. It was Susan who had phoned me for an interview.

That fateful day still stuck out in my goldfish-like memory. I'd been as nervous as a teenage girl taking a pregnancy test—not that I'd know from experience. My formative years had been spent with my heart turned inward and my head in a Harry Potter book.

But nervous I was. When I stood up from my seat in the waiting area, I had to make sure that my sweaty palms hadn't left a mark on my pencil skirt when I smoothed the creases out of it.

I was ushered into Gage's office, and the butterflies in my stomach had babies. I wasn't expecting the hottest smartphone application developer on the West Coast to be so, well, *hot*.

He stood behind a glass and steel desk, his tanned arms a stark contrast to the rolled-up sleeves of his blindingly white shirt. My gaze followed the buttons of his shirt up to his square jaw, full lips, a slightly crooked nose, and piercing blue eyes. They were almost the same blue as the glints in his coal black hair under the fluorescent lights.

His suit jacket was slung over the back of a massive black leather chair—presumably his throne—and his hands rested on his lean hips.

Easily, he gave off the impression of a man who was very successful, very driven, and who had a very large stick up his ass.

His hands moved from his hips to rest on the desk as he leaned forward. "Madeline Jones."

It wasn't a question. I already had the feeling that he made more statements than queries, as a whole.

Propelling myself forward, I put my hand out. "Most people call me Maddie." His grip was strong, and almost as hot as my face felt.

I had the distinct feeling that he'd already assessed me from my auburn head to the high heels pinching my toes, without ever moving his eyeballs. And found me lacking.

"I'll get right to it," he said, gesturing for me to sit in a clear Lucite chair in front of his desk. I wondered if having his guests look like they were sitting on nothing was a power tactic for him. With those X-ray eyes and demeanor, I didn't think that Brian Gage needed any more power trip strategies.

Apparently he knew my previous contract employer, who had blabbed about my business communication skills over single malt scotch at some networking event. He told Mister Gage about not having to write his own bullshit letters, and how my letters generally got better results.

Gage pulled out some of the letters that my ex-boss had shared with him and we discussed why and how I wrote what I did. I became more comfortable talking about my word choices and techniques of persuasion. Then he pushed some paper across the desk at me.

"This is the kind of thing I send to venture capital-ists and investors," he said.

My eyes widened as I read it out loud. *"My company needs money. I will make you money in return. Give it to me."*

"It's not working." He frowned.

No shit. "Have you considered saying please?"

"I've managed to attract a hundred million dollars to date," he pointed out.

"You've been lucky."

His expression was positively glacial. "I'm not *lucky*. I'm good."

That was Day One. Now I was on Day Forty of captivity, and the stick in his ass hadn't bent yet. And we were going to do trust exercises at some resort in the mountains. On the plus side, there would be lots of sticks around in case anything was dislodged.

"Maddie will send you the details," he said now, effectively dismissing everyone in the boardroom. They shuffled out, a few people bitching to each other under their breath. I remained in my seat until Gage fell into his chair beside me.

"This will be good," he affirmed. I didn't think he was looking for a challenge, and he wouldn't get one from me right now.

"Yes, sir. They seem, uh, enthusiastic. Gung ho." Okay, even I couldn't make that communication persuasive in the slightest. I used my toes to swivel myself in my chair from side to side. If I'd been alone I probably would have spun myself like a little kid.

"You can't lie worth a damn, Madeline."

"No, Mister Gage."

"Never lie to me."

"Yes, Mister Gage."

"You're lying to me now, aren't you?"

"No, Mister Gage."

"Maddie…" he growled.

I looked at him. "Yes, Mister Gage?"

The staring contest commenced. His gaze was opaque and penetrating, like a lizard waiting for the right moment to capture. Nope, wasn't going to blink. I could play this game, and win. My eyes watering, I lasted two long, silent minutes before I blinked.

A smug smile spread over the bosshole's face. My cheeks grew hot.

Retreat. Retreat!

2

GAGE

"I hear you're seeing Bobbie this weekend."

My mother was one of the few people who could make me pause my work. Then my irritation at being interrupted was accompanied by guilt over feeling annoyed. I reminded myself that both feelings were a colossal waste of time and energy, which was something I was loath to indulge in.

"She called you?"

"Of course! She's so excited to see you! You really don't call her enough, Brian."

I highly doubted that my sister Roberta, whom most people called Bobbie, was waiting for my arrival with breathless anticipation. Then again, she was helping to organize the retreat activities, so god only knew what I would be walking into.

"Don't forget to compliment her to her boss."

"Jesus, Mom, she's not trying to get a Girl Scout badge. My opinion doesn't mean anything." Except for the fact that I was bringing thousands of dollars to the hotel and conference center this weekend, booking a dozen rooms and pre-paying for food and liquor.

"And she's supposed to be an adult now," I added under my breath.

"She still needs our support, Brian."

I bit my tongue—literally. *Like I hadn't supported her in the dozens of jobs she'd had and lost over the years? Like I hadn't supported her by paying her rent more often than not?*

Somehow, at the age of twenty-eight, my younger sister was still flitting from job to job and from one loser live-in boyfriend to the next. She was habitually under-employed. Actually, she'd had an extremely successful career for a while as a sofa surfer and mooch—but our mother still thought she farted rainbow sparkles like a unicorn.

Every time Bobbie and our mother got together, they talked about how nobody understood her, and that was her explanation as to why she still didn't have her shit together. My mother, bless her gullible heart, always nodded and patted her hand in sympathy, then slipped her a hundred bucks to make sure she ate properly. I knew Bobbie was trying to turn her life around, but I would believe it when I saw it.

Mom might be proud of my little sister for getting a guest services job at the small mountain resort, but I was tempted to remind her it was only the most recent in a long line of jobs she couldn't keep.

Movement outside my open office door drew my attention, and I looked up to see Madeline talking to Aaron, my marketing director. Their heads were bent over an oversized piece of cardboard. As she dropped the end she was holding in order to talk with her hands, Aaron had to make a quick save.

He saw me through the doorway and raised an eyebrow. "You got a minute?" he called out.

I nodded. He had to hold on to the mock-up firmly as Madeline poked at it to make a point. I couldn't hear what she was saying, but whatever it was she was pretty adamant about it.

She stretched while she spoke, as if she were trying to make her words taller than her petite frame. Her clingy green blouse snuck a fraction out of the waistband of her black pants every time she leaned over to point at something, getting ready to make a wrinkled escape.

Her whole body was involved in her conversation with Aaron, which didn't surprise me. She had a tendency to read a lot of her words out loud, playing with the language and form. I'd almost gotten used to her talking to herself at her desk in my outer office area.

Madeline Jones was one of those people who seemed on the surface not to able to keep a serious thought in that wild red head of hers, but looks were deceiving. She was smarter than most people thought, including herself. I wouldn't have hired her if I hadn't believed that. Some people might have time to waste micromanaging fools, but I didn't.

But the way she rolled her big brown eyes at me drove me absolutely crazy. Most people deferred to me, or at least showed some respect. Her whole demeanor seemed almost flippant, from the way her hair bounced around to the way she took off her shoes and curled her feet under her while she worked. Her desk was a disaster area, and her handwriting impossible to read. She was good, however, at saying "please." Just not to me.

"Please?"

I shook my head, remembering that my mother was still on the phone. Aaron threw me a pointed, questioning look, and I snapped back to reality.

"Mom, I have to go. I'm really busy."

"Okay, if you see Bobbie tonight tell her I'll call her tomorrow."

I bit back the reminder that I might not even see my sister that evening, because she probably wouldn't remember. I'd been telling her for years that she should talk to her doctor about finding out if she was attention-deficit, but she always laughed and said she was just scatterbrained.

If she were any more scatterbrained, she'd qualify as the first human clay pigeon in Olympic skeet shooting. It had only gotten worse since my dad died, and that had been ten years ago. It was like he had kept her brain organized, and now she was all over the place.

It was one of the reasons I was anxious for our new app to launch. *Happit* was going to revolutionize the way people created and kept positive habits. I made a mental note to talk to Madeline about beta testing; I had the feeling she was a perfect candidate. The only thing she seemed to be consistent at was inconsistency.

After an abrupt goodbye to my mother, I sat back in my chair and felt like shit about practically hanging up on her. Well, there wasn't anything I could do about it now, and it sure wasn't the first time. Scrubbing my hand over my face, I sighed and stood up. My forehead creased as Aaron suddenly touched Maddie's arm.

"Aaron!"

Both he and Madeline froze mid-conversation to turn to me.

"I have a few minutes now," I called out, raising an eyebrow at Madeline.

When my eyes met hers, she blushed and tugged her arm away. The knot in my chest eased a little as Aaron made his way to my office and I watched Madeline return to her desk. Only then did I notice that her feet had been bare the whole time. The polish on her toenails was a soft pink.

"Yo! Gage!" Aaron sat in the chair in front of my desk as I stood there staring into space. He snapped his fingers and I looked down at him.

He slid a mock-up across the desk. "This is for the race sponsorship." I could feel his gaze on me as I scanned the ad. "Maddie's great," he remarked.

"Yes, she is." I wasn't sure about that color for the tagline.

"Has a good eye."

"Uh huh." I rolled back in my chair, assessing the ad from further away.

"Smart girl," Aaron added.

"Mmmm." Maybe if we moved the logo to the other corner...

"Banging body."

"Phenomenal. Wait, what?"

He sat there smirking at me with his arms crossed over his chest.

"Madeline is under me, Aaron," I reminded him as I wrote on a sticky note.

"Oh, *really*?" His grin grew. That was the problem with hiring friends. It was a little harder to instill respect in someone who'd beaten you at beer pong once upon a time. But I'd be damned if I let him poach Madeline for his department.

Aaron wasn't just an employee; he was an old friend. We'd met in a business class that he'd taken after a knee injury derailed his college football career. He prided himself on an effortless Afro and easily had the most tattoos of anyone I knew. Usually they were covered up by a preppy button-down shirt, which never seemed to fit his broad frame.

"You can't have her. She's mine. This is okay," I said, handing back the board, "but I made a few notes. See if you can get me a revision early next week. It doesn't need to be dry mounted."

"Do you hear yourself, Gage? 'She's mine, you can't have her!'" he mimicked in a brusque, caveman-type voice. "Og want." He uncrossed his arms and leaned forward in his chair, resting his forearms on his knees. "Does somebody have a little crush?"

"Crushes are for teenagers, Aaron. I grew out of that around ten years ago. I meant she *works* under me, and she's turning out to be a valuable asset."

"Ah, but you didn't say no, did you?"

Clearly he wasn't going to let this go until he got it all out of his system. Better here than at the retreat this weekend. I frowned. "Seriously? She. Works. For. Me. I don't dip my quill in the office ink."

"You don't dip your quill in *any* ink. Your quill might as well be back on the damn bird. Dude, have you had a girlfriend in the last five years?"

"I do fine," I said shortly.

Maybe I hadn't had a girlfriend in seven years, but there were a handful of women over the years that were happy enough to hook up once in a while. Although it had been a while, they knew the score and didn't play games, which I appreciated.

I wanted a woman who was confident, goal-oriented, and ready to commit—someday. Right now I was too busy.

And Madeline Jones—despite her objective attractiveness and the fact that she smelled like cinnamon—wasn't my type.

3

MADDIE

"Madeline Jones, checking in."

I parked my beat-up rolling suitcase by the front desk. It definitely looked out of place in the swank lobby of the "rustic" mountain lodge. Maybe it was time to peel my once-prized Harry Potter stickers off of it. But that suitcase had been my home longer anywhere else I'd lived.

The clerk smiled politely, tapping on her keyboard. I leaned against the desk with a small sigh and admired the river rock fireplace, open on all sides. It was so big it probably counted as an extra room in the hotel. It looked like a whole tree was burning inside it, but the heat it produced was already replacing the chill of the autumn air outside.

"You and Mister Gage are in Suite 203." Her smile broadened. "I hope you enjoy your stay, Miss Jones."

"I'm sorry?" I blinked at her. Did she say me *and* Mister Gage?

The problem with Mister Gage was... well, where did I begin? The main one was he elicited a strong reaction in me. Mostly it was impatience, but my heart was thumped a little faster when I saw him in the morning, and squeezed when I went home at night. I told myself it was anxiety, but the truth was that there was something compelling about him.

It might have been the way his arms flexed as he leaned on his desk. It might have been the curve of his lips as he told me to just call him "Gage." Or it might have been his willingness to hire me and give me health benefits. That would make any college grad's heart flutter—as long as I didn't mention it on the insurance forms as a pre-existing condition.

"Brian!" The courteous smile on the woman behind the desk expanded and softened as she looked over my shoulder. The tingling awareness crawling up my spine had already warned me, but Gage's staccato steps on the flagstone floor definitely signaled his approach.

"Hi, Pinky."

My head whipped around to look at him. The casual tone of his normally stiff demeanor surprised me, and the look on his face was even more bewildering. Added to that was the fact that her nametag said Bobbie, not Pinky, and I was totally confused.

"Problem?" he asked.

I nodded. "This nice lady says we are sharing a suite."

He frowned at me. "Yes, that's what I booked."

"But—"

"But what?"

Wow. He really didn't get it. "Isn't that, uh…?"

He raised a dark eyebrow at me expectantly. "Pinky" stared at the computer screen below the desk, pretending not to eavesdrop. I clutched the leather sleeve of his jacket and pulled him away from the desk for some privacy.

"Mister Gage, I can't stay in your suite!"

Why not?" His gaze pinned me just as effectively as the first time I'd met him.

"We just can't share a room," I persisted.

"Give me one good, solid, well-evidenced reason."

Heaven help us both. *Because I might accidentally on purpose walk in on you in the shower? Because I'm afraid I might call out your name in my sleep? Because I didn't bring any pajamas?*

"Because it's incredibly inappropriate, that's why!"

"It's a two-bedroom suite, both with en suite bathrooms. We only really share the living room."

"Oh."

"They insisted on giving me the best suite in the place for the business I'm bringing them this weekend, and it would have caused dissension in the ranks if I tried to offer it to Aaron or Nikhil or Susan. I figured you and I could share it, since we'll be working together this weekend anyhow. Is that a problem?"

"But I'm single!" I blurted out. It was an excuse, a reason, a label, and a philosophy all rolled into two words. Yeah, I was a damned efficient communicator.

Not only was I single at the age of twenty-four, but I was living with my parents in order to save money. I was a millennial cliché. A college degree in Rhetoric turned out to be, well, rhetorical when it came to the job market. I'd flitted through temp work while looking for just the right job, until it occurred to me that the better strategy would be to make the job right for me.

"I know you're single. What's your point?" He crossed his arms impatiently, his wrists flexing in the crooks of his elbows. I could smell the bruised leather of his jacket mix with the wood smoke from the fireplace.

"I'm a single woman working for you, and you're the boss, and you're so…"

"Single too?" His lips pressed together in a thin line. "Wait, is there someone that would object to us sharing a suite? A boyfriend?" His eyes widened as his arms dropped to his sides. "A girlfriend?"

My face heated. Like it was such an unbelievable concept that I could be dating someone? "No, but don't you see that's the problem?" It was bad enough that I already daydreamed about him too much, but now everybody at work would think we were sleeping together.

"Brian!" called Bobbie. "Is there a problem?"

"No, we're fine!" Gage replied calmly, a new tightness around his eyes. "Madeline, we're already late for dinner."

I shook my head. Clearly he didn't understand the optics of this situation. Maybe he was too powerful, too successful to consider the implications. But I shouldn't have been so surprised. For a smart man, he could very obtuse at times. For god's sakes, he didn't even say please in his letters to venture capital firms! There was direct, and then there was just downright rude. He'd hired me to know better.

Scowling, I left him in the middle of the lobby, firelight flickering on his face as I returned to the desk.

"Can you put me in a separate room?" I asked the clerk, who now watched me a little uneasily. It occurred to me that she'd called him Brian, not Gage. I could only assume that they had dealt together before if he also knew her by a nickname like Pinky.

Maybe she'd been the main point person for planning the retreat.

Maybe they were old friends.

Maybe they were fuck buddies.

Maybe I wanted to stab her in the throat with the cast-iron horseshoe sculpture on the table to my left.

She offered me a conspiratorial smile. "I don't blame you," she stage whispered, shooting a mischievous look at Gage. "He snores."

I heard a strangled "*Roberta!*" behind me. Not Pinky. This was getting worse, and my urge to *stab stab stab* grew ever stronger.

"But unfortunately," she continued sympathetically, "there aren't any other rooms. Between your block, another meeting, and the late season hikers, we're full up."

"It'll be fine," Gage said to her. Then he turned to me. "It *will* be fine. I promise."

I stood there feeling a little shaken, like the weekend was already out of my control. Making a scene with my boss was not the best way to start out this retreat. God, I wished I could retreat myself.

I could have been babysitting my laptop all weekend, but instead I was going to spend two days building towers out of office furniture. It was bad enough that I had to take a tourist bus to get out here. Hopefully I could get a ride home with someone. Reason number eighty-five why I missed having a car.

Gage's hands fell heavily on my shoulders, as though he was trying to keep me from running away.

"Bobbie, can you get someone to take her bags up?" he asked. "We're already late for dinner." Before I could say anything he steered me through the lobby to another foyer at the side of the building.

"You're late," he said. "If I'd known you were going to take the damn bus I would have given you a ride myself. I just got here, anyhow."

Four hours alone in a car with him sounded so tempting—and dangerous. A sign above the archway we were passing under said "Conference Center", and I heard some noise coming from the nearest room.

Someone yelled, "Hey, that's my eye!" It sounded like Aaron, our Marketing Director and, if I recalled correctly, an old college buddy of Gage's.

Gage's hands had unfortunately left my shoulders, but his continued light touch at the small of my back made me want to simultaneously lean back against him and walk faster to get away.

Susan, our HR person, popped her head out into the hallway and spotted us. "Thank god!"

I stepped to the side, gesturing toward Gage. "Yes, God is here."

Gage gave me a dirty look.

Susan grabbed my arm as I passed her. "Do the feeding," she urged me. "Do *not* eat." *What?*

Of course, my quizzical look could have been because there was a strand of spaghetti hanging from her black chin-length hair.

What the hell was going on in here—a food fight? That somehow didn't seem like Brian Gage's style for a retreat activity.

"Susan," he said calmly, his spine ramrod straight, "what is the meaning of this?" I knew him well enough by now to know that what he really meant was "What the fuck?" only he had too much self-control to say that in front of employees.

"This was the first activity, according to the sched-ule. Since you weren't here, the organizer and chef asked if we could still start on time so we didn't mess up the kitchen schedule for the lodge restaurant." She placed her hand on Gage's arm. "I was really hoping we could be partnered…"

I plucked some pasta from her hair. "I guess you couldn't wait."

She glared at me, her compulsion to fix her hair forcing her to let go of him.

He flinched as my hand touched his elbow lightly. I moved to his side to see a dozen tables each set up for dinner for two. It looked like spaghetti was on the menu.

And the tablecloth. And the floor. And Aaron's face.

At least I thought there was sauce on his face—it could easily have been red for other reasons, such as the pasta dangling from the collar of his button-down shirt.

"Uh, what *is* the activity?" I asked, almost afraid to hear the answer. "Executive food fight?"

Susan thrust a piece of paper in Gage's hand.

"Close," Gage said wryly. He read from the paper: "Welcome to your first test of personal communication. Divide into pairs, one at each table, and prepare to enjoy an intimate dinner. The only hitch is that one person will be feeding the other. The person doing the feeding will be blindfolded, and the person doing the eating will have their hands tied behind their back. It is up to the diner to communicate effectively how to direct the movements of their partner."

His voice slowed as he continued. "The diner will place the blindfold on their partner before having their hands tied behind them. Enjoy the extra surprise! *Bon appetit!*"

"Seriously?" I looked around the room. It looked like a junior high cafeteria acting out *Fifty Shades of Grey*. "What's the 'extra surprise'?" I wondered out loud.

Gage flipped over the sheet. "You may use *only* the utensil provided at the table for feeding your partner."

As we surveyed the carnage, the problem became self-evident. Aaron was being fed his spaghetti Bolognese with a turkey baster. Nikhil, our IT guy, was trying to coax his pasta not to slide off a giant pancake flipper. Another table was using a melon baller while a couple I didn't recognize at all was struggling with a corkscrew. Nowhere in sight was a fork.

"Oh dear god."

That's what Susan—who was now back at her table wielding a single, solitary chopstick—was warning me about. It didn't take long to determine the better role in this exercise. This was a new blouse, and I didn't plan on ruining it.

I dropped my purse at my feet. My hand shot into the air. "I call feeding!"

Gage looked down at me, his eyebrow lifting. Okay, maybe that was a little forward and unprofessional of me.

I stepped a little closer to him, fluttering my eyelashes as I looked up into his icy eyes. "I mean, Mister Gage, that this is a perfect opportunity to learn how to take directions from my boss."

"You take dictation all the time." His eyebrow had yet to descend. It was probably getting altitude sickness.

"Dictation is not communication."

"It isn't?"

Like I said, a little obtuse. Give a man a little money and power, and all of a sudden he thinks he knows everything.

"If you could have communicated effectively by dictating, you wouldn't have hired me," I pointed out.

"But you won't be able to see me, Madeline," he said in a low voice.

"Exactly, sir. You will have to choose your words very carefully in order to succeed." I sounded surer than I was, as the idea of being commanded and watched intently by him while being blindfolded made something squirm deep in my belly.

"I don't like to fail," he reminded me.

No kidding. I rolled my eyes then jumped as his broad hand swept over my forehead.

"You won't be able to do that anymore." His thumb traced the arch of my eyebrow, making my heart race.

"Yes, I will. You just won't see me doing it. You can't stop me. You'll have your hands tied…"

I lost my train of thought at a vision of a silk tie knotted around his wrists. The fact that he was lying down with his arms above his head in my imagination had absolutely nothing to do with dinner.

Gage frowned, his fists clenching at his side.

No, he would not enjoy being restrained or controlled. He was used to giving orders, not taking them. But as he loomed over me, I realized how much he relied on body language to communicate—and I was going to be completely blind to it. Only his raw, demanding voice would tell me what to do.

I shivered a little as Gage hung his jacket over the back of a chair and began rolling up his sleeves.

"I won't let you fail either, Madeline."

Gage and I stood together on one side of a round banquet table covered in a pristine white tablecloth, our chairs pushed back a little. The rest of the room was noisy with laughter and protests as everyone continued eating—or at least tried to.

"You will do whatever I say," he said, two black silk ties dangling from his hands. It wasn't a question.

4

MADDIE

He moved close to me, our bodies nearly touching. I kept my eyes on his chest as he gently draped one of the ties around me, cool and soft on the nape of my neck. The tiny hairs under my ears stood up at the feel of the silk sliding across my skin. Every sense I had was on high alert.

He smelled like fresh laundry, and a trace of something else lingered on his skin. It was almost like the scent of paper, or an overworked photocopier. I felt the heat from his hands close to my throat, and the hairs on his forearms tickled my collarbone for an infinitesimal moment.

My attention remained focused on the buttons of his shirt. I was very worried that if I met his gaze, my hyperawareness of him would shine out of my eyes like a flashlight.

"We'll just leave this here for now," he murmured, flicking one end of the tie against the underside of my chin. "Are you ready?"

Not even remotely.

I nodded mutely, but I let out a little gasp when his fingers touched my chin and tilted my face up. It was so tempting to screw my eyes shut, like a little girl trying to pretend that something didn't exist if she couldn't see it. I'd had plenty of practice with that before.

But he wouldn't let me retreat. He looked at me directly and without guile, as usual. What was a little different this time, however, was the way his eyes darkened into stormy seas.

"Trust me." His simple words wormed into my heart as his warm breath landed on my lips.

My voice cracked as I said, "Mister Gage." It wasn't an answer or a question, a protest or a plea. I honestly didn't know what I wanted to say, and whatever was building in me halted as he lifted the other piece of fabric to my eyes.

He smoothed his thumbs across the strip of silk over my eyes, spreading out from the bridge of my nose to my temples. The tie was held firm between his fingers—those nimble fingers that paused in my hair briefly before they met again at the back of my head.

"Is that too tight?" he asked as he pulled the half-knot.

The sound of the silk rubbing against itself whispered in my ear. I shook my head. His hands clutched my hair and held me still.

"I'm not done." His fingers tangled in my hair as he finished tying, pulling a few strands just enough to make me suck in a breath.

He froze. "Did I hurt you?"

"No." My nipples hardened into tight buds as his breath washed over my forehead. "I, uh, no," I repeated.

Gage had never touched me this much in the whole

time I'd been working with him. Just the memory of his hands in my hair was enough to make me wobbly in the knees.

He dragged his thumbs across my covered eyes again, like a parent wiping away their child's tears. Tracing his index fingers lightly over my eyebrows, he made an indistinct but satisfied noise.

"I can't see anything," I complained.

I was so blind that I flinched when his mouth dipped to my ear. "Good," he chuckled.

Reflexively I swayed toward him, like a flower toward the sun. He pressed his thumbs gently into my cheekbones, then his fingertips left a trail of fire down my jaw and neck. On the journey he slipped the other tie from where it dangled around my neck, and pressed it into my trembling hands.

"Tie me up," he ordered in a low voice.

Yeah, those were words I definitely never expected to hear from my boss's mouth.

I took the cloth from him. It was soft in my grip, supple but strong. He held his hands out in front, nudging my knuckles so I'd know where to reach. *Ha!* Knowing where he was? That was definitely not my biggest problem right then. On my first loop around his wrists I heard a voice break through our little bubble.

"Behind the back, Gage! No cheating!" I didn't even know who had said it, but we both realized our error.

"Okay, then. Hold on." He wound the tie around my own wrist for a split second while he spun around, and reached his hands back toward me again.

He had less flexibility this way, less range of motion. I had to step even closer in his personal space so he wouldn't have to contort his arms and shoulders too much. Without being able to properly judge my proximity, he touched my blouse just under my breasts when he reached back. I gasped as his exploring fingers curled against the material.

He laced his hands together into a fisted ball at his lower back. I sensed, rather than saw, the muscles of his back shifting underneath his shirt as he stretched. His deltoids likely came together in a mouth-watering inverted triangle beneath his shoulder blades. For one crazy moment I wanted to lean my face against him, to feel the heat and hardness of his body moving under my touch. Take shelter behind his broad back and powerful, unbending will.

Damn.

Instead, I fumbled with the tie, drawing the ends together like I was tying a simple bow. His head tilted, and his voice came over his shoulder and down upon me.

"Tighter, Madeline."

I paused, my hands wrapped around his strong forearms. They were warm and flexed in my grasp, presenting me with a dilemma. Grabbing his wrists a little stopped me from trembling. If I held on too tight, however, they might tremble more.

He spread his hands apart to demonstrate the ineffectiveness of my knot. "You can do better than that."

"Some of us didn't spend our summers sailing and camping," I hissed as I tightened the knot. My fingertips felt the silk dig into his skin just to the point where he flinched and grunted. "Good enough, *sir*?"

"I think so." He pivoted to face me.

We stood before each other, paralyzed momentarily by our respective handicaps. I could not see him. He could not touch me. When my stomach rumbled audibly, it occurred to me that I wasn't sure when I would get to eat, since *I* was feeding *him. Damn it.*

Susan's voice drifted closer to us; she must have just finished her "meal." "Here, I'll help you get seated." She must have only been talking to Gage, however, since she merely snapped in my ear, "Vending machines are down the hall."

I had to grope for my chair while Susan personally escorted the king to his throne. Thankfully we seemed to be seated right next to each other. The idea of trying to do this across a hotel banquet table would be ridiculous. I'd have to almost crawl over it in order to get any food in his mouth.

She pressed the Feeding Implement of Doom into my hand. "Good luck!" she trilled before fading out. Gage was silent beside me, but somehow I pictured him smirking.

I toyed with the utensil, my frown deepening. It was metal with a long neck, around a foot long, and a coiled bottom. "Okay, I give up. What am I holding?"

"A whisk of some sort."

"Fantastic," I muttered.

"We can do this, Madeline."

His confidence was admirable, if misplaced in this situation. "Do you have a plan?"

"Communicate."

"Oh god, we're going to starve to death. I'm going to be responsible for Brian Gage, gajillionaire godlike CEO, gnawing on the furniture in this beautiful rustic lodge."

"Rustic, my ass. Our suite is two grand a night."

His grumbling managed to ease the knot in my chest

—the one wound almost as tightly as the one at his wrists.

"Godlike?"

Damn, he'd caught that.

"Okay, effective personal communication, here we go!" If I got through this with my dignity, I would consider it a success. Maybe I could put it on my resumé. I rolled my eyes beneath the blindfold.

"Stop rolling your eyes at me."

My mouth fell open. "How did you know?"

"I can see your eyeballs move underneath the fabric."

"Okay, that's kind of creepy and disgusting." Plus, maybe he'd tied it too tight.

"Says the woman about to put her hand in a plate of pasta."

I pursed my lips. "This is not effective personal communication, Mister Gage."

"The plate is on your right."

I felt around for it, landing a little too close. He was right—my hand did dip briefly into the spaghetti. Then my flailing hand landed on his hard thigh. Actually, I was quite high on his thigh.

Without thinking I squeezed his firm muscles, my fingers splaying out and reaching up. A groan escaped him as he tightened under me.

My mouth went dry and I felt hot all over. "Sorry."

"Apology accepted," he said tersely. "But perhaps you could move your hand now. You're getting marinara sauce on my pants."

Ooops. So far we were failing this exercise, and it was only the first evening. I shuddered to think what was in store for us tomorrow and Sunday. The prospect of a hot shower and cool sheets was becoming more and more compelling.

Determined to get this done so I could head up to my room—no wait, our shared suite—I felt for the plate again and moved it to a better position. After swiveling a little in my seat to face Gage at a forty-five degree angle on my right, I brandished my whisk.

"Any suggestions on the best way to go about this?" I asked him.

"Carefully."

Great. I tossed the whisk from hand to hand, thinking about the way it was constructed. Eventually I tried scooping some spaghetti onto it, but heard it slide off back onto the plate. Pushing down to smush it in didn't work well either.

"Try twirling it," Gage suggested.

So I did. That strategy seemed to work better, as the whisk felt much heavier when I raised it from the plate.

Gage hummed. "That looks like a lot of pasta."

"I'll take your word for it." The hole in my stomach was deepening into a cavern as I smelled the food in front of me.

"Okay, you're a little turned around in your chair, right? So from where you're sitting right now," he said slowly, "I'm at your two o'clock. If you lift the whisk to about the level of your chin and stick it forward a bit, I can try to bend over and eat from it."

I bit my lip, and carefully raised the utensil. A piece of spaghetti slithered off to land in my lap. "Ew."

"Front and forward, Madeline."

I thrust my right arm out, hitting something that let out a yelp. With my other hand I frantically patted around to discover I'd stabbed him in the neck with a giant ball of pasta. His Adam's apple was slick with sauce, and a few strands had snaked inside his shirt.

"Agh! Why did you bend forward already?"

Fwip!

"Goddammit, stop waving it around!" he yelled.

I huffed but stilled my weapon hand. "You were supposed to wait until I reached out!" My left hand swiped pasta off him.

"I was trying to meet you halfway," he snarled. His throat, rough with the shadow of his beard, vibrated under my touch.

I walked my fingers down his neck to pluck some spaghetti off his collarbone. It would have been a lot easier without the blindfold. "That wasn't the plan. I reach, then you bend, remember?"

"I'm not good at waiting for other people to do something."

"No shit."

"Madeline…"

Leaning this close to each other, it wasn't hard to reach into his shirt and smooth my hand across the upper pectoral muscles of his chest. I was just looking for spaghetti, after all. More pasta fell off the whisk I held up in my right hand. Gage bent toward me.

"Don't move," he commanded. "I'm going in."

His attempt to eat off the end of the whisk made my grip waver a little. He chased it with his mouth, probably seething inside that he couldn't use his hands to hold me still. It was the first time Brian Gage was bending for me, and I couldn't see it thanks to the blindfold. Fuck my life.

"Keep your hand steady," he said sternly.

I tried to hold my whole body immobile and taut

while he bit, chewed, and swallowed. His attention was totally directed on the pasta, it seemed.

Though my right hand held the whisk up, my left palm rested over his sternum. Or was I supposed to move that hand? I curled my fingers in so that the knuckles of my fist pressed against his warm chest. Strangely, he didn't make any move to dislodge my hand, but maybe he was just afraid I would karate chop him in the trachea by accident. His heart thumped against the backs of my fingers like an impatient tattoo.

This was easily the weirdest dinner I'd ever had.

"Okay," he finally said, leaning back a fraction. "There is a napkin on the table at around twelve o'clock. Please use it."

Phew. I carefully placed the whisk back down on the plate, narrowly avoiding dipping my elbow in the sauce as I pivoted. Then reluctantly I withdrew my hand from inside his shirt, trying to ignore his quiet moan as my thumb briefly pressed into the hollow at the base of his throat. After I located the napkin I held it out timidly. With my luck I would smother him next, or poke him in the eye.

"I'm not afraid of it, Madeline."

Okay then. I stretched my hand out more confidently, stopping when I met resistance. My other free hand reflexively flew up to check what I'd run into this time, and I felt the curve of his nose and mouth.

He tried swiping his face across the napkin to clean up, while I took the opportunity to feel for more wayward sauce with my left hand. Really, my hand only trailed over his cheekbone because I didn't want him to be messy.

His breathing quickened as he nuzzled against the

napkin in my hand, the purr in the back of his throat still rumbling softly against my fingertips when he hummed. This would have been a good time for him to remind me about the company policy on sexual harassment. In retrospect, he might have brought it up when I practically palmed his crotch, but that was an accident —mostly.

"Wipe my neck," he directed hoarsely.

I swept my right hand over his chin and down his neck with the cloth, steadying myself with my left.

It was disorienting not being able to see anything. From what I could hear, the room had almost emptied out, the others clearly finished with the exercise. Vague sounds came from the hallway outside, but unless Susan was standing at the side silently waiting for us, my world at that moment consisted merely of me and Gage.

My left hand cupped his clenching jawbone, but he didn't shake it off. Wiping his neck with my right hand I tried to be judicious, but my left thumb dipped into the corner of his mouth.

I inhaled sharply as his lips closed around the first knuckle of my thumb, then sucked it in further.

5

GAGE

The moment my tongue touched her finger, her mouth fell open in shock.

She made a spectacular picture—the black silk tie around her eyes, dark against her bright hair, her cheeks stained by a telltale flush that didn't quite spread down to her chest. She'd been biting her lips nervously, pulling enough blood to the surface to make them rosy and full.

Okay, maybe Aaron was on to something. I just might have a small crush.

"Gage!" she gasped as I gently bit her thumb.

A frustrated growl built in my throat, and my shoulders clicked and ached as I tried to shift and stretch my arms. Madeline had definitely got the better end of this deal.

Her thumb slipped out of my mouth when she whipped her head around, as though she could see the room through the blindfold. We were alone, all my other staff having disappeared to either their suites or—more likely—the lodge bar.

"Is this, uh, effective personal communication?" she asked quietly.

"It depends. What exactly do you think I'm communicating?"

Her neck shifted as she swallowed hard. "Um… it's definitely personal."

"Mmm hmmm. Effective?"

She nodded and pressed her lips together. Her nostrils flared as she took in a deep breath, her spine stiffening.

"You're that hungry?" She let out a light laugh. "Really, Mister Gage. I'm sure the lodge restaurant can offer better than my finger." With a small, evil grin, she held out a handful of spaghetti. "Would you like some more pasta instead?"

My lips parted; she yanked back her hand and wedged it under her thigh.

"Are you suggesting that I am eating right out of your hand?" I asked, testing my silk handcuffs with little success at freeing myself.

"On the contrary, sir. Though I am very, *very* hungry," she admitted. "But I think it's safe to say that we've failed this exercise."

With that conclusion, I watched with envy her free, unencumbered hands reach up and tug at the blindfold. Then pick. And tug again.

"Jesus, what kind of knot did you tie here?" she huffed.

Eventually she gave up, and just pried her fingers underneath the silk at her temple to get it off her head. She blinked at me, her pupils constricting in the light. Her brow furrowed as she thoughtfully sucked her lower lip between her teeth. And let out a sigh.

"Mister Gage, I'm not sure about how trustworthy you are, after all."

Something twisted in my chest at her words, even though I believed she was probably teasing me. "Oh, Madeline. You're wrong."

She looked down to where she was rubbing her hands nervously up and down her thighs. When I slid forward in my chair and bent toward her, her gaze went from her own lap to mine. I pressed my knees against hers. It had been a while, but I was pretty sure this was considered flirting.

A grimace twisted her pretty face. "You like to be right all the time, don't you?"

"Don't you?"

"I know I'm not. Nobody's right all the time."

"Madeline, there's a difference between being right and being sure."

This time there was nothing to prevent her eyes from rolling in disbelief.

"Sometimes it's better to have confidence instead of certainty. You, of all people, should know how persuasive a little confidence can be."

And with more confidence, but less certainty than I truly felt for maybe the first time in years, I bent forward again to brush my lips against hers. She froze for a second, then her lips parted slightly to kiss me back. It was so brief I might have closed my eyes and only imagined it.

"You're sure?" she breathed, edging back and licking her lips. My body tightened again, frustrated and trembling in restraint and weariness.

I nodded. "I'm sure."

"Then I guess you're right. Thank you for dinner,

Mister Gage." She flashed an outrageously demure smile at me before rising from her chair. It was somewhat satisfying to see her grab the edge of the table for support on her shaky legs.

"You're welcome, Miss Jones. Are we done here?" I leaned forward and twisted my torso a little so she could reach my wrists.

"Yes, Mister Gage."

She picked up her purse and sauntered out the door. *What the hell was that?*

❦

As I blearily stared at the coffeemaker in the living room the next morning, I heard Madeline's shower start. I wondered what temperature she liked it at. Mine had been on the frigid side, both to wake me up and cool me down.

It had only taken twenty minutes to be freed from bondage the night before. It probably would have been sooner had I yelled for help. But I didn't. Yes, I was covered in red sauce with my hands tied behind my back, but that did not mean I wasn't smart, successful, and completely in control of my own world.

All right, I could admit it—perhaps not *completely* in control.

There was no point in explaining my predicament to the poor busboy, nor was it any of his business. But I slipped him a hundred dollar bill regardless and he refused to look me in the eye. That would have to suffice.

A few staff members waylaid me in the hotel lounge, and they took the opportunity to hoot at my stained shirt. With an impassive shrug, I let them have their fun. This weekend was supposed to be a little casual, after all.

I drew the line at their invitation to the pool before it closed, however. There was "mocking the boss" casual, and then there was "naked hot tub party" casual.

When I finally got up to the suite, I found a single lamp glowing in the living area, the door to one bedroom open, and the other one closed. After a quick cost-benefit ratio analysis, I decided that was a good thing.

After I raided the vending machine, I distracted myself with work before going to bed. No movement or noise came from Madeline's bedroom. It was like nobody was there. For all I knew, nobody was. At some point during my restless night, it occurred to me that she might have tried to share a room with a colleague at the last minute—like Aaron. The thought made me a little nauseous.

So while I lay in bed, my phone lighting up in the dark more times than I'd care to admit as I thought about texting her, I was in the novel position of not knowing what to say. It didn't seem like the right time for "please."

I still didn't know what to say when I woke up a few hours later. After two cups of coffee, my nerves had increased to downright jitters, but she hadn't yet emerged from her room. So I went down to the hotel restaurant to find some breakfast. Our first activity was due to begin at nine, and this one I was looking forward to.

The sight of Aaron and Bobbie laughing together at a table for four stopped me short. Bobbie's head was close to his, her inky hair stick straight in contrast to

Aaron's ridiculous Fro. I'd forgotten that of course they'd met each other before. Bobbie had even tried charming her way into a keg party back in the day. Aaron would have let her in, despite her being underage. I didn't. But I couldn't remember when they had run into each other since then.

I filled my plate at the buffet and joined them, effectively throwing a wet towel on the conversation. Literally —I knocked over a water glass when I put my plate down, soaking the tablecloth.

"Way to go, bro." Aaron shoved his chair back.

Bobbie gave me a perplexed look as she stood. "I'll take care of it," she said. "You okay, Brain?" We might not be the best of friends, but my sister still knew that this kind of clumsiness was not normal for me.

"I'm fine," I ground out while unwrapping my roll-up. I placed the fork by my plate and the napkin over the puddle. "I just didn't sleep well."

"Me neither," Aaron said.

I heard Bobbie let out an amused snort before she headed to the back of the dining room, where the kitchen was likely located.

My grunt was smothered by the scrambled eggs I was shoveling into my mouth. Next I started on the pancakes. Slowly I began to wake up, at least enough to jab my fork into Aaron's hand as he reached for a piece of my bacon.

"Dude!" He snatched his hand back, dramatically cradling it like an animal with a wounded paw. He might have begun to whimper if I hadn't shot him a dark look.

"You should know better, *bro*."

"Bacon is always fair game."

"Not today." I shoved a strip into my mouth.

"I know we're out in the woods, but you didn't need to find a *bigger* tree to stick up your ass, man."

"Fuck off."

"You sure you're okay?" My groove in my friend's forehead deepened.

I scowled and stabbed a sausage. "Why does everyone keep asking me that?"

Relatively certain that the small flood I'd created wouldn't drip onto his lap, Aaron scooted his chair back in and waved at my plate. "Usually you're a fruit and egg whites kind of guy."

"Plus," Bobbie added as she dropped a small stack of bar towels on the table, "You're wearing a sweatshirt." Aaron scanned me, nodding in wide-eyed agreement.

"So?" I'd dressed casually before; I didn't know why they were making such a big deal of it.

"And you tucked it in."

I looked down to see that I'd shoved the hem of my faded college hoodie into the waistband of my jeans. I must have been on autopilot while I was dressing, or still asleep. The latter was more likely.

"I'm hungry, since I didn't eat much last night," I said peevishly.

Aaron chuckled. Bobbie blushed, which made me wonder just how much she'd had to do with the Devil's Dinner. When I passed over the last sausage to narrow my eyes at her, she merely blinked and smiled beatifically. That shit worked on our mother all the time, but it didn't work on me. I was smarter than that, and had a longer attention span than a fruit fly.

"Bobbie's doing a great job here, huh Gage?"

Aaron's sidelong glance at my sister seemed to unnerve her. *Interesting.*

Now I felt unnerved, with a hard lump in my stomach—but that could have been the unhealthy amount of cholesterol I'd just inhaled.

"Good morning."

I jolted at the sound of Madeline's voice behind me.

"Good morning! Miss Jones, right?" Bobbie smiled.

Madeline rounded the table to approach the last empty seat with a silent "may I?" gesture. Aaron jumped up to pull out the chair for her, giving me a weird look. My legs didn't seem to work very well at that moment.

"Please call me Madeline," she said. She was polite and friendly, but her smile didn't reach her eyes. Nor did her eyes reach me.

Despite being dressed in black yoga pants, a fitted blue Henley and soft hiking boots, she looked about as relaxed as a Red Sox fan at Yankee Stadium.

Bobbie stuck her hand out over the table. "I didn't get a chance to properly introduce myself last night. I'm Brian's sister, Roberta—Bobbie."

"*Sister?*"

Maybe only I heard the breath whoosh out of Madeline's mouth. But it made my mouth curve up nonetheless, and I raised my coffee cup to hide my amusement.

"What's the 'Pinky' for?" she asked.

Bobbie threw me a grin. "We watched too much TV as kids. Our favorite was *Pinky and the—*"

"*Brain.*" Madeline smirked. "Obviously. Or, obvious now," she said, her gaze volleying between us.

"Yeah, sorry for any confusion. I realized later that you might have gotten the wrong impression." Bobbie looked meaningfully between Madeline and myself. "I, uh, didn't mean to step on any toes."

I choked on my coffee. Aaron reached over to hit my back, which didn't help anything.

"*What?*" Madeline gave a nervous laugh. "No, no toes! No problem! It's all good. It's a lovely suite."

"Okay, I just wasn't sure if you'd need both bedro— ow!" Bobbie yelped as Aaron and I both kicked her hard under the table. He shrugged at me when our feet met, as if to say "Sorry, dude. But she's *your* sister."

Madeline looked down at the wet tablecloth, clearly embarrassed.

"You want some breakfast?" Aaron asked her.

"No, I'm good. I had a granola bar from my suit-case. Thanks, though."

I cleared my throat. "Uh, did you sleep okay?"

Finally she looked at me. Well, looked through me, really. "More or less. I think I was a little nervous about what we're doing today. What *are* we doing today?"

"The ropes course," said Bobbie. "I'll be on site to supervise." There was pride in her voice, and I had to grudgingly admit that she seemed to be genuinely into this job. Maybe she'd keep it for more than a few months.

"*Ropes?*"

The expression on Madeline's face was unreadable as she stared out the ceiling-to-floor window framing the mountains. Maybe she was remembering tying me up the night before.

I was beginning to regret my unusually heavy break-fast. Not only was I worried that the weekend already ruined, but that she would be filing a harassment claim the second we got back to the city.

There was no point in trying to convince myself that I wasn't attracted to her. I wasn't an idiot. Madeline Jones fascinated me, from her wild hair to her inability to be on time. She was everything that irritated me about women, and most people in general, but yet… the way she blushed when she was with me, the way she teased me in private, the way she reacted when I touched her—all indicated that she wasn't totally oblivious or disinterested.

Yeah, it would be a pretty fucking dumb idea to get into bed with my employee. But it didn't have to be a bed. The couch would do. My car, my desk… I groaned inwardly, and when I rolled my eyes I realized that I was starting to pick up Madeline's habits. Acting on any mutual attraction would be a very bad idea indeed, and not one a rational, intelligent person such as myself should pursue.

It's not that I was impulsive, exactly, but I had a tendency to commit first and ask questions later. One of these days it was going to get me into trouble.

Or wedlock.

No. It would be better to keep her as an assistant and *Happit* guinea pig, then jump into a relationship that would be—at the least—unpredictable. My brain knew this. My blue balls were still processing.

While I was obsessing and squirming in my chair, Aaron and Bobbie had gotten up and said something about heading out to the course. Given the state of my jeans, I was thinking about "accidentally" dropping a glass of ice water in my lap.

It wasn't until Madeline shifted in her seat beside me that I realized she'd stayed behind, and we were alone. Even the rest of the dining room had almost emptied out. I checked the time on my phone. *Hell.* We were going to be late to the retreat activity—again. I took a deep, steadying breath.

"Madeline?"

At first I thought she hadn't heard me, so I opened my mouth again. Then she lifted her head to look at me —*really* look at me, and my unspoken words shuddered out with a sigh.

There were bags under her eyes and her smile was weak, but genuine.

I wasn't normally a man who waited, unless it was strategically necessary in negotiating a deal. But Madeline Jones seemed to have the ability to stop me in my tracks yet also make my brain and heart race at the same time. So I waited, and gave her the room to say what she wanted to say.

"Mister Gage?"

"Madeline," I repeated.

She cocked her head. "Why don't you ever call me Maddie?" she asked. I didn't think it was what she had planned to say.

What? I looked at her helplessly. "Because everyone else does." She was special. She knew that, right? She must have known that.

Her smile widened and warmed. My chest felt like a big pine log had caught in the lobby's giant fireplace, cracking and sparking from all the sap. It could have been the pancakes, though.

She reached out her hand. I waited.

"Can I eat your sausage?" With her gaze still locked on mine, she pinched the end of the fat breakfast link and drew it into her mouth.

The little tease sucked it into her mouth the same

way I had caressed her finger the night before. Her lips shimmered with grease, as I imagined her tongue was sucking its juices and rolling over the crisp fried casing.

She bit down gently, making me flinch. Then carefully she chewed.

Her hair, woven tightly at the back of her head in a French braid, left her neck totally exposed. The movement of her throat as she ate my sausage made me swallow at the same time she did.

Fuck, I was a dead man. Her communication was confusing and her message unclear. Either she was going to quit and sue me, or she wanted to suck me off under the table. But she was still beaming at me, which was a really good sign. My head was spinning.

"You owed me a meal," she said.

I cleared my throat. "I owe you more than that."

"The sausage will do. For now."

My mouth opened and closed. Then she rose from her chair, turned and bent over to grab a small daypack. My eyes closed and opened as I said a silent prayer for yoga pants.

"Your turn to get me on the ropes, *sir*."

Then she walked away—again. I untucked my sweatshirt and pulled it down over my hips as far as it would go, then went after her.

6

MADDIE

It took all my strength *not* to look back to see if Mister Brian "No Excuses" Gage was checking out my ass. I kind of assumed he was. To be honest, I wanted him to. I didn't *have* to wear yoga pants, after all.

At least with my back to him he couldn't see my face go hot at the thought of his gaze on me.

As it was, one of the reasons I stole the last of his breakfast was to stop myself from drooling onto the table at the sight of him in a well-loved college hoodie. It was such a departure from the suit and tie I was used to seeing him stalk around in.

Nobody would ever assume that Gage was a college student now, but I could see the remnants of his younger self in that sweatshirt. I imagined him pulling it on after a session at the gym, sleeping in it between cramming for exams, and sharing the snuggly warmth of the big pocket, his fingers mingling with mine. Oh wait—did I just insert myself in that little fantasy? *Oops.*

A brisk autumn breeze hit my face as I left the building in the direction that Bobbie and Aaron went, cooling my flushed cheeks and waking me up a little more. I desperately wanted to go back to bed.

I still couldn't believe that I was brave—or insane—enough to abandon my hogtied boss in a conference room, smeared with spaghetti. It was also unbelievable that the man could still look so... so... *fuckable* like that. I was chalking it up to the sheer foreignness of him being messy, frustrated, and not in control.

It was a relief to lose my clothes once I got up to my —our—suite, particularly as they were stained with marinara sauce. I thought about putting on my PJs, until I remembered that I hadn't brought any. My usual habit was to forgo them if I was going to be in a hotel room by myself. The terrycloth robe I found in the closet would have to do.

I spent a long time in the shower, baptizing myself with hot water. It beat down on the crown of my head as I faced away from the spray, sluicing down my back. The sheets of water in my hair warmed my back and shoulders, lifting the fatigue I'd been feeling and letting it run down the drain.

Then I wondered what Gage would be like in the shower, and my body tensed again.

Would he put his face in the spray or step away to let it pound his lower back? Would he wash his hair when he first got in, or stand planning his empire and then grab the shampoo as an afterthought? Did the crisp hairs I felt at his sternum go all the way down his chest, and further?

If I were there, would he follow the water's trail over the curve of my ass and down the backs of my thighs? If he did, would he chase it with his fingers or his tongue? Would he wrap his arm around me right under the spray, or push me aside and press me to the cool tiled wall? Would he wedge one long hard thigh between my legs and curve his hands under my ass to haul me up, or—

Oh shit. My reverie had gotten away from me. I found myself panting, my breath coming shorter and faster like trying to whisper while running. Something in me clenched and rippled. It was time to turn down the temperature.

By the time I got out, I was profoundly turned on and shivering like a Chihuahua in the snow. Pajamas would have been really good right about then—fluffy, fleecy, flannelly pajamas. The utterly sexless, baggy, wearing-a-hug, chastity belt kind of pajama.

Instead, the starchy sheets enveloping me only heightened my arousal, abrading my sensitive skin.

I burrowed my head back into the pillow, wiggling down with pointed toes until my chin touched where the flat sheet was neatly folded over the comforter. *Oh yeah.* I was so, so comfortable now. And so, so wet and aching, my chest almost burning from the effort to breathe properly around Gage.

My eyes were burning too, from the long day and maybe the pressure of the silk blindfold. What I needed was something to take the edge off, something to relax me and lull me into peaceful, dreamless slumber—like a spine-melting, toe-curling orgasm.

I closed my eyes, just as sightless as I was behind the blindfold Gage that had tied on me, remembering the feel of his hands in my hair, his breath on my face, his tongue memorizing my fingerprints.

Oh fuck.

At the same time that I broke down and dipped my

fingertips into the dampness at my center, I heard a noise outside my bedroom door, like a door closing. I froze. *How long had I been in the shower?*

When Gage hummed softly, almost sighing, I realized that the intruder was *not* Housekeeping with turndown service. I bit back a whimper as my thumb slid over my clit. Holding myself as still as possible, I keened inwardly until I heard the muffled snick of the door to the other bedroom close.

Only then did I close my eyes and let my orgasm go, like a balloon tugging free and floating up into the sky. Five minutes later, I was fast asleep.

Now I looked up at the bright blue sky, the taste of Gage's sausage still rich in my mouth, I contemplated the ropes course I was approaching. It was beautiful here, majestic even, the horizon studded with craggy mountains and patches of trees turning colors as it got colder.

But there was nothing majestic about trying to get across a giant spider web in an adult size Jolly Jumper. The small crowd of my officemates gathered at the base of a tall tower with giant staples in it for footholds, chattering amongst themselves. I paused about twenty feet away and wrapped my arms around myself.

This was all going to go very, very badly. I was five seconds away from pivoting on my heel and running back to the lodge before anybody saw me.

Then a warm hand landed at the small of my back, and I knew Gage had caught up to me. There would be no escape now. My arms dropped to my sides as I stared at the winding paths of taut climbing rope, suspended logs, slippery looking walls, and Bobbie showing Nikhil how to put on a harness.

I could do this. Yes, I could do this. The fact that I didn't *want* to do this was totally irrelevant.

So was the fact that I was afraid of heights.

Gage's hand slipped into mine and squeezed twice, like a beating heart. He tilted his head down toward mine. "I'm almost at the end of my rope, Madeline."

Was that a warning? A promise? A cheesy joke? My own heart stuttered as he walked ahead of me.

"Okay, everyone!" Bobbie clapped her hands loudly. "Welcome to our High Anxiety ropes course! Before we get going, I think your illustrious leader would like to say a few words."

Gage nodded and stepped out in front of the small group. "Thank you, *Roberta*."

I coughed to hide my laugh at the mocking formality in his voice. Now that I knew she was his sister, the family resemblance was clearer. She had the same blue-black hair, the same pale blue eyes. Black Irish, maybe? Was that the term for it? She and I were about the same height, a good six inches shorter than Gage, but where she shared her brother's angles, I had curves.

"Good morning! I hope everyone slept well?" His gaze took in everyone, but lingered on me as I joined the back of the crowd. I could see his eyes narrow on me where I hid behind Nikhil and Susan.

There were about a dozen of us, covering all the major arms and legs of Gage's company. Some people had brought his or her assistant or second in command of the department, but as I looked around, I realized that I was easily the most junior person there in every regard. I stayed at the back of the group, peeking between people.

"Have a good dinner last night?" Gage asked, and

got a few titters in response. "A few of you have sent me emails asking why we're here this weekend. That's a good question, since I'm sure most of you would rather be spending time with your families or friends, or at least sleeping in this morning."

Amen.

"When we expanded last year with new biometric apps, we were very successful—thanks to our R&D, marketing, and many other members of this team. But as we needed to hire more people as part of that expansion, we lost a bit of the cohesiveness that made the company so attractive to VC in the first place."

The urge to return to my cozy hotel bed—probably freshly made by Housekeeping—grew. I stifled a yawn with my palm.

"Now we've got *Happit* launching in the next six months, and you've all been working hard to get it ready," Gage continued. "I have a lot of confidence in this app, in *you*. But in private conversations with some investors, it has been indicated to me that we are being seen as too bloated now, and that our recent success wasn't due to hard work and innovation—that we got in at the right time, which made us lucky."

Oh yikes. I wondered which impudent investor's head was rotting on a spike somewhere back in the city. From my position behind Nikhil's elbow, I saw Gage's sour frown.

"Luck isn't enough. We need to be good. We need to be better than good. The reason our last app succeeded wasn't because of other new peripherals in the market that we tapped into—it was because we tried to envision the future as a team."

"Now, recently that team hasn't been as strong, nor

have our ideas—even mine," he grudgingly admitted. "And I'll level with you—there has been talk from some investors about pulling out; they think that we've already peaked."

A murmur of concern rippled through the group until Gage put up his hands. "Relax, nobody is getting fired or anything. But we can't rely on that golden egg."

"Or the king will kill the goose when it doesn't shit out another," Susan muttered under her breath to my left. Gage eyed her, but went on.

"So we're here because I want everyone to reconnect not only to what our goals are as a developer, but also reconnect to the drive and creativity that made us a success in the first place. Because we *are* going to come up with new ideas and run into new obstacles—I guarantee it. As a larger company now, we need to know how to work together to form solutions. So let's think outside the box, because there are no excuses for failure."

Of course there weren't. Commence eye roll. Gage didn't seem to get that failure just happened sometimes. It wasn't something people *chose* to do.

Ten minutes later we were walking like cowboys thanks to the uncomfortable harnesses around our groins, our chalk bags hanging like oversized testicles from our waistbands.

"You probably won't even need the chalk," said Bobbie. "But I know some people's hands get sweaty when they're nervous, so we're giving you the option. It can also help protect your palms from callouses and other injuries."

Injuries?

This "High Anxiety" course was increasing my anxiety. Fucking corporate togetherness. Fearless Leader probably would have seen more enthusiasm, participation, and better results if he'd let us play hooky from our desks on a Friday afternoon to play company Twister instead.

"Aaron!" Gage called out. "It's chalk, not face paint!"

Susan was still giggling at Aaron's mime act, as he'd swiped the chalk over his dark face and pretended to be trapped in a box. Bobbie punched him lightly in the arm with friendly expression as she brushed some of the dust off his face with her other hand. Something she said to both Susan and Aaron made them laugh and glance over at Gage. I frowned, hoping they weren't saying something awful about him.

He might be an overbearing, self-righteous tyrant, but he was my tyrant.

Bobbie gathered us all together. "We're going to start out closer to the ground today."

Oh, thank god.

She led us over to a group of trees that had marked and notched. "Our first exercise is a pretty basic one called the Swinging Log."

I looked down at the long log suspended on its side between two trees by cables. Precarious, maybe. But not impossible. What were we supposed to do?

"You're going to stand on it," Bobbie explained.

Doable, I thought.

"Together. All of you."

Uh, okay.

"At the same time, without falling off, for ten seconds."

And… we're done here.

7

MADDIE

I spun around to make a beeline back to the hotel, when Gage stepped in front of me with his arms crossed over his chest and his left eyebrow heading toward the high rope above us.

"Not a chance," he mouthed at me.

Fuck my life.

We got together in a big group and brainstormed ideas for how to firstly get on the log without falling off right away, then how to stay on. Should we all try at the same time? One by one? Would sitting on the log together count as a win? Sadly, no.

I had to admit that it was an interesting exercise. We each took turns getting up on the log and were thrown off within a few seconds. As it was suspended from strong cables, the rolling and swaying motions were intolerable.

Nikhil quietly tried to come at it from a systems angle. What was making the log move, and could we counter it? Susan believed that the right hierarchy of roles could turn the log into a stable base for us to stand on. She proposed beginning by straddling Gage on the log.

A snort escaped me. To his credit, Gage assumed she was joking. I wasn't so sure.

Experimentally, I climbed onto one end of the log, holding on to the tree it was cabled to for support. I leaned into the rough bark and as my core and legs fought to keep the log still underneath me. My rear end stuck out a bit, but for the most part I was stable—at least, until Gage came up beside me.

"You're onto something, aren't you?"

"Maybe."

He peered at me hugging the tree, then looked at the placement of my feet and the cable between the log and the tree.

"Can you hang on tight?"

My forehead bonked against the bark. "What do you think I'm doing here, playing tennis?"

"Smart ass. Then hang on."

I swayed as he clamped one hand on my hip, then stepped up on the log and turned in my direction. This could be a workable solution, if the anchor—me—wasn't at risk of falling off just from being touched by Gage. He inched up the log, getting closer to me.

"Steady," he told me.

I clung to the tree, my face burning as he held my hips firmly, almost curved around my body. My lower back was arched, my ass cradled by his thighs as he bent over me.

"Gage…"

"Let me try something. I want to see if I can stop you from wobbling."

Then stop touching me like that! I thought. I turned my

head as best I could to see the rest of the group huddled and still debating ten feet away.

Slowly he slid his hands from my hips around to my belly. His chest pressed against my back as he splayed his hands across my rib cage, his fingertips just a fraction of an inch away from the underside of my breasts.

"You're still unsteady," he breathed in my ear. His heat covered me like a blanket.

My laugh was almost as shaky as the log. "You think?"

He tilted his hips into my ass, and I gasped as I realized he was hardening in his jeans. "Is it the *log* that's the problem?"

I groaned, not even sure if he was joking. "Really? You want to do this now?" I muttered, but couldn't help wriggling my ass against him a little.

His muffled moan made sweat break out on my forehead, and my stomach muscles clenched under his long fingers.

I rested my forehead against the tree. My legs were starting to tremble a little with the constant demands made on my muscles, big and small. The heart was a muscle too, I recalled; it was definitely getting a workout. Our colleagues hadn't noticed us yet, though I saw Aaron glance over once or twice.

"Madeline, I said to stay *still*."

Flattened against my back, Gage stretched up and bit the nape of my neck. Even my ponytail stopped swaying as I froze in shock.

"That's better." *Wha—?* "Aaron! Susan! Madeline has an idea!" he called out, while I slowly processed the fact that he just treated me like a mare in heat.

The gaggle of people migrated over to us.

"Oh, of course!" Susan said with a sneer.

"I think the best approach would be for someone to get on the opposite end to stabilize the whole log. Anchored on both ends, it's unlikely to sway too much. Then one by one carefully step up and hold on to the person next to you," Gage said.

I heard the amusement in Aaron's voice even though I faced the tree. "Just like that, Gage?"

"Not exactly like *this*," Gage replied tightly. Not just his voice was tight, actually.

With a minimum of fuss, everyone ended up on the log—together.

"Nobody breathe."

"Dude, you're going to pull down my pants."

"Where's the guide? Is she timing us? Ten seconds must be over by now!"

"Bobbie!"

"I'm here. You guys did great!" Gage's sister moved around to my field of vision. "It looks like Maddie figured out how to, uh, not get thrown off."

Even with my face squashed against the tree trunk I could see her smirk.

"Okay, you can hop down now! Next up is the Leap of Faith!"

Gage waited until everyone was down before releasing me. Even then, he kept one hand on my hip as he dismounted. He moved close to my side, his other hand trailing along my arm to touch my fingers where they gripped the trunk.

"Take my hand, Madeline."

Sighing, I let him pry my fingers from the bark. His hand was warm and solid and easier to grip than the tree, but much more dangerous. Carefully I turned my feet around so I was facing him, then only flailed for a moment until he took my other hand.

The measured way he assessed me made me shakier than the log. He nodded at me, encouraging me to jump down and into his arms. His eyes were the color of the sky, crinkling a little at the sides as he broke into a grin. "I've got you."

"That's what I'm afraid of, sir."

§♣

"Next up is the Leap of Faith," Bobbie announced. "You will climb up this pole, using the attached holds."

My neck actually hurt when I tilted my head back to see how tall was the pole was. It was tall. Very tall. Trees on a mountain kind of tall.

I put my hand up. "I think I hurt myself on the last challenge."

Bobbie squinted at me. I would swear she and her brother must have practiced steely-eyed expressions in the mirror together as kids. Their family must have some kind of hereditary bullshit detector.

"Half your group has already gone." She pointed at their backs as they headed back to the lodge. A few stragglers were sitting on a nearby rock, their water bottles in hand. "We break for lunch after this."

"It's not a problem," Gage said, his hand on my back. "Is it?"

"I, uh… How high is that?"

Bobbie waved. "Forty-two."

"Feet?"

"And I just have to climb it?"

"Yep. Then stand on the platform at the top."

My head jerked back to look again. *Was there actually a platform up there?*

"It's a small one."

Regardless of how damp my panties might have been, my mouth was suddenly dry as sawdust. I tried to swallow. "On top?" I said faintly.

Gage nodded. "Then you jump, right, Pinky?" Bobbie nodded with him.

I gaped at him. *"Jump?"*

Together, they pointed to a red ball-like thing hanging about a hundred feet away in the air.

Now I really felt faint. My face went from over-heated to totally numb as the blood drained to my feet. "Jump. To that."

Bobbie rocked forward on her toes. "That's why it's called the Leap of Faith."

"Is there a priest at the bottom for last rites?"

Gage chuckled as Bobbie prepped my belay ropes and another guide roped him in at the same time. "You can do it."

Maybe so, but I sure as hell didn't want to. What was so bad about quitting while you're ahead? I felt irrationally enraged as they prodded me up the pole. Each rung up felt higher than the one before, which was technically true. But Gage was pushing me in so many different ways, and I wanted to push back.

Well, and pull him closer, but that was my own libido talking.

"You're almost there, guys!" Bobbie shouted from the ground, her voice carrying a little with the wind. "You just passed the third!"

"Third what?" I panted, clinging on to the pole. The

security of the belay rope hooked to my harness was not enough to make me feel better about any of this.

"Third story." Gage's voice drifted up from his position just below me. "This is the equivalent of about a four-story building."

Oh god. I wanted to vomit again. *Don't look down, don't look down!* When I got to the top, I felt stuck. Gage was just beneath me.

"You can do this, Madeline. Remember, you're totally safe; you're tied in to Bobbie. Just stand up really slowly, and jump for it."

My throat was tight. "You're fucking nuts, you know that? Both of you. All of you. Why would anyone want to stand on one square foot a million miles in the air and then plummet to their death? What possible purpose does this serve?"

Breathe. Had to breathe.

"Madeline, it's not that bad. I know you can do it. I have confidence in you."

"No, I can't."

"Yes, you can."

The big red balloon blurred as my eyes filled with tears. "I can't do it, Gage. Please don't make me do it."

I made the mistake of trying to look down at him. The wind ruffled his hair, but his expression was determined. There was no fear on his face, no hesitation— only confidence in me. There was also no ground underneath us. My brain barely recognized the safety net below. We perched on the pole like kittens in a tree.

"Madeline, there's only one way down." His voice rose and fell on the wind blowing around us. "And that's *down*."

I sniffled, but was too afraid to let go of the pole

long enough to wipe the tears from my face. "Then I quit."

"I won't let you."

"You can't stop me." No job was worth this. No position, above or underneath Gage, was worth risking my life over. My breath came faster and shallower, my heart pounding like a rabbit's.

"You're going to hyperventilate, Madeline. Relax."

"Relax? You want me to jump off a fucking four-story building!"

"You're not a quitter, Madeline."

I snorted, embarrassed when some snot escaped. *That* was worth using my sleeve for a moment. "Oh yes, I am."

"Quitters are failures," he said sternly. "I won't let you quit. Or fail."

"I'm actually really good at it."

He touched the back of my trembling knee, and was lucky not to get my foot in his face. "Don't you trust me? Would I really make you do something that bad?"

"I don't know," I croaked, and my stomach twisted as I realized it was true. Could I trust him with this?

"Maddie, I know you can do it. *Please*."

I shook my head.

"I'll make you a deal." His finger traced a fiery circle on the back of my thigh. Though his touch was gentle, frustration peppered his voice. "If you jump, I'll give you a raise."

"And if I don't?"

His finger traced the line of the harness between my thighs and around my ass, sending a shudder through me.

Oh my god.

The cool tears drying on my cheeks contrasted with the heat in my lower half. My clawed hands were aching, and I wanted nothing more than to just let go. Bobbie leaned back a bit at the bottom, boosting my position. The harness pressed into me like Gage's fingers, only a lot less forgiving.

"What if I quit, Gage? Will you let me quit?"

He was silent. When he spoke, his disappointment was evident. "I can't really stop you. But I don't want to lose you."

I meant quit the exercise, not my job. But my terror right now was taking over all rational thought. Gage was always pushing me.

"I could just order you to do it, as your boss," he pointed out. But I think he knew that if he tried it, I would quit my position in the company as well as my position forty feet off the ground.

Last night was the first time I'd really pushed back against his will, and today he was a big, dark bundle of nerves. Could I use that to my advantage? My mind went to the previous night, flashing on the feelings of power and arousal.

Gage shifted awkwardly, his knees banging against the pole. It was a subtle reminder that he was waiting to do the jump himself. And he would do it, no doubt. Knowing him, he would jump as hard and as high as he could.

Bobbie leaned back in the belay again, reminding me that people down below were also waiting for us. *Crap.*

"What's it going to be, Madeline?"

With a deep breath, I let go of the pole.

8

GAGE

F *uck!*
    With one arm crooked around the pole, I swiped at Maddie with my other hand and ended up with a handful of air. The guy on the other end of my rope was likely swearing at me and struggling, as it felt like my heart dropped into my harness.

Unlike a cartoon character, she didn't hover for a moment before gravity set in. Her arms stretched out toward the red ball but she was at least an arm's length away from reaching it. Bobbie screeched down below; probably frantically letting out a lot of rope quickly through the carabiner so she didn't get yanked up as Madeline went down.

I held my breath until I saw her bounce onto the net below with a grunt.

My body was starting to shake from emotional shock and physical fatigue, but thankfully my belay partner below sat back in his harness to keep me under control.

"I'm coming down!" I yelled in warning then began rappelling down the pole. Though I was irritated that I hadn't completed the challenge, my need to see Madeline was stronger. As I descended, I watched her crawl across the safety net to the edge. She was okay. *She was okay.*

Now that I knew she wasn't hurt, I wasn't sure if I wanted to shake her or kiss her. What happened to the confidence I believed she had? Was I wrong about her? Why didn't she just do it?

As my feet touched the ground, Madeline rolled off the net, landing on the hard ground with an "oof" expelled from her chest. Instead of unclipping the rope, I just unbuckled the harness and shoved it down my legs to shake it off.

I stalked over to her as she brushed dirt and pine needles off her tight black pants.

"What the hell was that?"

Against her pale face, her eyes seemed darker than usual and her cheeks were reddened from the wind. The harness had left puckered lines in her clothes, and her legs were a little shaky.

"I jumped!" she snapped. Her arm went over her head with her elbow bent as she tried to stretch out. The twinges in my arms would have to wait until we were done here.

"No, you fell. There's a big difference."

"I reached for the balloon."

"It was a half-assed effort, Madeline. I expected better from you." I didn't understand why she hadn't tried harder. Didn't she want to succeed? She had been so capable and confident on the swinging log.

Bobbie caught my eye, and she gestured that they were headed back to the lodge. I nodded at her then turned back to find Madeline's pointy little finger in my chest and her eyes a little watery.

"What do you want from me?"

I stopped short. That was a damn good question. Did I want her to succeed? *Yes.* Did I want her standing tall and proud? *Sure.*

I reached out to smooth back the tendrils of hair around her face that had escaped her ponytail. It was bad timing that my cock twitched as she pushed my hand away, her eyes flashing.

"That was unfair, cruel and unusual. God only knows what labor laws you broke coercing me to plummet to my certain death—"

"You. Didn't. *Jump.*" With each word I leaned closer, my lips closer to hers than was appropriate. Why couldn't she just take responsibility for her indecision?

"Yes, I did!" She put her hands on her hips, looking ready to stomp her foot like a little kid.

"You *fell*, Madeline. It's called the Leap of Faith, not the Drop of Doubt. Why are you fighting me on this? You failed. You gave up." Exasperation and disappointment burned in my chest. "God, I wish I could spank you right now."

Her lips parted on a gasp and her chapped cheeks bloomed darker. She stumbled back.

Wait. What had I just said?

I mentally played back my impetuous words. *Shit.*

"Mister Gage, I'm going to pretend I didn't hear that, ah, incredibly inappropriate statement," Madeline said shakily, looking down at the ground. Her hands went to her face, the backs of her fingers curved against her rosy cheeks.

Motherfucker. I hung my head.

"I'm sorry. That was, uh—there was no call, no justification for me to say something like that." I wanted to bang my head against that damned pole. But I didn't say there was no *reason* for it either.

This woman had me turned inside out. We'd been playing with fire for… well, I wasn't entirely sure who'd grabbed the matches first. Either way, we were close to getting burned. I turned away from her, thoroughly disgusted by my lack of discipline. My frustration had gotten the better—or the worse—of me, and I knew better.

Half a dozen deep gulps of mountain air did little to calm me. Everything was too bright around me—the trees, the sky, even the dirt under our feet. Closing my eyes, I searched for some control. How could I possibly rehabilitate this situation?

I had to face facts. I wanted her. I shouldn't, but I did. There was also a chance she wanted me too—if she didn't quit and sue me. But I also had to admit that I was being a bully, plain and simple, and this was not the time or place. My eyes still shut, I breathed in through my nose and out through my mouth a few more times to center myself.

When I opened my eyes, she was gone.

❦

Since clearly I became a raving lunatic in casual clothes, I skipped lunch to change back into a pair of dress slacks and a starched button-down shirt. As soon as I fastened the buttons of the crisp white cuffs, the steel of my everyday armor shielded me again. My back straightened; my will hardened.

When I looked in the mirror, however, there remained an unfamiliar softness around my eyes and mouth. It grew even hazier as I thought of Madeline.

I don't know how long I spent practicing grim expressions, but my face was almost back to normal when a knock at the door interrupted me.

"Room service!"

Bobbie was on the other side when I yanked the door open. A domed plate and a glass of water covered in plastic wrap sat on top of the cart beside her.

"I'm not hungry."

Her foot wedged in the door, stopping me from closing it on her. "No way, we gotta talk."

"My staff is waiting for me."

"*My* staff is waiting *on* them." She rolled the cart in, the heavy door shutting behind her. With two pinched, practiced fingers she plucked off the steel cover to reveal what looked like a club sandwich and some sweet potato fries. Then she ate one.

"I'm not tipping you."

"Big bro, all my life you've been giving me tips. How to do my homework, how to clean my room, how to get a job, how to dress for success, how to get a guy—"

I scowled. "I've *never* told you how to get a guy."

"No?" She smirked. "Good thing, because I think you'd give shitty advice. The point is—you're bossy."

"I *am* the boss, Pinky." Really, she wanted to waste my time with a childish squabble? I could go there. "You know what we're going to do tonight?"

Another few yam fries found their way into her mouth. My own mouth watered at the smell of them. "You've already taken over the world, Brain. But you're not the boss of me."

I leaned back against the back of the couch, my arms crossed over my chest. "And, we're ten years old again. Just when I thought you'd finally grown up."

I'd hurt her feelings. I had enough experience with it to recognize it in her eyes. The usual guilt and irritation rushed through me, leaving me even more on edge.

"I'm really trying here," she said quietly. "Didn't Mom tell you?"

"Yeah." I sighed, not wanting to hurt her further, but I'd been burned before.

It was hard to have real faith in Bobbie. She'd get a job then lose it. She'd move in with a guy, then end up in the ER with a black eye. In the past ten years, it seemed as though my sister was on the fast track to being a professional fuck-up. I told myself that she wouldn't have frustrated me so much if I didn't know she was capable of more. But I was tired of bailing her out and still she didn't seem to take accountability for her life. Well, until now.

"You like this job, don't you?" The pride when she mentioned her staff earlier was obvious.

Her smile was so wide it nearly filled up the room. "Yeah, I really do. But I think I'm also *good* at this, Brian. I like being outside, like being with people visiting. This place, being out here in the mountains… I don't know. I'm so insignificant and tiny compared to them, and they've been around thousands of years."

I raised an eyebrow. "You're comparing yourself to a mountain?"

"I just mean that I guess it's giving me perspective. My life is small and short, and I've been kind of wasting it. Crappy jobs, crappy friends, crappy men. By the way,

it's nice to see Aaron again. It's been, uh, a long time."
She blushed a little.

"He's always been around," I said. *But you haven't.*

"I never come to your office."

That was true. She rarely visited me at work, even
when she'd lived in the city. I'd always thought she was
just disinterested or couldn't be bothered. Now it
occurred to me that maybe seeing that kind of success
and productivity made her feel bad about herself.

But why should I feel guilty about what I'd accom-
plished, just because my little sister was a failure? I went
to school, I put the work in. It wasn't my fault she made
the choices she had.

"I had a good time catching up with him last night,"
she said.

"Aaron?" *To hell with it.* I was hungry. I reached for
the sandwich and took a big bite.

"He talked about Maddie a lot."

Smaller bites, I reminded myself, as I suddenly had a
hard time swallowing. "Did he?" Peeling the wrap off
the water glass, I asked casually, "What did he say?"

"This and that." She shrugged, acting just as casual
as I was—which meant we were both faking and totally
aware of it. "The kind of work she does, how you've
changed since she started, that kind of thing."

What? I downed half the water in one swallow,
chasing another bite of the sandwich. Damn, I hated
those little hotel glasses.

"How I've changed? What does that mean? I haven't
changed." Internally I was panicking. Was my attraction
to her making me soft at the office? Was it obvious to
everyone?

She held out her hands. "Hey, don't look at me. I

just met her. Aaron says that you're just more of an asshole now, for some reason. Actually, the words he used were 'whiny little bitch.'"

Oh. I chewed on the sandwich, thinking about that. Bobbie poked around the suite, presumably checking on Housekeeping's work or counting towels or something. Her voice echoed in my bathroom.

"He says you like her."

It was a good thing she couldn't see my face at that moment. I swallowed then tossed the crust on the plate. I was done. "She's very likeable," I said mildly as I wiped my fingers with the napkin.

Bobbie's head appeared from behind the bedroom door with a smirk on it. "He thinks you *like her* like her."

So juvenile. But not untrue. "What, were you guys gossiping all night or something?" Her face turned red and she hid behind the door again. *Wait a second...* I stalked into my bedroom. "Just how much 'catching up' did you do?" I was so unsettled that I was using finger quotes like a douchebag. "What *were* you doing all night?"

"Sleeping!" She bounced on the edge of my neatly made bed with a secret smile.

"With Aaron?"

She stopped bouncing and looked at the floor. *Oh, fuck.*

"He's my oldest friend!" I felt queasy, a little violent, and a lot relieved that Aaron wasn't into Madeline after all. But my sister—*my little sister*—wasn't much better. I put my hand up and shook my head. "No way. Not happening."

"Aw, that's kind of sweet. But you can't protect me all the time. I'm a big girl now."

"Fuck that, I need to protect Aaron! Does he even know what you're like now?"

She threw a pillow at me. "Asshole!" My reflexes were faster than hers, so she missed me but got nailed when I hurled it back.

"Seriously, Bobbie, do you think that's a good idea?"

Her shrug was pointedly casual, which made me worry that she was already in deeper than she should be. "Maybe not, but it can't hurt. It's not forever, you know. Not much is."

Our father's death had affected us in different ways. She went the rebel without a clue route, and I campaigned hard for the overachieving arrogant ass of the decade award. We'd both been pretty successful so far. I couldn't control what she did; I'd already discovered it was a waste of time and energy to try. It took enough of my time and energy to keep having faith that she would get her shit together.

"Don't fuck him over, Pinky."

"Thanks a lot! Did it ever occur to you that *I* might get hurt?"

No, it didn't. But that was because while I had little faith in Bobbie's ability to see things through, I knew she had a core of steel and a tough skin despite her tiny size. In contrast, Aaron was a big old chocolate teddy bear, just built like a linebacker.

She snorted. "I could say the same to you, you know."

"What do you mean?"

"You do like Maddie." She narrowed her eyes at me. "*Like her* like her. I could see it today."

I doubted her ability to see anything of nuance with me. Bobbie and I had never been super close; she bonded more with our mother. Even after our dad died, I'd never gotten the chance to be the man of the family, since the family didn't seem to care much about me. Being a "Junior" didn't help.

It was around then that I started to go by Gage instead of Brian. I could see the pain on my mother's face when she called me Brian, like I was a sad reminder of my dad—which, technically, I was. So I'd spent the past twenty years trying to make myself worthy of attention, for some fucked up reason that likely didn't matter anymore.

"I like her too, Brian." Bobbie nodded in approval.

I bowed. "Oh, thank you."

"I know you don't care what I think. I'm just telling you. But she seems smart and funny. And she doesn't seem to put up with too much of your bullshit. Actually, she's probably too good for you. Does *she* know what she's getting into with *you*?"

Both my middle fingers went up.

"Seriously, you'd better not be using her," Bobbie warned as she followed me.

Now that hurt a little. "What kind of an asshole do you think I am?" Truthfully, I was more worried about Maddie manipulating me, if she knew how much she was getting under my skin. "And besides, we're not dating."

The smirk on my sister's face looked disturbingly familiar. I'd seen it in the mirror a few times. "That's what you think," she said.

"Thanks for lunch," I said, holding the door open with one hand and rolling the room service cart out into the hallway. I left the "now get the fuck out" unsaid. Even if Bobbie didn't know me that well, she knew me well enough to not be offended. It was too bad, because there were times when I *really* wanted to offend her.

"Okay, okay, I can take a hint." On her way out the door, she paused to slip her arms around me in a quick hug. It was like being attacked by a koala—you knew they could be dangerous, but their cuteness disarmed you.

"It's still nice to see you, Brain," she said.

I reflexively dropped a kiss on her soft black hair. "Yeah, thanks Pinky."

The sandwich sat like a rock in my stomach after she left, but a cursory glance at the mirror showed that dippy expression from earlier had been replaced by a scowl. Good enough.

What Bobbie said made me wonder, however. If I had been grumpier lately, then why would Madeline be interested in me? Was she into assholes?

Sure, I could be moody, but show me a wealthy person who wasn't. Lots of money meant lots of problems and little time to deal with them. She had to deal with me all day long. In fact, she probably deserved a raise.

I just didn't understand why she chose to be so disorganized and flighty, though. Didn't she want to make her life easier? Didn't she want to succeed? Nobody ever achieved anything by half-assing it. Perhaps she just needed to be pushed. She needed a boost, a tool to help her commit.

Damn, I really had to get her to try *Happit*.

Her hesitation on the pole had mystified me. It was so simple. Jump for the red ball. There was a safety harness. There was a net below. Yet she'd been petrified.

Was it the height thing? Would she have jumped if she couldn't look down?

The evening before, when she wore the blindfold, she'd been more assertive, more impudent. An idea began percolating in my head.

Maybe Madeline needed to close her eyes to her fears and insecurities—literally.

Maybe she needed to lose control in order to appreciate the value of mastering it. Then she could let go.

9

MADDIE

Gage managed to avoid me for the rest of the afternoon. We broke out into small group work, and while I was with Aaron and some PR people, he was huddled with Nikhil and tech R&D. In what seemed like both a handful of minutes and endless hours, the day was done and people began to talk about dinner.

I hesitated when Aaron and Bobbie asked me to join them for dinner in the village further down the mountain. If I was honest, I wanted to see what Gage was doing. I wanted to ask about his afternoon, and tell him about mine—as an employee, of course, conferencing with her boss.

Oh hell, who was I kidding? The man had me wrapped around his ankles like a stray cat.

Without any communication from him, though, I didn't see a way to adroitly avoid going out for pizza for Aaron and Bobbie, and now Susan too. It wasn't until we met in the lobby with our coats on that I finally spotted Gage.

He'd changed out of his casual clothes and was back in office attire, his jaw tight and his black hair sticking up in a few places as though he'd been running his hand through it.

Standing by the ever-burning fireplace, my body heated up quickly until I was looking forward to the cool air outside. Then he saw me, and if I hadn't been watching him so closely, I might not have noticed something loosening in his expression—like an elastic band stretched too tight then easing.

Bobbie waved him over, but there was no need; he was making a straight line for me, his gaze never wavering from me. In fact, he may not have even noticed her gesture, so intent was his focus on me. I undid my coat, suddenly roasting beside the fire.

He stopped in front of me, blinking. "Madeline." It wasn't a question or admonition, but almost a compulsion to softly say my name. The sound of his voice made me quiver, but I remained mute.

"We're going down to that pizza place in the village," Bobbie explained. "You want to come?" Aaron and Susan chatted in the background, while I held my breath waiting for his answer.

"I don't know," he said slowly. "I'm a bit tied up here."

My lips parted then curved into a smile. Of course, he would have to make a rope joke. His eyes danced at me, as if daring me to say something. Anything. His magnetism had paralyzed me once again. His affect on me seemed to be magnified at this altitude, like thinner oxygen.

"All you do is work," his sister complained.

He was unperturbed, until Aaron moved closer to us

and brushed Bobbie's hand with his fingers. Gage did a double take, his Adam's apple moving under his dark evening shadow of scruff as he swallowed whatever he wanted to say. I reached out and touched his hand to calm him, but instead the sensation of the dark hairs at his wrist against my fingertips made me all kinds of unsettled.

"It's okay," he mouthed at me, twisting his wrist around to capture my fingers with his and squeezing lightly. It all happened within a few seconds, like a magician's sleight of hand.

I'd gotten over the emotional maelstrom the Leap of Faith had wrought in me, and come to peace with the fact that I wanted him. If he made a move on me, I would be inclined to turn into pudding in his arms. Yes, it was a big, dumb decision. And with him, there would be no going back.

"Slave driver," Bobbie muttered.

"He doesn't ask me to do anything I don't want to do already," I said firmly. Not once did my gaze flicker over to his sister as I reassured her. Gage and I were in a bubble. "Let me know if you want to, um, pin anything down later."

Like me.

His smile was so wide that his teeth flashed white like a wolf's in the firelight. "Oh, I will."

"Let's go, I'm starving!"

Bobbie's interruption popped our little bubble. She prodded me out the door, Susan and Aaron following behind us. The tingle running up my spine told me that Gage watched us go, and the dampness in my panties told me that I couldn't wait to get back.

The pizza was good, but I barely tasted it. The

conversation was lively, but I was subdued. Bobbie gave me a few strange, measured looks, but I couldn't possibly explain to her that I was struck dumb and senseless by the thought of fucking her big brother.

Yeah, I couldn't imagine that going over very well.

The red wine we shared helped my mood a little, but by the time we got back to the hotel, my shoulders ached with tension. Trying to foist off Susan's questions about working so closely with Gage didn't relax me much. It was pretty obvious that she had a crush on him, but as far as I could tell, it wasn't reciprocated.

At least, he hadn't rocked his erection into her ass and bit her neck like a stallion in heat. He'd saved that for me.

The memory of earlier made me blush. I peeled off my coat and folded it over my arm in the elevator, but my body continued to simmer with every step I took down the hall towards our suite. The door shutting behind me sounded so damn loud. I threw my coat over the back of the couch as I toed off my shoes. The light was on, but Gage's door was closed. The door to my own dark bedroom gaped open.

I let out a shuddering sigh, unsure if his absence was a relief or disappointment. *Maybe it was a good thing*, I thought as I turned on the shower in my en suite. Getting involved with my boss would be a phenomenally stupid thing to do, especially in this job market. The hot water helped my stiff muscles but did nothing to alleviate the arousal pooling in my belly. It had been a long ass day.

After a quick shower, I padded back into the bedroom, reaching up to rub my hair a little with a white towel.

"Madeline."

"Agh!"

Gage sat on my bed, leaning against the rustic looking headboard. The towel fell to the floor; my hair licked my back with dampness.

When he leaned over to flick on one of the bedside table lamps, I saw that though he was still in business clothes, his feet were bare and his shirtsleeves rolled up and buttons undone halfway down his chest.

On his lap, in his hands was a black silk tie, like the blindfold we'd used the night before at dinner, and a length of climbing rope. He twisted both together around his hand.

"Gage, what the actual fuck!"

My heart pounded in fright, and I was paralyzed by embarrassment and astonishment. Fresh arousal closed in on me, squeezing my insides just like the rope that was biting into Gage's long, straight fingers. He folded his thumb over his palm to hold the end of the tie then began idly wrapping it around his hand like a bandage.

"You scared the shit out of me!" I yelled, deciding that the best defense was a good offense.

With a trembling hand, I crouched down to grab the towel that had fallen to the floor. Seeing as all my other defenses against Gage were shot, right now the towel was my only option other than retreat. As a shield, it did diddlysquat against the wicked gleam in his eyes as he surveyed me.

"Can you at least turn around?"

He stopped winding the rope, twisting his torso to look awkwardly at the wall, then back at me with a smirk.

"Then close your eyes like a gentleman."

His eyes snapped shut, his lips still crooked and mocking. His thick lashes carved inky shadows at the top of his cheeks, and his eyeballs twitched under the smooth skin below the gashes of his eyebrows. Without his gaze to distract me, I noticed the crease across his forehead deepening.

"How was dinner?" he asked as he unwound the length of silk from around his palm. It curled onto his lap like an apple peel.

Quickly I retrieved the hotel robe from the closet and pulled it on. "Fine. They have a wood-burning oven, and make a damn fine thin crust. *Really?* You want to talk about the pizza?"

"Not really."

I tightened the belt as much as I could and held it with my hands in case of slippage. "Okay, it's safe."

His eyes were dark even when he opened them. "Is it?"

The black blindfold draped around his wrist like a cuff, and he looped the rope between his hands like it was soft yarn.

"What are you doing here?" I asked lamely. I knew why he was there. We both knew that I knew it.

"We didn't finish our little talk about committing yourself to something earlier. It occurred to me that maybe you don't understand the relationship between that commitment and power."

His hands spread wide, making the rope snap together in the middle. I jumped despite myself. My breath caught in my throat. I was stupid to believe we weren't going to arrive at this moment. It had been dancing through both our imaginations for the past twenty-four hours like a giant pink elephant in a tutu. Maybe even twenty-four *days*.

"What do you want from me?" I'd asked him that earlier at the ropes course. At the time I'd been frightened and belligerent.

He cocked his head, considering the question. "*Everything.*"

Well, that was clear as mud. *Everything? As in my body, my soul, or my 401k?* "What are you expecting in return?"

"Everything."

My breath whooshed out of my chest. "You know you're a bit of a control freak?"

"I've been told that before." *Yeah, understatement of the century.* "But there are advantages to being in control, you know."

I hummed noncommittally.

"Let me ask you something," he said.

"Do I have a choice?"

He gestured for me to sit on the bed—my bed, which he appeared to have little intention of moving from. His gaze held me still as I waited for his big question.

"Did you like tying me up last night?" he asked.

I gaped at him. That was his question. That was what he asked me. Tying him up.

"Yes. You, me, this." He held up the black silk tie; apparently I'd processed his bizarre query out loud.

My eyes widened and my lips parted. "I, uh…"

"Yes or no, Madeline."

"No," I blurted out.

Tilting his head, he looked at me curiously. His attention unnerved me. Twisting my fingers in my lap, my gaze flew to the blindfold and rope he'd just dropped on the bed beside his hip.

"Why not?" he asked.

"Honestly?"

"I told you before—never lie to me, Madeline."

"It's not that I didn't like tying you up," I said slowly. *I mean honestly, what self-respecting underling wouldn't?*

"But?"

"It didn't seem fair, me being blindfolded and your hands—" I waved my own hands between us.

"How so? That was the point of the exercise, wasn't it?"

I didn't understand. "To be unfair? I thought it was to 'communicate effectively?'" I made air quotes while rolling my eyes.

Gage made a snorting sound in the back of his throat. "It was about flipping the power dynamic. You didn't have the ability to see me, to interpret my cues. Body language still talks, Madeline."

"You don't say." I folded my arms over my chest, the robe pressed against my bare breasts. The pull of the fabric parted the robe to reveal more of my thighs. He had a point. I'd definitely felt vulnerable, despite knowing that he was restrained at the time. I hadn't realized how much I interpreted from his facial expressions or the way he moved, until I was denied it.

Yet, if Brian Gage thought that simply manacling his hands reduced his power, he was delusional. With a single raised eyebrow or a brusque demand, the man could compel me to do almost anything—except jump off a three-story building. Was that what this was about?

"Where are you going with this, sir?"

Arched eyebrow time. Damn, did he know what that did to me?

"I want to try something." He ran his palms over his outstretched thighs, like he was brushing dust off his pants. Then he held up the rope and silk tie in front of me.

My insides clenched deliciously. It was a good thing I was sitting on a towel, more or less.

It was one thing to fantasize about doing inappropriate things with Gage, but another entirely for him to sit on my bed and promise them, expect them—in the very immediate future.

I waited. He swung his legs off the bed then shuffled down to where I was sitting at the bottom of the bed. The starched cotton of his shirt rustled against the sleeve of my robe, and his spicy, intoxicating scent drifted toward me.

My lap was utterly fascinating, my bare knees pressing together under the robe. I couldn't look in his eyes, afraid of what I might see. Gage's intensity intimidated me at the best of times. Now naked and faced with—let's face it—sex toys—I assumed I would just go up in flames.

I shifted on the bed, my robe coming further apart. Beside me, Gage dangled the silk tie between my legs, tickling the inside of my thighs.

Holy Jesus.

"Which is the more powerful sense? Sight or touch?"

"Sight," I answered, without thinking.

"Why?"

I paused. "Knowledge. I learn more from seeing things. You know how sometimes people ask whether you'd rather be deaf or blind? I'd rather be deaf. I guess I'm a visual person."

He let out a thoughtful hum. And reached for my hand. The heat of his fingers around my wrist made me jump. "But then you wouldn't be able to hear music."

"I could read, watch movies with subtitles."

"Okay, let's test your theory. I'll tie you up and you blindfold me. We'll see where things… go, and then you can tell me who has the greater handicap."

"Handicap in what?" My voice was low as his thumb strummed the inside of my wrist like the fret of a guitar.

"This." His fingers circling my wrist, he held my hand up to his mouth and kissed my palm. I trembled.

"Gage…"

His lips moved over my wrist and the inside of my arm as he pushed up the sleeve on my robe. Little pinpricks of fire broke out all over me, like a jagged wheel was being run over my skin. In my other hand, he placed the wad of silk.

"I want to kiss you, Madeline." He shook his head. "Correction—I'm going to kiss you."

Never let it be said that Brian Gage wasn't direct. I swallowed hard, my mouth dry. "Th-that's very efficient communication, sir. But…"

"But?" He splayed the tie across my hand and pressed his palm against it. The thin silk was a useless barrier against the heat of his body.

"But isn't this a bad idea?" *Oh god, this was happening.* I felt electrified but still, like an exposed wire waiting to spark against another.

"It absolutely, positively is," he agreed. We were on the same page, just of a naughty book. Still, I hesitated.

"You have to commit, though, Madeline. This time,

you have to go all in, or not at all." He leaned toward me, his breath tickling my neck. My head tilted ever so slightly and my eyes closed, my body unconsciously begging for his touch.

With his hands wrapped around my fists, he shifted us to face each other. Only our hands touched but I felt his nearness on every inch of my body. I looked in his eyes and saw total, unflinching determination.

What would it be like to feel that kind of certainty? I wondered. I lived a lot of my life by the seat of my pants, but it was an approach borne out of anxiety, not confidence.

"A leap of faith," I murmured to myself.

His eyes widened, then crinkled at the sides as a knowing grin transformed his face. An intense, serious Gage was heart-stopping, but a gleeful Gage was downright dangerous.

"*Please*," he said. "See, I know how to ask now."

Well, when he put it that way… *How's this for commitment, sir?* The teasing thought danced through my brain as I touched my lips to his. I could go "all in," as he said, but my cards weren't great. Would he call my bluff?

Yes, he would.

Lightning quick but like a gentle puff of air, he pushed me back until I lay on the bed and he hovered over me. He raised my hands above my head, our fingers still laced together. His darkened gaze drank me in, and he groaned before capturing my mouth again.

My nipples hardened against the inside of the robe, which was slowly slipping open with every move I made, every fevered wriggle. The knot I'd tied was not up to Gage's Boy Scout standards.

He kissed me, over and over, until my lips were

tender and the dark shadow of his beard rasped against my neck.

"Give me the blindfold," I gasped as his tongue dipped into the hollow at the base of my throat.

"Fuck it, I'll do it myself." He knelt back, draping the rope over my quivering, exposed abdomen like a back-up belt. His hands flew to the back of his head as he secured the material over his eyes.

I sucked in a breath as he loomed above me, the blindfold in place. He reached out, his hands grasping and his fingers curling in his search for me. He licked his lips and I gasped as he found me.

With more grace than I thought possible, he swiveled us around so that he was sitting up against the headboard and I was straddling his knees.

"Time for me to tie you up," he said, squeezing my thigh.

This was almost certainly a terrible idea, and it thrilled me. I wanted him to tell me what to do. Gage was wrong—I didn't want power over him. Maybe this was something he couldn't conceptualize, but I liked someone taking charge, taking care of me, and relieving me of my already-pathetic decision-making ability.

Part of me wondered what spurred this on in him, what pushed him over the edge of whatever container his attraction for me was held in. Why make a move now? To punish me for my hesitation on the pole earlier? To get me back for my impudence the night before?

Did it matter? I was hot and wet and ready to climb him like the ropes course.

I shrugged with false nonchalance. "I'll try anything once."

His frown disarmed me almost as much as his grin did. "That doesn't sound very committed."

"I should be committed," I mumbled to myself. *Enough teasing*, I thought. "Are you sure you can do this without seeing?" I asked him.

He parted my robe, running his knuckles down my body from my collarbone to my navel. "I can see you just fine, Madeline."

Oh. God.

I bit my lip as I ground my throbbing core onto his knee. Those pants were definitely going to the drycleaner on Monday morning.

He whipped the length of the rope over my head, almost like a lasso, catching me around the shoulders.

"Such a good girl," he crooned as he tugged on the ends to pull me in. He sat up to capture my lower lip between his teeth, right where I had just bitten it. "You. Taste. Amazing," he said between light kisses—*too* light.

"You're teasing me." I wriggled against his legs.

"Madeline…" he warned. He was trying to look stern, but totally failed. I tried to look unaffected, but was similarly unconvincing.

So I reached for the buttons on his shirt, and he untied the belt of my robe like he was unwrapping a Christmas present. My fingertips dragged through his very, very happy trail as I opened his shirt. He let out a hissing noise when my knuckles skidded over his abdominal muscles.

"How does it feel to *not* see what I'm doing to you, sir?" Did the element of surprise frustrate him or turn him on?

"Fucking amazing."

Turn him on, apparently. The bulge in his pants grew.

"*Oh,*" was all I could say when he peeled the robe off my shoulders. Rather than take it off, though, he pulled it halfway down my arms and tied the ends of the sleeves together loosely, effectively putting me in an Egyptian cotton straightjacket.

"Do you know what it was like to have my hands tied last night?" he asked me darkly, those same hands hot on my breasts, squeezing and weighing them. "To watch you hang on my every word, every instruction— blind as a new kitten, and know that I couldn't touch you?"

I moaned. He was certainly touching me now. "Fuck, Gage. *More.*"

He plucked my nipples with a maddening delicacy. "Then you left me there with my hands tied behind my back, Madeline. Helpless. Frustrated. Hungry."

Forget the drycleaners. His pants were a complete loss. I tried to rub back and forth on him, desperate for some friction. My nipples rose in hard points against his palms. I had never been so turned on in all my life. Granted, my life had been fairly short until then.

There was so much freedom in being invisible to him. I felt like I could revel in my arousal, let all my inhibitions go, and he couldn't see the expressions on my face. With a blindfold on, he wasn't my boss. He was just… Gage.

My gasp was loud as his thigh found a hidden spot on me. His hands went to my hips, stopping my ascent. "Easy. Not yet."

I warmed all over, my brain turning to mush once he kissed me again.

No light brush against my lips this time—his tongue swept inside my mouth, taking my breath away along with all my inhibitions. His kiss was as demanding and uncompromising as he was, and all I could do was try to meet him halfway. His hands slipped under the robe around my lower back, his fingers digging into the fleshy dimples above my ass.

"How far are you prepared to go?" he whispered against my lips.

10

MADDIE

"I'll do whatever you say, sir. " All my good sense had been overcome by arousal. I was his to command.

"Good girl. Open my pants."

With what—my teeth? My eyes widened at the large bulge under the fly of his charcoal wool slacks, but I was still restrained by my terrycloth straightjacket.

"I can't, my arms—"

"Oops, my bad. I'll help you." He let go of me just long enough to slip open the button at his waist and unzip. His erection, barely contained by his stretchy black boxer briefs, swelled forth.

My mouth went a little dry as I looked down. Any rational thought I had then left my head as he squeezed himself and groaned.

"Fuck, Madeline. You make me crazy."

Before I could even take another breath, he tugged down his briefs and pulled out his cock. He was long and thick, dark with engorgement and shiny at the tip. His fist wrapped around it like it was second nature, moving up and down while he stared into my eyes.

"Rise up on your knees," he ordered.

I did, lifting my breasts closer to his mouth. I wobbled a little, struggling to keep my balance with my arms behind my back.

"Ah!" I yelped as he leaned forward to take a nipple into his mouth. He rolled it on his tongue then sucked hard. A line of fire shot from my breast to my pussy, making me jerk. "The other one too," I panted.

He let it fall from his lips with a wet pop as he shook his head. "Still think that sight is the most powerful sense, Madeline?"

Maybe he was right. I could see everything he was doing to me, but I felt naked and needy and totally helpless.

My position above his lap, my knees on either side of his thighs, opened me up but left me powerless to chase the sensations vibrating through me. I huffed in frustration, growing even more irritated when he just laughed softly at my need.

"Take a leap of faith, Madeline."

He opened my robe to fully expose me. His forehead furrowed above the blindfold. "Fuck, I wish I could see you right now."

I wished he could, too.

He trailed a finger from my quivering belly to the damp curls at my core, before his wrist twisted to slowly ease two thick fingers into me. "How does that feel?"

I groaned then tilted my hips to follow his hand.

"No." He pulled out his fingers, leaving me clenching and grasping for him. I wanted to scream with frustration. "You need to commit to this, Madeline."

"I am! Just... *more*, Gage."

There. Committed.

"Fuck this," he growled. "I need to see you."

He tugged off the blindfold, dragging his fingers through his dark hair and blinking. The blue of his irises barely adjusted, swallowed up by his arousal.

"Beg me to fuck you, Madeline."

My breath was short in my chest, my body burning. Gage's eyes weren't the proverbial windows to his soul— they were one-way glass, where I saw my own desire reflected. It was too much.

"Please, sir." But I closed my eyes as I said it. "Please fuck me."

With a satisfied grunt, he slipped out from underneath me and grabbed my ankles, yanking my legs so that I flopped onto my back with a surprised cry. Lying back on the discarded robe, I was able to get my hands out of the sleeves, but when I reached for him I felt the swift burn of him pulling the rope out from underneath me.

"Gage!"

"*Madeline.*" Swiftly he doubled the length of rope, then grabbed my hands and pushed them above my head. He wrapped it around my wrists then looped it in between them like handcuffs.

Oh god, he was tying me up. And unlike my lame knots, it appeared as though he *had* been a Boy Scout at some point.

He knelt between my legs, his hot, hard length bobbing between us as he braced himself over me. The lapels of his shirt fell around us like white curtains, tickling my ribs. He ran his thumb over my throbbing pulse, just where the rope rubbed my wrist.

"Do you want to quit?" he asked.

I shook my head. If I wanted to, I could probably

bring my arms down in a circle around his neck in an embrace. But I wouldn't, not yet.

Despite being restrained and physically dominated, Gage's position over me didn't scare me. I wouldn't say I felt confident, exactly, but not intimidated either. His intensity was overwhelming, but there was a freedom in being passive, in lying here and taking whatever he wanted to give me. His gaze swept over me then pinned me down just as neatly as his hands did. Dark with desire, his eyes held me, reassured me.

"Do you trust me?"

I nodded, my throat aching.

"Out loud, Madeline." His voice was low as he bent down to run his tongue down my neck.

"Yes!"

"Yes, what?"

What more did he want? My head swam. "Uh, yes, sir?"

He growled. Okay, that wasn't what he wanted. Holding the rest of the rope in one hand like I was on a leash, with his other hand he flipped me onto my stomach and bent my arms until my hands reached down my back. I felt a twinge in my shoulders and triceps, but it was like a good stretch at the gym, not painful.

I was still processing that feeling when bent my knees and wound the rope around my ankles, my heels almost brushing my ass.

"Ungh!"

The stretch in my quads surprised me, but again it didn't hurt. If anything it felt good after the strain on my muscles today.

I turned my head, trying to see exactly what Gage was doing. He looped the rope between my ankles just as he did my wrists, then tugged gently until I was curved like a bow. My lower back arched, my belly pressed into the bed, and I hung from his grasp like a marionette.

This was different from the spaghetti dinner experiment the night before.

"Do. You. Trust. Me?" he said in my ear, making me shiver.

He was kidding, right? "Well, it sure looks that way!"

When I wriggled, the ropes tightened to the point of biting.

He smacked my ass with one hand, the other still holding the rope. "You have to commit, Madeline. Don't fight it or it will hurt. Give yourself over to me and trust that I'll take care of you."

Now I felt intimidated. I had thought that being tied up meant not making any decisions, and now he wanted me to choose this, choose him. This leap of faith was just as frightening as jumping off a forty-foot telephone pole. I knew that I could say no, knew that I could quit. Of course, Gage did not want me to quit, but he would release me the second I said "red light" or whatever.

I relaxed my muscles, easing my body into limp submission. I had to make the decision to be an inactive participant, willing but disabled. It didn't matter if I was blind or restrained or if I had industrial-strength earplugs in.

I would be *his*.

"I—I trust you." *Don't make me regret it*, I prayed inwardly.

He sighed as I melted into the bed. My knees spread apart, as did my elbows, until I almost resembled the shape of an X.

"Oh, Maddie. You are so fucking gorgeous."

He moved behind me, slackening my bonds. Then he took the end of the rope and tied it to the knotty pine and wrought iron headboard. When I pulled on it, the only effect was to bow me more and tighten the rope cuffs around my wrists and ankles.

"Relax," he said, stroking my shin.

I rolled my eyes. Easy for him to say—he wasn't tied up like a calf at a rodeo. He was right though; the more I fought it, the more uncomfortable I would be. I had to trust him.

He slid his hands between my hips and the quilt and scooted me a little closer to the headboard, then lay down on the pillows, perpendicular to me. My thigh rested on his shoulder as he wedged himself in between my legs. I wasn't sure what I was expecting, but his tongue stabbing into my core wasn't at the top of the list.

"Gage! Shit!"

With one hand he reached underneath me to find my hot little "on" button, and flicked the switch, while he luxuriated in the arousal spilling from me. The flat of his tongue dragged over me roughly from my entrance to my crack, making me shudder and arch my back. As the rope tautened again, Gage pressed his hand into the small of my back.

"Just open up for me. I'll make you feel so good," he promised. Then he dove back into lapping up my juices, the strong point of his tongue leading where the rest of him wanted to follow.

I drove my forehead into the bedspread with a tight sigh, beyond frustrated that I couldn't touch him. He was right; seeing him wasn't enough.

With one curled finger, he found a place inside me

that made me feel frantic. I squirmed, warning him with a whine. "Oh god, noooo… I'm gonna—"

"It's okay, Maddie. Just let it go."

He added another finger to tease at that crazy spot on the inner wall behind my clit. My body was overloaded with sensation—his fingers beckoning, his tongue catching, his nose nudging, his hand branding me.

"Oh fuck, I'm coming!" My chin rose off the bed, my teeth grinding together and my head tilting up and back as I fought to control the sensation ripping through me. It was unlike anything I'd ever experienced.

This was what powerlessness felt like. It was freedom and fear wrapped up in one stomach-clenching moment.

I couldn't help flailing a little, making the rope bite enough to add an extra layer of intensity to my orgasm. Gage didn't relent, not even slowing his ministrations until I was panting and boneless.

Barely aware that he'd swiftly undone my bonds, I tried to catch my breath.

My arms and legs fell to the bed, embarrassment flooding my body. The bed rebounded a little as Gage got off and disappeared into the other room. It would have been a perfect time to escape, to slink away in a blaze of mortification—if my limbs could receive any messages from my brain.

He returned with a damp facecloth, which he gently dragged over my oversensitive body. It made me shiver, but didn't cool me down. I raised my head to see his semi-hard cock bouncing a little at the top of his pants. He looked a little uncomfortable and a lot fully dressed. My heart was still pounding in my chest like a drum.

"And that was just the foreplay," he said.

Holy shit. Were we really going to do this? We wouldn't be able to come back from having sex.

Then again, it wasn't like it would be easy to forget that he'd just discovered my G-spot.

"I want you, Madeline."

I rolled onto my side to watch him take off his clothes. He removed them so efficiently that I was almost surprised when he didn't fold them into neat piles. Every inch of skin, every taut muscle and hair revealed on his body took another breath from me, until I was panting with anticipation. *Again.*

He knelt on the bed beside me, his thighs cradled by my curled up body. I could feel the heat of his body, could smell his skin and the arousal glistening at the tip of his cock, bobbing just out of reach of my mouth. I swallowed hard.

"Condom?" I managed.

His entire being stiffened, then sagged. "Goddammit." He sighed. "I don't suppose you have one?"

I tilted my head back to look at him. "Just what kind of girl do you think I am, Mister Gage?" It was kind of a rhetorical question, I realized as he surveyed my naked, blushing body on the bed.

"A prepared, responsible one?"

I hated to dash the hope in his voice. "I already told you I wasn't a Girl Scout." But it was so tempting… I reached out to wrap my hand around his hardness, making him hiss. Not all of him had wilted. And I definitely wanted to return the favor… I squeezed tighter, making him moan.

He rocked his hips into my touch, his eyes closing briefly. "I suppose one of us should be responsible, then."

"I could—" I was surprised to find his fingers on mine, prying my hand away.

He shifted back off the bed, crouching to the floor to look me in the eye where I lay. "No."

Oh.

Maybe he could detect my own disappointment or insecurity, because he placed his hand over my mouth to silence my protest. "I want you, Madeline. Jesus, don't ever doubt that. But the first time you make me come, it's not going to be down your pretty throat or in your fist."

His words made my body clench in reaction. But I nodded.

He touched my face. "You understand, Maddie? I'm all in. And I want to be deep inside you, not spilling into your hands like a teenager."

I licked my lips. "I want to taste you."

His groan filled the air between us. "You're killing me, here. If you—" He broke off, brushing his forehead against the bedspread. "I might just lose control and say 'fuck it.'"

"So?"

"So, I won't be reckless, not with you."

"You're never reckless, Gage." Although, I wasn't sure how to qualify the last hour.

His jaw twitched. "Yeah, well, this is not the best time and place to start."

His gentlemanly behavior touched me, even if the hot, hard heart of him didn't. He gathered me up in his arms and carried me into his bathroom, which had a bigger tub than mine did, with jets. In a moment, the faucet was on at full blast, the tub filling with water and the room muggy.

"It's okay, Madeline," he said softly, kissing the top of my head. I smiled. Of course it was okay—I was in his arms.

He helped me into the tub, where he'd already thrown all the hand towels and facecloths to soak up the hot water. Those, he draped over my arms and legs like he was prepping casts for my broken nerve endings.

"Maddie, you did so great. I'm so proud of you, baby." He soothed me with his voice, hands and lips—and a tube of cream that he smoothed over the tender parts of my body. The smell of the cream mixed with the earthy smell of his skin, and I wanted to drink it all in.

His touch was reverent and so light it almost felt like he was leaving butterfly kisses all over my body. Despite the delicacy of his care, when I looked in his eyes he left deep marks within me.

This could become a habit. "No excuses next time, okay?" I said.

"No excuses," he promised.

11
GAGE

Within five minutes of Madeline passing out, it was obvious that rest would not come for me until I took care of business. The tub was still warm, so I stripped and slipped into the water. Once I lay back with my knees up and my hand fisting my cock, it didn't take long to finish.

Once I slipped into bed beside her, my skin still hot from the bath, my brain refused to shut down even though my body was spent.

I kept staring at Madeline, taking the opportunity to memorize the curve of her ear and the exact color of her lips. Her courage and commitment impressed me more than the soft lines of her body and the sounds and taste of her climax. When I finally fell asleep, it was to dream of her as a mermaid trapped in a fisherman's net.

When I woke up Sunday morning, the coolness of the sheets beside me indicated that Madeline had been gone for a while. I fished the robe out of the closet and shoved my arms in the sleeves, determined to find her.

I didn't have to look far.

She was dressed in her matching robe, sitting on the couch with her feet on the postage stamp coffee table and her laptop open. The smell of coffee lingered in the room, but twenty bucks said that the full cup by her feet was stone cold. Absorbed in her screen, she didn't even hear me come up to the back of the couch.

"What are you doing?"

"Aaahhh!"

There went the coffee, as her flailing foot connected with the mug. We both watched the liquid arc out and land on the floor like a rainbow. She swiveled around and glared at me.

"You have to stop sneaking up on me like that." She shut her laptop, her arms not so casually resting on it.

I shrugged. "I can't help it if you don't pay attention. What are you doing?" It had looked like she was online, but it was mostly text-based.

"Nothing."

The robe had fallen open to show off her legs, and if I leaned over the back of the couch and looked down I could peek into the gaping vee above where she'd belted it. Her hair had dried into a wavy auburn mess while she slept, which I swept into my hand and wound around my fist. Her head tilted back when I tugged, so she looked at me almost upside down.

"Tell me?" I wouldn't force her, but I was curious. "I want to know about you. *More* about you."

She wrinkled her nose in thought. "I hate the color pink."

"Okay. Random, but a good example, I guess." I moved around the couch, avoiding the coffee-soaked carpet, and sat beside her on the loveseat. There was no need to sit so close, but I liked the way her thigh melded to mine. "What else?"

"I have an irrational fear of spiders and I like sleeping alone." She arched an eyebrow at me.

It was probably foolish to smile so much this early in the morning, but I couldn't help it. "I'm sure you could get over it if you tried."

"The spiders?"

"The sleeping alone." I tapped the laptop. "So what were you doing?"

For once, her face was easy to read. *Should I tell him? What would he think?* The indecision in her expression worried me. Was it something really bad? Was she into something horrendous, like human trafficking or—god forbid—decaf coffee?

"It's personal," she finally said, tracing the seam of her laptop with her fingers.

I manacled her slim wrist with my fingers, frowning at the faint mark left there by the rope. *Damn it.* I'd been too rough the night before. "I'm pretty sure we're past a business relationship now."

She exhaled heavily—whether in relief, recognition, regret, I couldn't tell.

"I'm adopted," she confessed.

I blinked. "That's… fine?"

What was the big deal? Why was she clinging to her laptop like it was a nuclear briefcase?

She sighed. "Do you know how lucky you are to have a sister?"

"That's debatable some days." I snorted. Maybe *I* was adopted. It would explain why I seemed to have little in common with my mother and Bobbie, who were two of a kind.

She punched my thigh. "Seriously. I would have loved to have grown up with someone to share things with—other than five other foster kids that changed more often than underwear."

"Share, fight—six of one, half a dozen of another…" I stopped mid-shrug. This was clearly important to her. I pried her hand off the laptop and laced her fingers with mine. "Uh, do you want to talk about it?" Part of me wanted her to say no. I wasn't good with situations I couldn't clearly fix.

"Meh. My father died, I guess, and my mother couldn't deal. Actually, she did *deal*—mostly Ecstasy, and some meth. When she went to jail, I went to foster care."

It was a sad story, but I had a feeling it would get worse. "How old were you?"

"About four. But I guess I didn't talk for a while—I don't really remember." She tried to rub the frown from her forehead, like her fingertips could erase the memories. "I only found out recently that she wasn't actually…"

"What?"

"Dead." Her voice was lifeless. "She just signed her rights away instead while she was in prison. She didn't even wait to get out. Poof!" Her hand expanded like an exploding fist bump. "*Evanesco!* No more daughter."

I couldn't even imagine that. My mom drove me crazy, but I knew she loved me to distraction—literally. She was like a kitten with a laser pointer.

Madeline smiled, but it looked fake. "At least I was lucky enough to get adopted. I knew some kids who ended up aging out."

"Did it happen quickly?" I tried to picture Madeline as a small child.

"I was fourteen."

Fourteen? What? I didn't know much about the foster system, but that seemed like a long time to be in it. Or had she been in an orphanage? My imagination went to a weird place where she asked for more gruel, and I shook my head.

"Your mother is still alive then?"

She shrugged. "I guess so. She stared at her lap. "I've been kind of trying to look her up."

My surprise must have shown on my face, though, because hers shut down like an airport in a thunderstorm. Why would she want to search for the woman who basically abandoned her? For that matter, how could anyone give her up like that? I couldn't even give up a tell at poker.

Her hunched shoulders widened the gap in her robe lapels, drawing my attention. My cock stirred, drawing her attention. "When do we have to check out?" she asked, her gaze on the tent forming in my robe.

"I paid the day rate for everyone today. We have the rooms until six o'clock, but there's still another retreat exercise today."

She cocked her head, her gaze shifting from my lap to my face. The freckles around her eyes stuck out against her creamy skin. She was one of those women who looked better without make-up. Or clothes.

"Do you really think this retreat thing is working out?" she asked.

That gap was just too tempting. She shivered as I traced her collarbone with my index finger. "Are you questioning my leadership, Madeline?"

"Not at all, *sir.*" She sighed. "What form of group torture is planned for today?"

"I'm not sure of the details, but it's some kind of assertiveness exercise."

She rolled her eyes. "Yeah, I don't think you need help with that."

"But maybe you do. And I know you changed the subject. If you want to talk about, uh, your past…" Most conversations I'd had with women about their "pasts" involved numbers, not notaries.

With a pat to my knee, she effectively and patronizingly closed the topic. "Don't worry your pretty little head about it." With a sly smile, she slid her hand further up my thigh.

"Believe me, my 'pretty little head' is not exactly 'worried'."

I leaned in to kiss her. She tasted like toothpaste, my guess that she hadn't touched the coffee validated. With one hand, I moved the laptop to her side on the couch. It had left her thighs warm, but I suspected she was even warmer in other places. She sighed softly into my mouth, deepening the kiss. If she was trying to distract me… well, it was working.

"Madeline," I whispered against her lips. "We can't—"

"Why not?"

My eyes squeezed closed as her hand wandered into my robe. "*Christ.* I wish we could, but we've got something at nine." And I wanted to take my time with her. With protection.

"I found something at nine o'clock already," she said archly, reminding me of our failed strategy at the dinner table two nights before.

My whole body was stiff with need, my blood coursing through my body but going nowhere near my heart.

"Believe me, when I take you it will not be with a clock ticking down."

With black spots starting to bounce in my vision, I regretfully peeled her hand away. My kiss was an apology, a promise, and a rain check.

"Shower with me?" she said shyly.

God, she wasn't making this easy for me. "You're too tempting." *I should get a medal for this.* "Rain check, definitely."

When I prodded her towards her bathroom and I headed for mine for separate showers, I found myself wishing for a violent thunderstorm. It was somewhat ironic that an hour later, I was wishing for lightning to strike me.

12

GAGE

"**Y**ou want me to what?"

Bobbie spread her smile around the group, but then it turned evil as she looked at me. "Stand still, and your employees get to take turns hitting you with this bat."

Oh yes, there was no doubt that she was enjoying this exercise.

I looked around at the people circling me in the conference room. Aaron was just grinning like a big doofus, Susan was whispering in a huddle with Madeline, and Nikhil looked like he was about to piss his stupid hipster skinny pants.

The rest of them were staring at the floor as though it held the answer to some kind of year-end bonus riddle. *Note to self: bonuses will be determined by performance in this game.*

I stood in the middle, like a sick game of Spin the Bottle. Or a piñata.

"Ideally, you will try to *not* hit Brian with the bat," Bobbie explained to everyone. "You are encouraged to use verbal communication to assert yourself and your concerns about your department. However, sometimes assertiveness can lead to aggression, so this—" She whipped it forward and bonked me on the head with the foam-covered baseball bat. "—is a kind of back-up. Use it or don't use it, but be clear about your objective."

My objective was going to be bludgeoning her to death with that stupid thing. Aaron's grin was creeping me out, until I remembered with a groan that he'd played baseball in college.

"Each person gets two minutes to air their thoughts, so think before you speak and consider what your priorities are. You can say a lot in two minutes."

I saw Madeline nodding in agreement out of the corner of my eye. I prayed that she would take the high road, as a professional communicator. Then I noticed her pulling the long sleeves of her blue sweater down over the pink marks on her wrists from where I'd tied them. *Oh shit.*

"We'll take a break for a few minutes now for people to brainstorm. Feel free to consult with your colleagues. Maybe you have shared problems or concerns, or issues that cross several departments. The purpose is to improve your communication and air your frustrations in a safe environment."

This was considered safe? For whom? Now not only was I going to be treated like a human piñata, but I also got to sit quietly in nervous anticipation. Bobbie absently whacked the bat against her thigh as the group splintered.

"I'll get you back for this, Roberta," I growled.

"It's just part of the retreat, Brian," she said innocently. "You signed off on this program two weeks ago."

I must have been mesmerized by Maddie's ass when I gave it the green light. There was no way in hell I would voluntarily submit to, well, submitting. I wasn't a very good bottom—I already knew that. Even at the end of a Nerf bat.

Bobbie bumped my elbow. "Chill out. Would you rather be blindfolded? Because I can arrange that."

A shudder went through me, and it wasn't a sexy one. "No."

Bobbie gathered the gauntlet together and reminded everyone that any contact had to remain below the neck and no junk punches. After my sister made a joke about not wanting me to lose the ability to create new employees, Madeline turned crimson and a few others sniggered.

At first it went smoothly, without violence. Susan brought up some very useful concerns she had about health benefits, including adding massage and physiotherapy.

"Okay, why?" I asked.

Susan gifted me with a toothy smile. It seemed even brighter against her lipstick. "The body is a temple, Brian."

Damn, how was I supposed to respond to that? "What, it's open to strangers leaving tributes? For all that you people call me God, I don't see a lot of fruit baskets at my door."

Susan's giggle grated on my ears. "Ergonomic studies show that computer workers, which most of us are—" She made a vague, all-encompassing gesture. "— will suffer more back and neck problems, which can lead to reduced productivity and increased health care costs for the employer. I learned about it at the last Human Resources course you sent me to."

Her mouth said Human Resources, but I had the feeling that the flirtatious sweep of her straight eyelashes was trying to convince me to part with a whole different kind of human resource. *No, thank you.*

"I'll consider it," I said dismissively.

"Brian, maybe that kind of disdain is what prevented Susan from speaking up before now," Bobbie pointed out. The rest of the group nodded, and Madeline put a sympathetic arm around Susan.

Apparently I was the bad guy. Was I that much of an asshole at the office?

We went through a few more concerns with staff members, none of which were accompanied by swings and all of which could have been dealt with in an internal memo, in my opinion. This "exercise" was starting to feel like a waste of time.

Nikhil babbled about client architecture and biometric profilers, to which I listened carefully and made mental notes. His nervous twitch turned the bat into a weapon for self-injury as he thwapped it against his knees over and over again.

Aaron was the only person who really tried for a home run, but I'd prepared myself for that. I'd get the fucker back another time. He wouldn't know where or when, but it would happen.

Unfortunately, he would have to follow up with an email with his issues, because I was practically spellbound by the flush creeping up Madeline's cheeks as she watched me fend off the bat. Her eyes widened and darkened with each successive hit, and her lush lower lip fell open a little when I grunted at one that fell across my belly.

Maybe my Madeline had a naughty streak to her. I couldn't wait to find out.

Aaron handed the bat to her, and she swung it low by her hip with a loose wrist. She was the last at bat, and the room fell silent. As she was the one who worked most closely with me, it was as though everyone suspected that her assertiveness would morph to aggression very, very quickly. I almost expected dollar bills to be changing hands behind her as bets mounted.

There was a sparkle in her eyes as she met my gaze, though. Hopefully I was the only person who recognized the signs of her arousal. But because I had shit timing, however, my cock swelled. I gave her a pointed look, then I glanced at the bat and downwards, hoping she might break the rules and junk punch me anyhow to deter my erection.

Let's face it—popping a boner while being walloped by my employees would be hell on my authority.

Madeline pointed the bat at me casually, like a cocky player pointing to their planned trajectory. Then she covered a lascivious smile with her free hand, pretending to cough. *Bad girl. When would I get my turn with the bat?* I wondered.

"Let's see. Mister Gage, I'm concerned that you work too hard," she began.

A chorus groans rose up, and I heard someone sounding suspiciously like Aaron yell out "wuss!"

"Um, okay?"

"You see," she continued, "I feel like I need to be in the office when you're in the office, so your ten-hour days turn into *my* twelve-hour days."

Oh. "I'm glad that you're not actually that inefficient."

The bat connected sharply with my right kneecap, buckling me for a moment.

"Is that aggression or punishment, Maddie?" Bobbie called out. "Remember, we're trying to use our words, not the weapon."

Madeline lowered the bat, tapping it against the floor thoughtfully. "Sometimes I also feel that you're too inconsiderate of people's lives, like you didn't even think about whether we could easily attend this weekend. You just assumed we would drop everything to come. And I don't think I was the only person afraid to speak up."

A murmur of agreement bounced off the walls.

I looked to Bobbie. "Is this assertiveness or the airing of grievances?"

"You push too hard," Madeline continued with a light bunt to my thigh, her bottom lip captured by her lucky teeth. "You expect too much."

"I don't expect anything of you that I don't expect of myself." She hit my forearm, and it connected with the bone more solidly than I'd expected.

"You expect too much," she repeated, blowing her a lock of hair out of her face. "That whole 'no excuses' thing…" She mocked my tone, triggering another wave of snickers and one random "you go, girl!"

I held up my hands and looked to Bobbie, who was just watching in amusement. She was no fucking help whatsoever.

Maddie's eyes were blazing at me as my gaze returned to her. "Sometimes excuses are reasons, Mister Gage—and good ones. Everything doesn't fit into your little box. You can't control everything, and you sure as hell can't control me!"

She finished with a loud and solid second-base hit to my hip. The room was frozen as she dropped the bat. Her chest was heaving, but she wasn't winded.

Emotion wracked her body as she turned away from me and the rest of her co-workers. I couldn't tell if she was embarrassed, angry, remorseful, or all of the above. But I couldn't fault her honesty, not when that was the purpose of the exercise. Nobody dared speak or move, even Bobbie—until I began slowly clapping.

Swallowing my own feelings of shock and umbrage, I held up my hands and gave a pointed nod to everyone in the room to encourage them to applaud as well.

"G-g-good job, Maddie," Bobbie stammered. "Great, uh, communicating."

Madeline put her hands to her face, still facing the wall. The tips of her ears were bright pink, and her shoulders rose and fell as she struggled to recover her, well, whatever.

Her words echoed in my head, rattling around until they dented my pride and patience. I wasn't that controlling, was I? I just wanted her to try hard, to succeed and to be confident. Was that so wrong?

"Now it's time for your last exercise—primal screaming."

What the fu—?

Bobbie handed out pairs of foam earplugs.

"Why the hell couldn't I get these before?" I grumbled.

"Because then you wouldn't have listened to your staff."

The problem was that I'd been listening to my *staff* a

little too much that weekend. I was irritated that this retreat did not work out as planned. Granted, there were elements of the weekend that worked out better, such tonguing Maddie into a spine-melting climax, but I did not achieve my professional objectives. *That* bothered me to no end.

Bobbie slipped her phone out of her pocket and checked it with a nod. "I want you to think about every-thing that drives you crazy about work. People, tasks, computers, anything that you feel you can't control. And then take a deep breath, and let out that emotion in one long, loud scream—straight from the heart. Now, I've been asked by the kitchen that you not stay in here for your primal screaming. I encourage you all to spread out around the property so you can find privacy. Don't worry, everyone has been warned, and nobody's going to call 911 on you," my sister joked.

People filed out the door, leaving her and Aaron, Madeline and myself. Aaron winked at Bobbie, and she just smirked at me as I rolled my eyes and tugged Made-line behind me.

"What the hell was that?" I asked as we stepped out a side door, bypassing a few lodge employees on a smoke break.

Her gaze was on her feet as we walked down a path behind the hotel. "Honest communication."

I stopped us at a ridge of tall lodgepole pines, over-looking a steep drop down the mountainside. Dead, golden needles carpeted the ground off the trail, old tree roots certainly hidden beneath. If we screamed here—which was an inane exercise, I thought—our voices would drop over the edge into the peaceful valley below.

My hand went to Madeline's chin to pull her gaze

up to me. The corners of her lips quirked a little, and there was a hint of a smile in her eyes. If she was truly angry with me, it had faded. This girl kept turning me upside down. Fit into my little box? Ha! I'd like to fit into her little bo—

She put her hand on my mouth as I let out a harsh sigh and bit back my thoughts. "Time to scream, *sir*."

I narrowed my eyes at her. "We're not done with this, Madeline."

"I'm sure we're not." She pulled away from me, put in her earplugs, and turned toward the ridgeline.

After watching her take several deep breaths in preparation, but no sounds coming out of her mouth, I was worried she was about to hyperventilate. Her shoulders sagged as I came up behind her and touched her back.

She swore. "I'm not good at screaming. I don't like to yell like that."

I wondered how much screaming she'd done as a child—a lonely, abandoned, scared little girl. My stomach twisted at the thought. I understood her reluctance; I didn't like screaming either. It seemed so…out of control.

My hand slipped into hers. "I'll make you a deal," I said. She tilted her head at me, while I squeezed her fingers together. "Instead of a 'primal scream,' pretend you're coming harder than you've ever come before."

The wind lifted her hair off her burning cheeks as she stared at me. "What?"

I leaned in so she could hear me through the earplugs. I sure as hell didn't want anyone else overhearing. "Scream like I'm plunging my rock hard cock into you. Scream like you are *so* wet and *so* hot you'll die if I don't touch you. Like I have you tied down, spread-eagled and blindfolded, your body on display and mine to take however and whenever I want—and I've already been eating you out for hours. You can't take any more. Imagine that my dick is stretching your pussy to the point of pain and bottoming out deeper than anyone has ever been inside you." Inwardly I winced at the thought of anyone else inside her, regardless.

Her pupils dilated at my words. If I touched her through her yoga pants right then, she might go off like a rocket. It was so tempting…

I brushed my lips against hers, drawing more feelings out of her. I wanted to make her squirm, wanted her to be so turned on that she might even find a true release as she let it all out. Keenly, I wished I could control *all* her orgasms.

"Scream like you've never come before, and your body and soul are completely mine."

Now she almost *was* hyperventilating, and I moved my palms to her chest. It just so happened that her tits were in the way; I couldn't help that. I kissed her again, deep and slow, my thumbs brushing against her raised nipples. She shuddered and gasped into my mouth.

"Gage! Fuck!"

"Exactly, baby."

Dropping my hands, I stepped back a little and turned her toward the trees. I stood close to her but a little behind, so she wouldn't be puncturing my eardrums. Her chest rose and fell, her eyes screwed shut against the magnificent scenery.

"Let it go." I drew my thumb up the back seam of her tight pants, deeply tracing her crack from her thighs to her sacrum. In response, she inhaled sharply then filled her lungs completely, ready to scream.

As she opened her mouth, her arm shot back and she grabbed me through my pants—hard.

"Aaaaaaaaaaaaaahhhhhhhhhhhhhhhhh!

13

MADDIE

I tried not to laugh at the pained, offended look on Gage's face as we returned to our suite. Yeah, I knew that what I did was stupid, but it was spontaneous. Really, he'd brought it on himself for trying to manipulate me.

He wanted me to commit to the exercise, right? Well, I committed.

He threw a glare over his shoulder at me when we arrived at our door, and he reached in his pocket for his keycard. I blinked at him, oh so innocently, and then did stupid thing number two.

"So, how do you think the *staff retreat* went?" I asked.

He shoved open the door. Only a few steps after I followed him in, he spun me around and hauled me up against the closing door.

With his thigh wedged between my legs and his nose nudging mine, he flattened his hands around my skull above my ears. I was held completely still by the strength of his body and his gaze. *Oh shit.* Maybe I had gone too far in teasing him.

"Too soon?" I offered him a timid smile.

His response was to lower his mouth to mine, consuming me in a toe-curling kiss. When he thrust against me, boosting me up so I was off-balance and riding his leg, it was possible that my toes really did curl.

"Tell me, Madeline, when my assertiveness becomes aggression."

He slanted his mouth forcefully over mine until my teeth bit into my lips, and then he licked any soreness away with surprising tenderness. The pressure he was putting on my aching core made me dizzy, and far too close to actually coming for my comfort.

That silly primal scream seemed to bring out the primitive in us, for sure. With a kiss he swallowed his own name as I tried to cry it out, and I clung to his shoulders for security.

The passion in his kiss was almost frighteningly fierce. I'd shown my trust in him the night before, but he still unnerved me at every turn. Was I crazy for thinking about getting involved with this man? Even if he wasn't my boss, he was, well, bossy. But I couldn't help the shiver that ran up the back of my knees at the thought of him commanding me to come, and how helpless I was against his dominance.

In every way, this was a bad idea.

I was his assistant. I was nearly ten years younger than him. I flew by the seat of my pants while he probably organized his sock drawer. He was rich and I was, well, not. If this was a smutty book he'd be pulling out a contract and introducing me to his playroom.

Yeah, right. I was a recent college graduate too, and even I knew better than to sign anything like that without a lawyer. Then again, that chick also managed to get through college without a computer—which made the book fantasy, not fiction.

The twirling sensation in the pit of my stomach wove through my spine like a needle and thread. His hands moved from my head to under my arms and clamped on the back of my neck like a collar. I tried to wrench my head back to catch my breath, but I was flat against the door. I jerked my head to the right, and his lips landed on my ear.

"Gage, stop! Red light! *Red light!*"

Like a switch had been flipped, he lowered me to the floor gently and released me. I missed his arms around me, but savored the breathing room. My heart thumped like a lab rat at the sight of a white coat, and slowly my feet recognized the floor underneath them. Brian Gage didn't need to do much to unsettle me—or make me his fucking slave.

It should have scared me how ready I was to throw my inhibitions out, to let him do anything and everything to me. Like I'd told him, I'd try anything once. Well, except autoerotic asphyxiation. I wasn't too crazy about that idea. I rubbed at my throat, still feeling his touch there.

He stumbled back until he hit the couch, breathing heavily. His gaze was square on my trembling lips, and he swiped the back of his hand over his own.

"Jesus, Madeline. What you do to me…" He shook his head, at a loss for words.

Me? What I did to him?

"Ditto." I glanced over to my bedroom. "Uh, we should pack. Are we heading home soon?"

He'd insisted that I ride with him. At the time, the idea made me nervous. Now it excited me—and made me nervous. *Oh god. Four hours in the car with him—alone, in that fucking sexy car. Maybe I should try to get a ride with Susan,* I thought to myself.

He exhaled heavily then stood straight and tall, calm and collected—if not totally cool. His mouth twisted as he glanced down at the noticeable bulge at the front of his slacks.

"Yes, go ahead and pack up. We'll have a quick roundtable discussion downstairs with lunch." As I stepped toward my room, he said, "Don't worry about packing for me."

"I wasn't going to! You can handle your own dirty underwear, sir."

When I looked back he was trying to discreetly adjust himself, muttering something about his dirty underwear that I didn't quite catch—and wasn't about to investigate. Something told me I'd already pushed my luck enough today poking the bear.

I closed the bedroom door just as he looked up at me. I'd never seen that expression on his face before—confused, almost bereft, and downright voracious. He looked like a starving man in front of a steak dinner, but finding it behind glass.

Well, I thought as I stuffed my own soiled panties into the front pocket of my suitcase, *glass wasn't that hard to break*. You just had to be careful not to get all sliced up in the process.

A second, completely unnecessary hot shower and an hour later, I rolled my bag down to the lobby. Bobbie waggled her fingers at me and, unlike upon arrival, this time I smiled at her easily across the front desk.

"It was so nice to meet you!" she gushed.

I shook her hand with genuine pleasure. We'd gotten

along the night before like the proverbial house on fire, at least before I returned to the hotel and her big brother practically set me *on* fire. The way she grinned reminded me of Gage, and the memory of his talented lips made me blush.

"I'll be coming to town more often on my off week- ends to, uh, get out and see stuff," she said, her own cheeks darkening.

"You mean see Aaron and get off," I needled her. Two glasses of red wine the night before and we had turned into over-sharing goofballs. Thankfully I didn't have much to over-share… then. Now I would have to watch myself around her a little. She was a few years older than me but I saw the potential for a friendship, which pleased me. It also made me nervous, as it was one more way to be entangled in Gage's life.

"You have a wicked swing." She laughed and mimicked my stance with the foam bat. "You want to take it back to the office with you?"

A snort escaped me. "Yeah, I don't see that going over well. What was it like growing up with him?" I had a hard time imagining him as a kid. A brooding emo adolescent, maybe, but not as a small child.

"When I was about twelve I called him Keyser Söze for almost a whole year." I burst out laughing at her reference to a mysterious fictional titan of tyranny. She spread her hands out on the desk. "No, I'm serious. It drove him up the wall."

"I'll bet." We exchanged numbers, and she promised she'd call me for coffee when she was next in town. I wouldn't expect it and I wouldn't hold her to it; but, as I wheeled my suitcase over to the conference center, I realized that I hoped she'd be in touch.

I was the last one to arrive, missing lunch, since my bathroom indulgence made me later than I'd planned. Hovering at the back, I tried to ignore Gage's long pause and X-ray vision.

"As I was saying, since we're all here now—"

My eyes rolled up so fast I almost got vertigo. Seriously? If he didn't want me to take a second shower, he shouldn't have gotten me so... dirty.

"It's been pointed out to me," Gage continued, "that a group assessment of this weekend is not the most expedient idea. What I will do, then, is compile a list of questions about the retreat and your experiences here, then distribute it to you at the office. You are free to print out your answers instead of email, if you want to stay anonymous."

Thank god, I thought. Despite the fact I would probably end up in charge of this, at least Gage was starting to understand that keeping the staff happy meant not putting them on the spot all the time and expecting spotlessness. There were a few people who refused to make eye contact with him as he glanced around the room.

"If you have any further suggestions on how to improve our productivity and creativity, I'm open to hearing them. Each one of you is valuable to this company, but together we are worth a fortune."

Not bad. He looked to me for help with a big finish, to which I shrugged. I was better at bullshitting onto a keyboard, not verbally. Well, okay, maybe a little.

Gage cleared his throat and stepped forward, trying to look casual as he leaned against a table. "In any case, thank you for coming this weekend," he said in a surprisingly humble tone. "I know that you all have other things you'd rather be doing." Again he looked over at me, but again I was helpless—and blushing at the knowledge that he would probably rather be doing *me* this weekend. "I appreciate your commitment."

The room was silent.

"And you have tomorrow off," he added.

The room was no longer silent. There were a few tepid cheers, but only Aaron had the balls to clap the boss on the back in thanks. As the room emptied and Gage's lips pressed together in a flat line, I felt a little sad.

If he just relaxed a little, he'd probably get to know his staff better, and they'd work harder for him. All for one and one for all, that kind of thing. Right now Gage's benevolent dictatorship was limiting his reach and ability to connect with his team—and me, if I was honest.

My attraction to my boss had been physical at first, and who could blame me? Week by week, I'd started to fall for his intelligence and dry humor as well. He had high expectations, but that was because he actually thought the best of people's abilities to achieve them. He had a lot of confidence in us, in me—way more than I did. That's why I felt so rotten when I disappointed him.

While shrugging his coat on, he walked over to where I leaned against the wall. When he looked at me, I didn't see the fire that I'd grown accustomed to that weekend, only a kind of defeated look. It broke my heart.

Brian Gage had so much to give, if only he'd stop taking.

With only the two of us left in the room, I slipped my hand into his. Susan had already left, but I'd resigned myself to the prospect of driving home with Gage anyhow. He glanced out the open doorway to the empty hall, then bent down to kiss me.

"Thanks," he murmured against my lips.

"No problem, sir."

The way our lips curved against each other in smiles felt strange, but not bad, like kissing with braces.

He sighed then gallantly grabbed my suitcase. "Shall we?"

It was more than just the question of hitting the road. Invested in it were also the questions of "Can we date now? Do you want to try to be together? Do you want me like I want you? Can we manage to be boss and employee and lovers at the same time, without fucking everything up?" It was a lot to take in with two little words.

Why did the shortest statements always seem to hold the heaviest meaning?

Gage flinched in surprise as I stood on my tippy toes and kissed his cheek. I reveled in the feel of his coal-black scruff against my tender lips, since he hadn't shaved that morning.

With his leather bomber jacket on and the shadow on his jaw, he looked like an ordinary man—a ridiculously handsome, virile, driven, intense ordinary man. I had my suspicions that he was, in fact, extraordinary. And I couldn't wait to find out.

After a quick goodbye to Bobbie and thanks to her staff, we made our way out to his sexy, low-slung car. As we pulled away from the lodge and headed to the curvy ribbon of road going down the mountain he visibly relaxed, sinking into the leather seat with a sigh.

"Mister Gage, have you ever had road head?"

14

GAGE

Madeline Jones should come with a warning label: *Do not operate heavy machinery while under the influence.* My hands tightened on the leather-wrapped steering wheel.

After a pause, I replied easily, "Yes, I have had road head, Madeline."

"Oh."

"Have you?"

"It's a little harder for women," she said. "Logistically speaking."

I tilted my head to consider the angle, the seat, the center console, and figured she was right. And then shifted in my seat, cursing my stupidly responsive dick. "I meant, have you given, not received."

"Oh."

I didn't have to look over again to tell that she was blushing. But she didn't answer the question, and I didn't press her. Instead we decided to try working.

I'd dictated to her for the first hour, all of which of course she rearranged and paraphrased and repeated back to me, as she usually did. The edge of her laptop dug into her belly as she tried to work in the low-slung seat, and she had to hold her elbows at a strange angle in order to type.

On my right side, her hair bobbed back in forth like a candle's flame as she worked, then asked me a question, and continued. It was nice to have company for the drive, and in my peripheral vision I caught the smiles she thought she was so secretly aiming my way.

"Music?" I asked.

She glanced at my phone in the cup holder. "Anything good on there?"

When she reached for it I wrapped my hand around her wrist, stopping her. Call me paranoid, but I didn't let anyone touch my phone except me. My whole life was on that thing. She inhaled sharply, but didn't jerk her hand back right away. The slim bones of her wrist felt birdlike in my grasp.

"What do you like?" I asked, clearing my throat and peeling my fingers free. "I've got lots of stuff."

She shook back her hair and pressed her fist to her chest. "I totally heart Scandinavian death metal."

Quickly I brought the car back under control before it veered into the other lane. "Uh, I don't have that."

Her laughter filled the small space, and her hand drifted over to touch mine on the wheel. "I'm just joking."

This time I took my vision off the road just long enough to see her trying in vain to suppress her giggle. The smug twinkle in her eye made me chuckle with her.

"I almost had you," she said.

"Yeah, you're an expert in persuasion, remember?"

"Not always," she reminded me. She bent over the phone, her fingers scrolling through playlists. "Jazz?"

I shrugged, wrinkling my nose automatically. "Anything newer?" She named a few bands I'd never heard, making me feel unbelievably old and uncool. "Okay, not that new."

"You want retro as in my parents' CDs or retro as in those big record things?" she teased me.

"Watch it, Madeline. I'm not a hundred years older than you."

"Classical?" she suggested.

I raised an eyebrow at her. "You *want* me to fall asleep at the wheel?"

"Point taken." *Scroll scroll.* "How about the Beatles? Hey, did you ever see them in concert?"

She giggled when I growled at her.

By the time the fool was on the hill, she'd started to drift off. The album ended, and without shuffle turned on, silence filled the car again. Within moments of peaceful stillness and the rhythmic sound of the tires slapping the highway, she was out like a light. I was jealous, but couldn't hold it against her.

For a retreat weekend, I didn't feel very refreshed. In fact, I felt exhausted.

It was surprisingly hard work resisting my own desires all weekend. I'd never had to work so hard at it before. Never had I felt so impulsive or so close to being out of control—and all over a woman.

But something in my chest twisted as I looked over at Madeline, and over the previous forty-eight hours I'd accepted that I wanted her. I wanted her, and I was going to have her—any way she would let me. It was a good thing I was an excellent multi-tasker.

In the quiet car, with her breathing quietly beside me, it seemed like as good a time as any to fantasize about her. I imagined her in my shower, on my kitchen island...

The tires on the cement made a rhythmic white noise, though muffled by solid German engineering. My eyelids felt heavier as we bore down the road. After the third time I found myself shifting in my seat to stay awake, I decided to pull over at the nearest rest stop.

She woke as I stopped at the far edge of a picnic area, bereft of cars.

"Do we need gas or something?" She straightened her legs, her toes stretching underneath the glove compartment.

I swiveled in my seat toward her. "Are we going to do this?"

"Do what?" She peered at me. "Road head?" she squeaked.

"No." I smiled. She may not like pink, but her blush was very becoming. There were several places on her body I yearned to see all rosy and warm. "Though I would definitely take a rain check on it, if you're offering."

"I thought *you* were offering," she joked.

"Touché."

"I wish."

With a gentle click I undid her seatbelt. "There's always making out."

Her gaze was riveted to me, curious and open and she let me twist my hands in either side of her open coat. I pulled her toward me, thrilling at her small gasp.

"Making out? How old school of you, sir."

"Tell me you don't want this," I said.

She looked me straight in the eye and repeated, "You don't want this."

"Liar."

I kissed her. Each time I kissed her I fell further under her spell. My body had been in a constant state of tension all weekend, and my soul wasn't far behind. She kissed me back, but hesitantly at first. Her lips drifted across mine in the lightest of touches. Was she unsure?

When I drew back a little, she glared down at the console between us, and I realized that her timidity was due to the obstacle in the car, not in her mind. Hauling her to my lap was a great idea in theory, but impractical unless she wanted to almost sit on the steering wheel.

I opened the car door and got out. She watched me as I walked around the front of the car. Her eyes were still on me when I opened her door.

"Back seat. Now."

She raised a delicate eyebrow at me, but the corner of her mouth also perked up. "I'm sorry?"

Oh right, the magic word. "*Please.*" This is why I'd hired her, after all. I wasn't always the best communicator.

I stepped back to offer her assistance. When she took it, the electric feel of her skin against mine unnerved me, and like an idiot I dropped her hand. She climbed out of the car and closed the door behind her, then leaned against it.

"Are you sure this is a good idea?" she asked.

I rubbed the back of my neck. "I don't know. What are we doing?"

"Dating?" she guessed. "But what about work?"

I tilted my head as I considered it. "What about it?"

"Do you think we can still work together and see

each other? I mean—you *are* my boss. Everyone probably already thinks we're sleeping together since we
shared a suite this weekend." She put her fists on her
hips. "Really, Gage, that wasn't the smart—"

I covered her mouth with my hand. "Let it go. As for
the office, are you going to charge with me sexual
harassment if I do this?"

Her eyes widened when I reached inside her coat
with my other hand and palmed her breast. Her nipple
hardened underneath her sweater and bra. Wordlessly
she straightened, reaching up to tug my hand away from
her face.

"Only if you do that *at* the office."

"I want you." I simply could not be blunter. "What
do *you* want?"

"A raise?"

I doubted that she meant my own pulsating erection.
My hands met at the small of her back; she was trapped
between my body and the car behind her.

"Are we negotiating?"

She shook her head, her cinnamon-colored curls
floating around her shoulders. "I am not trading sexual
favors for money," she informed me. Her tone was extra-
ordinarily prim, considering the fact that you could
barely get a piece of paper between us.

I grinned. "I don't want your money."

"What? No, I meant—ugh!" She reached up to
smack me on the side of my arm.

"Madeline, as you noted earlier this morning with
the assistance of a foam bat, I am very good at putting
things into boxes. I'm sure we can successfully compartmentalize our relationship outside the office and still
perform at work."

She blinked up at me, her eyes shining. "You had me at 'compartmentalize.'"

"Smart ass."

My mouth covered her smile as I pressed her back against the car. Immediately she welcomed me inside, the tip of her tongue touching mine in a long, slow kiss —the kind that kneecapped you like a gangster. It was a good thing I could brace myself against the car, because her taste, her smell, the feel of her body were all threatening to fell me.

I'd never dated a lot, much to my mother's—and her friends'—disappointment. In college I was a geek playing video games, and when I started making money I wanted to stay in control. That meant control of everything, including my libido.

Maddie's hands skimmed down my back to the hem of my leather jacket. Her fingers traced along the waistband of my pants, making my skin crawl in the best possible way.

"Back seat?" she whispered against my lips.

I hadn't planned to *take* her in the back seat, only... borrow her a little, make out like lust-ridden teenagers. Looking around, I saw a lonely picnic table, a trash can designed to keep out wildlife, and a lot of trees. There was nobody around...

"What would we do there?" I had ideas of my own, but wanted to hear hers. It was still a fairly sleek car, not exactly a station wagon.

She tugged my head down, her mouth close to my ear. "I still haven't gotten my hands on you yet," she said. *Oh god.*

"No, you haven't."

"I bet you I can make you come without even touching you."

Something in my spine rattled. "Miss Jones, you can be very persuasive."

"That's why you hired me."

"Has anyone ever called you 'spunky'?"

She squinted, her hands stilling maddeningly on my fly. "Maddie, Madeline, Mad, Kid, Maggie, and Red," Her hand moved further down the front of my pants. "But no Spunky… yet."

"Smart ass," I said again with a groan, inwardly cursing as an SUV pulled up about twenty feet away. The heat of her body was driving me insane. I wanted to be inside it. But it would have to wait.

"You're being repetitive." She tsked.

A young couple fell out of the nearby vehicle, catching my attention. The woman then pried a crying toddler out and took it over to the grass. With a sinking heart, I shook my head and reconsidered my plan. "No back seat."

"Awwww."

Her pout utterly disarmed me. Then she shocked me a little with her next words.

"You're right. I think we need to back up a bit."

Her words clogged my ears, not quite making it to my brain. Normally, when I wanted something I went for it—all in, no excuses.

Conversely, Madeline's spontaneity and feistiness belied a casual, noncommittal attitude, which stuck in my throat even more. I wanted her to give me all of herself, or at least one hundred percent of whatever portion she was offering.

"Back up? Madeline, I've already tied you up and

made you come like a freight train," I reminded her in a low voice.

Her face went bright pink with embarrassment. Her forehead bonked on my chest, her hands still on my waist. "Ugh, I know," she muttered. The memory made me dizzy, distracting me briefly. The arch of her back, the rope on her wrists, the succulent taste of her—*oh yeah*.

"What do you want?" I asked her again, deadly serious. I tilted her chin up, not letting her hide while I tried to ignore the aching bulge in my pants. It got more painful when she pressed her knuckles against it.

She kissed the left corner of my mouth. "I want you to want me." Then she kissed the right corner. "I want to be wanted, just for me."

"I do," I replied shakily. Actually, it alarmed me how much I desired her. It threatened to make me lose control, to unman me. Just telling her that gave her power over me that I wasn't entirely comfortable with.

The screeching of the nearby child and the white noise of the cars on the highway numbed my ears. Madeline took up the entirety of my vision; everything else around us was blurry and unimportant. I only knew the sun was shining because of the way it lit up her hair like a fiery halo.

But when I gazed into her eyes, I realized that her need wasn't just about lust. There was a shadow of insecurity, of uncertainty about what or who she was. Knowing now that she was adopted, I tried to remember what she had said about her birth mother. The memory, despite it being so recent, slipped through my synapses like a computer worm.

Her hands slid up between us to briefly cup each

side of my neck. "So let's go home, and then tomorrow —" She smiled lazily. "—Or the next day, since my boss gave me the day off, we go to work. We just don't let work get in the way."

"You mean *us* get in the way of work."

"Either way. We'll give it a shot." She shrugged.

Her confidence overwhelmed me.

15

MADDIE

Three weeks after the mountain retreat, Gage and I had managed to separate our work and personal lives so successfully that we were acting like we were in high school and sneaking around like Romeo and Juliet.

We'd flirted relentlessly, had lunch together more days than not, dinner a handful of times, and logged a few epically hot make-out sessions on the leather couch in the corner of his office after everyone had gone home. For all that I complained at the retreat about working long hours, it seemed less of a hardship when my boss's exacting hands and lips were on me.

But we still hadn't gone any further than second base, leaving me perpetually hot and frustrated. Honestly, I wasn't sure who I was getting more attached to—Gage or my battery-operated boyfriend.

At my, um, employer's request, I began testing *Happit* on my phone. In the past week, I'd successfully scheduled my self-love sessions into a routine. And I'd been on time for work—mostly.

"Did Nikhil see us leave together last night?" I asked

Gage one morning, my hands clutching the side of his door tightly.

I wasn't sleeping with the boss—yet, but I still didn't want to have a reputation. We'd spent too long talking at the end of the day, then even more time on the couch not talking. By the time we left, my stomach was growling and I was breathless from kissing. I hadn't noticed that Nikhil was still there as well, until he waved as we passed his open office door.

Gage beckoned me to his desk.

I glanced behind me, but nobody was there. *Phew.* Wait, why was I sighing in relief? I could walk into my employer's office without guilt or shame, couldn't I? For god's sakes, my desk was right outside the door! Rolling my eyes at myself, I went up to his desk, careful not to put my hands down and smudge the freshly cleaned glass.

He crooked his finger again, a smirk toying with his beautiful, addictive lips. Damn those lips. I was powerless against them.

"Well? Did he?" I rounded the desk to where he sat in his big cushy chair like a real billionaire. Someday I had plans for him and me and that chair.

So much for stealth dating. Everyone probably heard my loud squeak as he tugged me on to his lap, my arms flailing as the chair back reclined underneath us.

"What are you doing?" I scrambled to get off him, but his arms were wrapped around me like iron bands. "Someone might see us."

"Who cares?"

"I care! Jesus, Gage. I thought you wanted to compartmentalize! You know, no 'us' at work?"

We both glanced over at the couch that we'd been entwined on the evening before, necking like teenagers.

"I think that ship has sailed," he said, his fingers walking up my spine and his lips on my neck.

"Hmph." I clambered off, almost falling on the ground in my effort to get away his Kryptonite mouth.

His smile was ten kinds of amused as he watched me adjust my skirt. "What, do you want to meet under the bleachers after school instead? Should I put a note in your locker?"

"I just thought we were backing up a bit."

"No, Madeline, we're just going slow. Too slow," he added with a scowl. "By the way, I want to expand your job description."

"To what?" I eyed him suspiciously.

"I'd like you to start coordinating all the office communication."

"I thought I was only supposed to write your letters?"

"It was clear to me from the retreat that good communication is important for the company's success, internally as well as externally."

"But…" I didn't know what to say. Was it a promotion? I narrowed my eyes at him. "Is this a way to give me a raise so I'll owe you sexual favors?"

He held up his hands. "No, not at all. I just know that you can handle more responsibility."

I snorted. "Yeah, sucking you off under your desk is a huge responsibility, Gage." Which I had not yet done, regardless.

His glare was truly frightening, and not for the first time I cursed my impudent tongue. "Talk like that again, and I'll blister your beautiful ass."

Shocked into silence, my gaze flew to the floor. The way my belly flipped at his words startled me, but it was a sensation I was getting used to. Gage made me want to try all sorts of things; he already had. I dreamt sometimes about his rope tricks at the lodge and how he'd unraveled me.

"Come here," he ordered. My feet moved before my brain did. When I was close enough, he grabbed my hand. "Look at me, Madeline."

I looked up. He was totally serious, and refrained from pulling me onto his lap again. Instead, he kissed my knuckles but still kept me at arm's length.

"I wouldn't ask you to do it if I didn't have full confidence in your abilities. You are smart and capable. It's time for you to recognize that and take some control over your life."

I was horrified to find my eyes filling up, and tried to blink it back. My throat was tight. "Ironic advice from a man who just threatened to spank me."

"That was a promise, not a threat. I respect you, and I expect the same consideration."

"How does—" I whipped my head around, but there was still no activity in the outer office area, so hopefully nobody listening to us. "How is spanking me respectful, *sir*?" I hissed. My insides fluttered, and I realized I would have to change my panties at lunchtime—again. I had begun keeping extra in my desk.

"Oh, it's not," he agreed grimly. "It's a last resort. But I imagine you would respect me more for punishing you for your smart mouth if said smart mouth is running yourself down."

My mouth fell open as I backtracked over his words again. "God, no wonder you need me to communicate for you." Was that supposed to be some kind of compliment?

"Exactly."

I wanted to bang my head against his desk. Or bang him. The two impulses were constantly at war within me these days. "I need to get back to work," I said.

"By all means." He dropped my hand after nipping the knuckle on my middle finger. "I've already sent an email to Susan about changing your job title and official description."

Wonderful.

The rest of the week dragged, and the next one after that. Susan was only too happy to dump a ton of personnel information on me so that I could get to know every staff member on paper, for the purposes of effective internal communication.

And now I was being copied on almost every single email that went around the office, including banal stuff. In fact, Gage pointed to the banal stuff as what I could work on streamlining within the system.

My desk was a mess, my inbox was exploding, and the only time I spent on Gage's couch was for a catnap on Thursday at lunchtime. He didn't even join me, just sat there in bemusement at his desk, working through lunch and probably watching me sleep. It might have been creepy if he hadn't also put a blanket over me and made sure nobody came into his office and disturbed me.

Because it never rained but it poured, in addition I was starting to get somewhere in my search for my birth mother. Unfortunately, Jones was a pretty common last name, so I'd found at least a dozen people in adoption registries online and through correctional services that had the same name as my mother. Now all this extra work was distracting me from my goal, which was very frustrating.

I was used to letting things like work and school float around me, like I was dragging my hand in a lake while sitting in a canoe. Now Gage had handed me the oars and demanded I row. By Friday afternoon, I was absolutely, one thousand percent ready for the weekend.

"Maddie!"

I looked up blearily from my screen to see Bobbie's smile and shock of black hair. My mouth curved involuntarily. "Hi! Have you got the weekend off again?"

We'd traded a few emails and text messages, mostly on a superficial level. One quick coffee while she was in town the weekend before last was the only face time we'd managed, but I was enjoying getting to know her.

"Yep." She looked thoughtful. "I probably won't come as often when the snow hits, so I'm making it count now."

"I'm sure Aaron appreciates it," I said mischievously. Then I glanced back at the closed office door behind me. "Does Gage know you're here?"

"Nope, and let's keep it that way if possible. I don't want to hear the lectures about how a four-hour drive is too far for a 'booty call.' I just came to pick Aaron up."

I couldn't help laughing, imagining Gage's reluctance to believe that his little sister and his best friend were capable of hooking up. I could already see the worried scowl on his face and the deep crease above the dark slash of his eyebrows. That line on his forehead had been deepening all week.

"Your secret is safe with me. How's it going with you guys?"

"Amazing." She sighed, clasping her hand over her heart dramatically. "I haven't had a lot of luck with guys before. I've dated too many dickheads. Maybe it's because I knew Aaron before, but we're getting along like a…"

"House on fire?"

"Couple of horny minks."

"TMI, Bobbie!"

We giggled together then hushed when we heard movement behind Gage's door.

"How's it going with big bro?" she whispered to me, jabbing her thumb in his general direction.

"He gave me a promotion. I think." I still wasn't sure if he was just spanking me with extra work, euphemistically speaking.

Bobbie raised her eyebrow in an eerily similar manner to her brother. "I guess that's one way to get a *raise* out of him." Then she jerked her pelvis forward and made a crude gesture. I almost choked in embarrassment.

"It's not like that," I protested, my face burning. It was almost true.

"Sure it's not." She must have seen my face fall, because she quickly said, "I'm just teasing. Actually, I think you're good for him. You got him to take the stick out of his ass."

I had? He was still a little too rigid and had high expectations, but I also loved getting to know the man who texted me silly jokes and had ordered my lunch all week. And he remembered to get my salad dressing on the side. I supposed from his sister's perspective, Gage was mellowing.

She didn't see the heat in his eyes when he looked at me. That heat threatened to spark into a raging fire soon. I knew there was a chance I'd get singed, so I'd been keeping some distance and myself protectively doused. Well, okay, my dampness seemed to be pretty constant with Gage around, looking at me all sexy-like.

"Hmmm. Taking stuff out of his ass is more of a fifth date thing, actually," I joked. "We've only been on four." *Officially*.

Bobbie clapped a hand over her loud snort, sending us both into giggles again. Her eyes danced with merriment. "TMI! *TMI!*" she echoed my earlier protest. We both froze, tamping down our laughter when we heard louder movements in Gage's office. "I'm out," she whispered. "Coffee Sunday before I head back?"

I nodded. "Text me."

A smile lingered on my face even twenty minutes later, when Gage poked his head out his door to find me. "You almost done for the day?"

Hell, yeah! I was done for the *week*. Almost… "Just about. Have you got a second?"

"For you, I have a whole minute." He flashed white teeth at me wolfishly and lured me into his lair.

Leaving my heels abandoned under my desk, I padded into his office in my stocking feet and locked the door behind me. The sound of the click made him whirl around in surprise.

"Miss Jones, whatever are you doing?" he asked archly.

"It's time for a performance review, sir." I'd been

thinking about what he said about taking control over my life. I had a tendency to be spontaneous, to act first and think later. This was one of those times. "Since you threw me in the deep end, I'd like to show you what I've learned about effective internal communication."

MADDIE

He stared at me, his expression dubious. "Effective internal communication?" he repeated slowly.

"Remember when I said I could make you come without touching you?"

Now his expression was just downright incredulous —and immediately turned on. His pupils were dilating, I saw as I stepped closer to him. Those damn fiendish lips parted, his breath shaky as it moved over them. I didn't have to look down to know that he was probably growing harder in his designer wool pants.

With a lot more bravado than I felt inside, I began unbuttoning his shirt. He remained still as a statue, as though afraid of spooking me.

"I don't think you can do it," he finally said as I slipped the last button through and opened his shirt.

He was probably right. It was an impulsive, stupidly provocative thing for me to promise on the drive back from the mountains, and I was glad he hadn't taken me up on it at the time. I surely would have failed. The thought lingered in my head like a sinus infection, though, and I'd spent a little time at night reading online ways to talk dirty.

Because Brian Gage made me want to be dirty.

My fingers moved to the fastening at his waist, until his hands wrapped around mine to stop me and hold me back.

God, he had a gorgeous body. For someone who sat behind a desk ten hours a day, he sure didn't look it. Over lunch one day he'd told me that he got up early— like dark o'clock early—to work out, which at the time I thought was just insane. Why give up sleep to sweat? But now I could see the results, and would wholeheartedly encourage his healthy routine.

He was lean without being skinny, built without being bulky, and the faintly olive tone of his skin made the ridges of his abdominal muscles stand out like speed bumps. His nipples had pebbled up under my perusal in the cool air of the office, and when I dared to take one in my mouth he shuddered. Goosebumps spread across his sternum.

"God, Maddie."

It was so rare for me to hear my nickname in his voice that it sent shivers up my spine. The few times I remembered hearing him say it were intense moments, his voice hoarse with emotion.

"You're still touching me," he pointed out.

This was true. He groaned as I hooked my first two fingers in the waistband of his pants and led him over to the couch. "Have a seat. Wait!" Before he sat down, I deftly undid his pants, his hot length bulging against his boxer briefs against the back of my hand. My throat went dry. "I'll be right back."

I pushed him down to sit. Then I dashed out to

retrieve the scarf I'd stuffed inside my laptop bag and, thinking quickly, a spare pair of panties from the zipped front pocket. Remembering to lock the door again when I returned, I found him sprawled on the black leather, his white shirt hanging open and his arms stretched out over the back of the couch. His legs were spread a little, and his dark trousers and briefs almost hid the impressive bulge below his waist—almost.

He looked like what he was—a powerful, insanely hot, dominating, fuckable billionaire.

Seriously, he looked like a book cover that I wouldn't want people to see me reading on the bus. And he was mine, at least for now. My heart jumped and my stomach flipped when my gaze skimmed over his perfection to find his blue eyes twinkling at me.

"Do your worst, Madeline."

"Oh, you really shouldn't have said that," I said. Before he could react I wound my scarf around his head in a makeshift blindfold.

"Hey!"

"You're the one who said that being able to see wasn't that important, Gage. Tit for tat." I tweaked his nipple.

He gasped then chuckled with obvious amusement. "Okay, then. I still don't think you can do it." He was ready to triple dog dare me, from the sounds of it.

Swallowing the nerves swelling in my throat, I plopped down beside him. I'd missed being close to him that week, and for a brief moment I drank him in. This could either be really fun, or really dangerous. Or both. Leaning close to his ear, I blew a soft stream of air down his neck. His shoulders hunched in reaction.

"I'm not touching you," I sang.

"Your breath is. I still think it's cheating," he complained, but he couldn't stop the grin from taking over his face.

"I haven't told you the rules yet—how could it be cheating?"

He tilted his head toward me in acknowledgment. "So what are the rules?"

I was making this up on the spot, more or less. I tapped my fingers against my lips, thinking quickly. "Rule number one: I cannot touch you with any part of my body."

"Okay. I can't see you or touch you? This should be interesting."

"Rule number two: you can touch yourself. In fact, I would like to see that."

He smirked. "I bet you would."

My core spasmed. I squirmed a little on the couch, rubbing my thighs together underneath my plain black pencil skirt.

"Is there a rule number three?" he asked.

"We can both talk." I paused. "That's about it."

"So basically you want me to jerk off while you talk dirty to me?"

His shoulders pressed back against the sofa and he slouched a little. The bulge at his center expanded as he spread his knees a little wider.

"Gage, you make it sound so… hot." A bubble of delight grew in me. Maybe I could be spontaneous *and* have control. The revelation made my mind spin off into different directions. Which rabbit hole would I dive into?

"Okay, I'm game," he said simply. Without any hesitation or modesty, he reached into his pants and pulled out his cock.

"Well?" he said expectantly.

"Gage, I'm impressed."

His chin rose, but his cheeks reddened a little. "You damn well should be."

"Not every man can wear a pink striped blindfold and make it look sexy."

He growled at me. There was something hedonistic about a powerful man dressed in a suit and tie, holding an impressive erection in his hand.

"I'll tell you what, *sir*. Why don't you imagine that I'm taking off my clothes here in front of you? I'm unbuttoning my tight little skirt and letting it fall on my hips a little. Oh, you can see my little pink panties!"

His moan gave me the courage to go on, and his hand slowly moving on himself gave me confidence.

He didn't need to know that I was actually wearing granny panties.

"God, I love your cock," I told him. "It's so long and thick. I'm not even sure if it will fit in me." I cranked my intonation up a little, to sound younger and more innocent. "It's so big! It might hurt my poor little pussy."

"Fuuuuu—" His hand moved faster and he flopped his head back against the couch. "Madeline, you're in so much trouble after this!"

"My sweater is getting so itchy, Mister Gage. Do you mind if I change in your office?" Without taking my sweater off, I shoved my hands underneath and experimentally squeezed my breasts. "You should really turn the air conditioning down, sir. My poor nipples are so hard and tight—you can see them poke through everything I wear." I shivered audibly for effect, watching him also tremble.

"You're a bad, bad girl, Madeline," he said in a low voice.

"I know. You're going to punish me, aren't you, sir? Oops! My skirt fell off! Now I'm just in my panties, and they're *so wet*. I bet you want to bend me over your desk, don't you sir?"

His hand sped up, and the muscles in his jaw popped as he ground his back teeth together. The crown of his cock was slick with arousal, and I wasn't joking about my underwear—they were soaked. I didn't dare take off my skirt, either, for fear that I would actually try to mount the man against my better judgment. My thumbs brushed over my hard nipples, making me moan out loud.

"You can bend me over your desk and peel my damp little panties off, down my quivering thighs. I know that's what you're thinking about, isn't it? You said once you wanted to 'blister my ass' for misbehaving."

"Ungh."

"I'm waiting, sir. I'll take my punishment and count the blows. Go ahead, raise your hand and spank me." Deciding to improvise, I smacked my hand down on the thick leather armrest. The loud noise made him jump and hiss, his hand tightening on his weeping cock.

"One!" I whimpered a little after I counted. Focusing on his erection made me sigh again, for real this time. Wow, this was really kind of fun. Gage looked painfully aroused, teetering on the edge and frustrated beyond belief. He shifted in his seat, panting my name.

As I inhaled deeply, Gage's left hand rose unconsciously and as I yelled out "Two!" he slapped his palm against the couch.

I jumped and gasped in honest surprise, my heart sprinting towards something dark but playful. My mind blanked for a second, and I had to remember what I was doing and why I was doing it.

"Is my ass getting all hot and pink, sir? I can feel my juices running down my thighs. Did you know that would happen? If you spank me one more time, I might come," I teased him.

His hand rose in the air again, his rosy lips twisted into a devious smirk. I eyed his throbbing cock. It really *was* impressive, and the evidence of his arousal made my own body heat up to a rolling boil. How far did I want to take this?

If this was going to be a real demonstration of control, I could try to persuade him *not* to come—that he wasn't allowed to come until I said so. That idea was intoxicating. Then again, the prospect of watching him lose control made sweat trickle underneath my bra and my throat tighten.

Would he be more frustrated by the lack of control or the lack of orgasm? Either way, it was hot, and more than a little empowering. I decided that he might have been on to something with the whole 'taking control of your destiny' thing.

His breathing was ragged now, and his strokes lighter and slower. He was trying to calm down, I figured. Gage didn't want to give me the satisfaction of being right, which made me even more determined to win this little game. I wracked my brain to think of the kind of stuff I'd read in smutty books.

"Oh god, sir. My pussy is all tingly, what are you

doing to me? I promise I'll be good! I'll respect myself and not say nasty things. I'll do anything you want. Just let me come, *please*."

Apparently I wasn't above pretend begging, although the throbbing lower down in my body was very, very real. With a shock I realized that dirty talk was doing it for me, too.

"You'll come when I tell you to, Madeline," he said harshly. "You have to take your punishment before you get your reward."

My belly clenched at his words. My punishment and my reward seemed to be the same thing, and I was perilously close to losing control myself. I shook my head, trying to slough off the haze of lust that was fogging up my plan.

His flat hand hovered above the couch, waiting for my prompt. He held it high and even in the air, but I detected a faint tremor in it. This naughty game was affecting us both way more than I had expected it to. Two flushed spots high on his cheekbones were blending into the pink of the scarf around his eyes, and he bit his lower lip again before soothing it with his tongue.

"Such a good girl with your panties around your knees and your ass in the air for me," he crooned. He sounded genuinely grateful, if not also choking with arousal. "Just one more, baby," he promised. "One more and then I'll take care of you."

My breath hitched and my mind raced. He was turning it around on me. I was just as horny from his dirty talk as from my own. What should I do? I gulped back a sob that was *almost* totally fabricated while I stalled for time.

Damn you, Google! You didn't prepare me for this.

"I don't think—"

"Last one, Madeline." His right hand tightened around his shaft, his brow furrowing at the top of the scarf as he concentrated.

I was out of time, and my thighs were actually sticking together now from my own arousal flowing. My chest felt tight, my voice small. "Please, sir! I swear to god I—"

His hand came down with a thundering crack before I was really ready, making me cry out in surprise. "*Ahhh!*"

My body jerked with an uncoiling sensation, like a spool of ribbon unfurling. It wasn't quite an orgasm but something had reacted deep within me, confusing me.

"Maddie! Fuck!" He grunted, arching his back, his thighs flexing. *Control. I wanted more control.*

In a totally spontaneous and thoughtless move that I would later regret, I thrust my hand between his legs and clamped my fingers around the base of his huge, angry cock. Under my hand I felt his hot balls tighten and his cock pulse, and then his hand clutched mine in violent shock.

"Fuck! No no *no!*"

He went rigid, his breathing harsh and the tendons of his throat sticking out as he shook with the force of his almost-orgasm. I'd held him back, leaving him high and dry. The redness in his face had spread down his chest, and his flat, ridged belly contracted hypnotically as he chased his climax.

I'd heard that men could come without, uh, coming, but it was startling to see it in action. With pincer-like fingers he pried my hand off him. I swallowed hard as he yanked the scarf off his head with his other hand.

"Ow."

He held my hand hard. The expression on his face was even tighter. I offered him a weak smile, which he didn't return. The way his lips curled up wasn't so much a smile as it was a grimace.

"What. The fuck. Was that?" His eyes had darkened to murky sapphires and he was practically hissing.

Oh shit oh shit oh shit. "You told me to take more control, right? Besides, I broke the rules and touched you, right? And you said before that you wanted to come inside me the first time. So it's only fair that you—"

"My god, Maddie. You're in for it now."

17

GAGE

I was having a heart attack. Except in my dick. If there was a medical term for extreme cock blocking, I was suffering from it. A myocardial infucktion.

When I tried to focus on something other than the cramping in my balls, I saw Maddie's red face in front of me.

Fool me once, shame on me.

Fool me twice, get carried over my shoulder to get your brains fucked out.

But still, it was my fault for taunting her in the first place. I'd spent the last two weeks trying to tease out of her a sense of self-awareness, of commitment to work and to a budding relationship. Madeline was by turns skittish and brashly seductive, which was a heady combination.

The only problem is that the dichotomy mostly went to my little head, not my big one.

My big head with my big brain had theorized, "Ah, maybe she'll start realizing her potential if I push her to succeed." She'd complained that we were acting like we were in middle school. Well, adding to her work duties was more or less the grown-up work equivalent of chasing her around the schoolyard at recess and knocking her down.

I teased her because I liked her, but I'd had enough of this pussyfooting around. I had different plans for her pussy.

And I really did like her. She made me nervous, she made me laugh, she made me horny, and she made me crazy. Perhaps in the morning, she would make me breakfast along with the crazy.

With a wince, I carefully zipped up my fly. My legs were stiff when I rose from the couch. Correction: a lot of me was stiff when I rose from the couch.

"Uh, Gage…" I guess she saw the look in my eye, probably wild and crazed with lust and frustration. "What are you doing?"

I stalked toward her. "Tit for tat? Did you actually say that?"

The laugh she offered me was weak to the point of fraudulent. The way she backed away from me as I approached her was almost penitent.

"Okay, I'm sorry." She held up a shaking hand, almost blocking her own burning face. "I went over the line. I've never done anything like that before, I swear. But you seemed okay with it, until…." Her ass hit the edge of my desk, and she halted with a flinch. I closed in on her, never taking my eyes off her.

"Until you put my balls in a vise?" My hands went to her hips. If I held her tightly enough, hopefully she wouldn't see that I was still quaking. "What's the matter, Madeline? Don't you want children someday?"

Her eyes nearly popped out of their sockets, then

narrowed. She wasn't sure if I was joking or not. I wasn't sure, myself. "I'm sorry. I'm so, so sorry. It was a stupid—"

"Inconsiderate," I added.

"—split-second—"

"Reckless."

"—decision."

She touched my bare chest, making us both gasp. Her fingertips branded me. Until now I'd thought she would be mine, but now I was realizing that I was hers. She owned me. The truth was, she had me by the balls —literally.

There was no fear in her big brown eyes, though. She actually looked... playful. A bubble of pride welled up in my chest at my girl's self-confidence.

"You're a bad girl, Madeline." It was hard to scold her with a stupid grin on my face.

She nodded slowly, licking her lips. "Do you want to spank me, sir?"

God did I ever. I tilted my head at her, pretending to consider it. My hand drifted around her hip to her ass, right above where she leaned against the desk. When I pinched her, the resulting sound went straight to my cock.

"What do you think, Madeline?" I dipped my mouth to her neck, lazily sucking on her carotid artery like a vampire. I was determined to leave a mark this time. Thankfully, the tension in my pants had almost gone down to Defcon 3.

"*Ah!*" She bent her head back to allow me access down the long line of throat and into her tight little sweater. She was a hot secretary fantasy come to life in my office. I was a lucky, lucky bastard.

"Uh, I guess I got carried away," she said.

With a grunt, I bent down and looped my arm under her knees, hauling her into my arms bridal-style. Her hands flew to my chest.

"*What?* Put me down!"

I may have worked out regularly, but I wasn't nearly flexible enough to kiss the woman while holding her like that. So I simply smiled and said, "No."

She slapped at my bare chest ineffectually. "Jesus Murphy, Gage. Nobody actually does this! What are you *doing?*"

"Just what you said. You're getting carried away."

❧

My heroic gesture had to be abandoned once we reached the outer office. The reality was that she had to get her stuff and we both had to put our coats on. But after we gathered our things and headed for the elevator, I didn't let go of her hand.

I locked my fingers around her wrist like handcuffs, down into the lobby and out onto the street. She shuffled behind me, trying to hike her laptop bag further up on her shoulder.

It was only around six o'clock, but it was cool and already dark. Patches of the wide sidewalk in front of the building and the asphalt beyond glimmered with recent rain, and mist still threatened to permeate the evening. Cars and streetlights lit up the streets, rushing home as fast as possible on a Friday night. Who could blame them?

Madeline's hair seemed to double once we got outside, curling wildly around her face. My gaze skimmed over it as it shone in the amber light. Her free hand went to it.

"Oh god, I look like a clown, don't I?"

"No, you look beautiful."

Flustered, she tried to smooth her hair back, but her bag fell into the crook of her elbow. I took it from her and swung it over my shoulder, then pressed my palm to her fiery halo of hair.

And still I didn't let go of her other hand.

"Gage?" She blinked up at me and raised our clasped hands to her warm cheek.

"Time for a vote," I said, taking a deep, damp breath. "I'm taking you home and we are not coming up for air until you've screamed my name at least twice. Yay or nay?"

"Yay." Her voice was steadier than her breathing.

About fucking time. "Yay," I said flatly, but my mouth was wide with pride.

It only took a few minutes to hail a cab, and once we were settled in it I smoothed my free hand over her knee. She shivered, despite the heat going full blast in the taxi.

"What about your car?" she asked, her head resting back against the seat and turned to me.

I didn't want to let go of her hand. I didn't want to let go of *her*. "I'll pick it up tomorrow. Maybe."

She squeezed my hand silently. We stared at each other. Shadows in between the oncoming cars' head-lights slid over her face like a strobe light, leaving me wondering if she was blushing or not.

"Are you going to tie me up again?" she asked quietly.

I touched her cheek. She *was* blushing, if the heat on

her face was any indication. "Do you want me to?" I'd rather tie her down—forever. I wanted to be balls deep inside her and set up a summer camp there.

She didn't respond.

"Madeline, please answer me."

"I just want you."

Oh god. "Can you go any faster?" I said to the driver. He smirked at me, but barely revved the engine. Lazy jerk was trying to pad the fare.

I felt for my money clip in my pocket, which I then raised it to the scratched little plastic window between the front seat and back of the cab. He glanced back then did a quick double take at the wad of bills with wide eyes, before jerking his gaze back to the road with renewed enthusiasm.

We pulled up in front of my house within five minutes. Unfortunately, that was the point that I lost Madeline's hand, as she broke free to slide out while I paid the driver.

He'd just driven away when I joined Madeline on the sidewalk. She stood there, unmoving, staring at my house. Her arms were crossed over her chest.

"What?" I asked.

"You have a white picket fence."

"Yeah." The gate screeched a little when I opened it. "Come on." I had to prod her out of her paralysis, and she walked robotically before me up the path.

It wasn't until we were taking off our shoes in the foyer that she turned on me with a pointed finger and an accusatory tone.

"This can't be your house."

"This is my house. I know it's a little small, but—" I wasn't about to apologize for it. I liked my house. I shoved her laptop bag against the wall by the console table and began to help her with her coat.

She spluttered, jerking her head around while I extricated her from the sleeves. "You don't—it's not —Gage!"

"Madeline?"

"Don't all billionaires live in penthouses in the sky? All white and lots of modern art?" She waved her hand above us as I hung her coat from an antique hall tree.

I raised an eyebrow at her in disbelief. "You know a lot of billionaires?"

"No, but—"

"I bought this house when I was just a piddly millionaire, and I see no reason to leave it. It was a good investment and I don't need more right now. Besides, it's cozy." Although the size of a shoebox, it was still a million dollar house—mostly because of its location in an older area just adjacent to the downtown core.

"Cozy? Investment?" she echoed.

"Besides, I'm not a billionaire."

Her mouth fell open. "What? You mean I've been taking orders from just a *millionaire*?"

I would have been offended had I not seen the corner of her lip quiver with suppressed laughter.

"I have a lot of *extra* millions, though. But I never got that whole billionaire bullshit. More money, more problems. I suppose that if I added up everything I owned and the company's holdings, plus last year's IPO value, I might just crack a billion. But that's all on paper. I'm not diving into pools filled with dollar bills like Scrooge McDuck."

Why did everyone think that billionaires had castles in the sky and more dollars than sense? I couldn't help rolling my eyes, having had this conversation with my mother more than once before.

Maddie looked around. "Yeah, I guess you don't have a pool."

"I'm sorry to disappoint you."

"On the contrary, I love this."

I believed her. Her eyes shone as she spun around, taking in the flagstone floor, the wrought iron chandelier above us, the oak staircase, and the symmetrical darkened front rooms sitting like eyes at the front of the house.

"You have wainscoting," she whispered.

"Are you drooling?"

She gulped, peering into the living room on the right. "How many fireplaces?"

Ah, my Madeline has a thing for interior decoration. Maybe it came from years in a foster home. Saddened by the thought, I decided to play with her a little.

"The hardwood floor is original. I put these tiles in for contrast."

She stared at her feet, her toes curling against the uneven stone. Her breathing picked up. "What kind of wo—"

"Maple."

She sighed.

I lowered my voice seductively, going in for the kill. "There's beadboard in the laundry room."

She pounced on me, her mouth fusing to mine. With impatient hands she pushed off my jacket. It dropped to the floor in a heap, nearly tripping us as she pinned me against the archway on the right. When her hands moved from me to feel the chair rail running along the wall, she whimpered.

Her eyes were nearly black with desire as she caught her breath. Her mouth was already rosy and swollen from our kisses, and I hadn't gotten nearly enough of her taste yet.

I rested my forehead against hers. "Do you want to see my playroom?"

18

MADDIE

"Playroom?"

My body was hot, but my brain went cold. Jesus, more ropes. Handcuffs. Maybe one of those crazy benches or a lit-up display case of canes and floggers. Damn, I'd been reading too many smutty billionaire books.

I wouldn't deny that something deep inside me quivered at the thought, but it also frightened me a little. The intensity of what I felt with Gage at the lodge still made me uneasy. I wanted him enough to follow his lead, but how far would I go down the rabbit hole?

He spun me around and marched me toward the staircase.

"Up. Now. Go down the hall."

When I was a couple of rises ahead of him, I glanced back. "You're a bit bossy, you know that?"

"Better believe it, baby."

I rolled my eyes as he openly ogled my ass. I heard him shed his jacket and tie while we walked up the stairs. At the top, I paused as he unbuttoned his shirt halfway. The lump in my throat was hard to swallow.

When he took my hand, he pressed his open mouth first to my palm, then the pulse point on my wrist. I was sure it was fluttering like a freaking butterfly.

"I want to show you my playroom. It's important to me."

Oh god. "Um, okay." *I could do this. I could totally do this.*

He led me down the hallway in his little dollhouse. Another time I would have run my hand along the banister at the top of the stairs, its patina velvety with age. Or I would have probably noticed the vintage glass doorknobs at each room. But all I could see was the bright white of his shirt like a truce flag as I trailed behind him.

He stopped us in front of a door at the back of the house, and I hesitated. Actually, we both did. Gage rubbed the back of his neck. The direct, motivated, successful billionaire was nervous—and *that* made my knees close to knocking together.

"This is probably the most… personal, private part of me," he explained haltingly, his gaze penetrating me. "Someday I would like very much for you to join me in here."

Do not hyperventilate, I told myself. *You are a mature, sexually active adult with an open mind—and past rope burns to prove it. You just role-played in the office, for god's sakes. Do not embarrass yourself.*

Instinctively, I squeezed my eyes shut as he reached for the knob, and the door creaked open. When I opened my eyes to slits, it was first to look up at the exultant look on Gage's face. Then I faced the playroom. I hadn't realized I'd been holding my breath until it whooshed out of me.

"Gage, you are sick and wrong. Just no. *No.*"

"What?"

"How can you have Pac-Man but *not* Ms. Pac-Man?" I pointed to the array of arcade games lined up against the far wall. "That was clearly the better game!"

"I beg to differ." With his arms crossed over his chest like that and his jaw looking like it had been set in concrete, there would be no persuading him.

At least he had Mortal Kombat and… was that a Dance Dance Revolution platform? It was covered in Japanese writing.

"Please tell me you have an Xbox."

"Baby, I have everything." He pointed to the giant beanbag and large—but not huge—television in one corner. Gage was almost glowing as brightly as the screens on the old consoles. Their sound had been muted, but the lights blinked in the background like dozens of little disco lights.

I wanted to laugh at myself for my idiotic fear. Whips and chains? Come on. I began giggling as I imagined myself bent over and tied to a bubble hockey table.

Boys and their toys. It gave a whole new meaning to "joystick." At that ridiculous thought I bent over a little, my hands on my thighs, trying to cork up the laughter.

"What's so funny?"

"Oh god, you are."

He stiffened, probably unused to being seen as a source of comedy. Well, it was past time to change that. Finally I managed to control my giggle fit, which probably half due to relief.

His annoyance came out in a strange sound from

deep in his throat. When I flung my arms around his waist, he felt as though made of steel. I wanted to melt him down in a fiery forge and bend him into sinuous shapes. Cradling his carved jaw in my hands, I pulled him down for a tender, apologetic kiss.

"I would love to play with you, Gage. But you should know that I take no prisoners in Mario Kart."

He sighed against my lips, multi-tasking while devouring me. "That is one… of… the sexiest… things… I've ever… heard… come out… of your mouth."

I sagged against him with a shiver. It didn't take much for him to move me back out into the hallway and close the door to his "playroom." Nor did it require a lot of effort to pin me against the wall next to it, the ridged doorframe digging into my spine.

He held me up and stroked me into submission at the same time. His fingers were sturdy matches, striking against my surface of my skin until my arousal flared. It threatened to burn us both down.

The bulge of his erection dug into my belly, reminding me of the hours, days, weeks of foreplay leading up to this moment. "Bedroom?" I murmured.

He led me down the hallway to another door, this one wide open. I paused just after I stepped inside.

"What?" he asked from behind me, running his hands up and down my arms. I fought a shiver. The man made me tremble so much that it probably seemed as though I had malaria.

"I like your room," I said simply as he reached to the wall for the light switch.

It was surprisingly peaceful for such a powerful man. A strange sensation pulled in my chest as I took in the calming blue paint, the tiny fireplace and the window seat looking out into the dark night. With shameful shock, I realized it was jealousy. I was almost vibrating with envy.

Brian Gage lived in a dollhouse—one that would have been my dream house as a child. I had used shoe-boxes and secondhand toys to create little domestic fantasies while he was—well, okay, he was in high school, but he still had a home and a family. And I would bet my last paycheck that he never appreciated it.

My throat closed up a little as I gazed over his stacks of books, expensive-looking clothes tossed on a chair, and then finally the bed that dominated the space. Almost incongruous to the style of the little house, the headboard looked like an experiment with recycled wood pallets.

"Kickass bed."

He shrugged. "Bobbie went through a Pinterest phase. I didn't want to hurt her feelings, so I kept it."

I couldn't take my eyes off it. It was so… raw. With a jolt I realized that the metal details on the edges were big metal eyebolts, screwed in tight, with carabineer clips hanging from them. That was the moment that my shyness threatened to derail us.

"Gage, I'm not really—uh, well—"

He cradled my chin, tilting my face up to him. "Not really what?"

"Sexy?"

He actually laughed out loud. The embarrassment flooding me was probably how he'd felt moments before in the game room.

"I beg to differ," he said.

Blushing furiously, I lowered my gaze to the

gleaming hardwood floor. "Seriously. I know you think I'm—well, okay, all that crazy stuff in the office was just wild. It was me being silly. I don't have a lot of experience with the…" I trailed off when he peeled off his shirt. It was so easy for him to distract me.

"With what?"

"Um, the basics."

"Basics?"

"You know, getting naked and putting Tab A into Slot B."

He hummed, snaking his arms around me to unzip the back of my skirt. It fell around my ankles in a small dark puddle. He reached for the opening of his pants.

"If you think we're working with tabs and slots, then we have a problem." With a restrained sigh, he eased his "tab" out of his fly.

"Fuck, Gage, I don't know what I'm doing!" My eyebrows felt like they were near my hairline. After he lifted my arms like I was a doll and tugged off my sweater, he traced his finger across the crease in my forehead.

"I have full confidence in you, Madeline."

His gaze drank in my cream-colored bra. I hugged myself, goosebumps spreading across my upper arms. He smoothed over them with his palms, as though calming an agitated animal. Twice, three times he ran his hands over me then pulled me close.

My heart thumped so hard he likely felt it echo against him.

"You weren't this shy in the office earlier," he noticed out loud. I squirmed as his hands trailed up and down her back.

"That was different," I mumbled, my breath

bouncing off his bare chest. "This is your home. It feels more—I don't know, intimate."

His semi nudged between us, looking for attention. I let out a little gasp as the glistening tip of his cock painted my belly just above the waistband of my panties.

"Make no mistake about it, Madeline. This *is* more. I want more, and this is it. I need to be inside you, and I need you to give yourself over to me. Can you do that, sweetheart?"

My lips trembled until he nipped them. "You're the boss," I said shakily, closing my eyes. I hated making decisions, and this was a big one. Maybe it had already been made for me, which I honestly wouldn't have a problem with.

"Right now I'm not your boss. I'm just me."

"Just him" was intimidating enough, what with the BDSM bed and vintage Nintendo.

"And Madeline, I really, really want you." He thrust his hips against me, to make his point. His point was hot, hard, and throbbing.

"I-I want you too." It was foolish to try to deny it. I would let myself be his and think about it in the morning—or maybe the next week. I could only hope that I would be enough for him.

Gently he unhooked my bra and pulled it off me. "You're so beautiful." He bent to take one of my aching nipples in my mouth, soothing the heat and fanning the flames at the same time.

"Yes!" I hissed, my hands going to his hair as he switched to the other side. He suckled and nibbled, teased and tugged until I thought I was going to scream. Just when I was about to cry "enough!" his lips made their way up my chest and neck again, landing in the tiny crease underneath my ear lobe.

"You have to say the words, Maddie." His voice was husky and close.

I looked into his eyes, reading his urgency and heartfelt sincerity.

Gage might be a demanding sonofabitch, but when he went after what he wanted he usually got it. And at that moment I was his singular goal. That intensity of focus made me want to run away, but then I might not be able to come back.

"*Please*. Please take me, Gage. I want all of you." I was hot all over from desire and supplication.

The words "make love to me" flashed through my mind, startling me into sudden silence. Was that what I truly wanted? Was I falling in love with him?

Thankfully he didn't seem to notice my distraction. He hooked his forefinger under the elastic of my panties at my hip then traced its path down to my center.

"You're wet for me, aren't you?"

He slanted his mouth over mine at the same time his long, unrelenting finger pushed into me. Swallowing my gasp, he circled his finger around until I nearly buckled from the heady intrusion. I kneaded his shoulders like a kitten finding a resting spot. Thankfully for my wobbly legs, his other arm was crooked around the small of my back, keeping me upright.

"Is that good?"

"So good," I panted.

I let out a small whine when he slipped his fingers out of my underwear, then licked them. Somehow we'd moved toward the bed, our lower legs brushing against the mattress. The worn denim quilt cover reminded me of his tight ass in jeans—an endangered vision only seen fleetingly, like the spotting of a clean-shaven hipster dude.

His hands firm on my shoulders, he pushed me down into the soft cloud on his bed.

19

GAGE

All Madeline wore was a blush and panties. She was breathtaking. I fervently wished I could see her in this outfit every fucking day. A new kind of casual Friday, maybe.

"What are you leering at, sir?"

"You, baby. I could eye fuck you all. Day. Long." I kneeled on the bed beside her. "And remember, I'm not your boss here."

"Could have fooled me," she muttered.

"Ahem. I think I demonstrated my willingness to give up control earlier in my office, don't you think?"

She flushed scarlet. "I said I was sorry—"

I bent down, my knee on the bed, and placed my hand over her mouth. "Stop. It was amazing. Well, *almost* amazing. I should return the favor."

Her eyes widened in alarm at the thought of me withholding her orgasm now. "But I won't," I reassured her. "There will be no stopping us now. No games, no baby steps, no slacking. I am all in, and I want you to give me everything you've got."

Her eyes fluttered shut, making me remove my hand so she could speak—but she didn't. When she opened her eyes, they were nearly black with want. "I'll try," she promised hoarsely.

"Do or do not. There is no try."

The laughter erupting from her chest made her body wobble in miraculous, wonderful ways. "You're such a geek."

This wasn't news to me, nor should it be to her after I showed her my playroom. I shrugged. "I've been accused of worse." At the back of my bedside table, I found a small strip of condoms, which I tossed on the bed silently.

She wriggled back on the bed as I approached her. I couldn't tell if she was nervous or excited, or possibly both. Madeline Jones made my head spin—spontaneous one moment, shy the next.

Shy Madeline let me peel her damp panties down her legs, but spontaneous Madeline announced I was still overdressed, before proceeding to remedy that fact.

Shy Madeline burrowed her face into my neck when I teased her to the edge of orgasm, but spontaneous Madeline sucked my fingers clean.

Shy Madeline left the condom to me, but spontaneous Madeline rolled me over and straddled me.

"What do you want to do to me?" she asked.

I smirked at her. "I love multiple choice tests." My hands roamed over her, from the curves of her tits and ass to the sinuous line of her back and shoulders. Her breath came quick and sharp as I outlined the possibilities with my fingertips.

"No kinky stuff tonight, okay?"

My hands froze near the perfection of her bellybutton. "Did I hurt you before?" *Oh shit.* My need for control and commitment had already fucked this up.

"No. God, no!" She bent to kiss me then looked me straight in the eye. "I just need a good, old-fashioned fucking," she told me.

"Old-fashioned, huh? I thought you said no kink," I teased her.

I was divining at her entrance as she hovered above me. Her arms and thighs were shaking a little, but I doubted it was from fatigue. I gripped her hips—not to pull her down on me, but to reassure her.

"I just want to be with you," she said. But she still looked a little nervous.

"We can stop if you want, Madeline." God knew I didn't want to, but I would. It was easier to live with blue balls than with bad decisions.

She shook her head, biting her lip before she bent over to kiss me. With her mouth, she committed to me. Her lips parted and her breath mixed with mine. The taste of her, cinnamon and coffee and caramel, punched through all my neural receptors. I grew harder, aching to penetrate her blistering heat. We were both at the top of the tower and ready to jump together.

Raising her head, she looked behind me. "Next time I'm going to tie you to that, sir."

Oh fuck.

"Next time I'll let you. But I don't think we need the rope to keep us together tonight.

Then she lowered herself on to me, taking every inch of me inside her until I felt as though we couldn't be any closer. Holy Jesus, she felt amazing. She was so excruciatingly snug and hot that I had to close my eyes to regain some control.

"Maddie, *don't move.*"

I was embarrassingly close to blowing my load, just at the feel and knowledge of being embedded within her. Her whimper forced my eyes open.

"Gage, I need to move." Her voice was tight, her mouth stretched a little at the corners.

Ironically, her urgency stopped me dead, a panicky feeling rushing through me. "Am I hurting you?"

"God, no. I'm so full, I feel like, *ungh.*" My eyes nearly crossed as she squeezed me. "Your tab is too big for my slot," she complained.

My cock swelled further at her words, which made her groan again. "Sorry." I grinned, not really sorry at all. My hands still clamped onto her hips, I encouraged her to move, relatively certain now that I could hold out.

She moaned with relief as she rose up a little and started weaving back and forth. "That feels better."

"Yeah?" I gritted out, realizing that I might have been prematurely convinced of my self-control.

Her hair fell around her shoulders as she rode me, a flush crawling across her chest. Automatically my palms went up to meet her breasts, making her move a little faster.

"Jesus, Gage, I'm too close," she panted.

Thank god I wasn't the only one poised on the edge here. There would be time for finesse later. I would *make* time. She'd said she wanted an old-fashioned fucking, and this would be over soon enough judging by the tightening in my balls.

I slid my right hand down over her belly to where we were fused together, my thumb unerringly sliding over her clit.

"Fuck!" She tossed her head from side to side. The

lower lip she'd been chewing on earlier fell, her mouth open and breathing harshly. "I'm sorry! Oh god, I'm coming already!"

As I felt her spasm around me, the knife of my own climax severed my control. "Fuck, Maddie!"

I reached up for her and dragged her down to me, swallowing her gasps while stars exploded behind my eyes. And in my balls. And in my ass.

There was a whole goddamn planetarium laser light-show happening in my body.

Her skin was hot as it pressed against mine, but my roving hands felt tiny bumps rising on her arms. She shivered, tumbling off me gracelessly onto the pillowy bed.

"One sec." I got up to remove the condom, and when I got back she was splayed out on her stomach and she'd put her head under a pillow.

"What are you doing?" I asked her.

"Need the cool side of the pillow," she replied, her voice muffled a little.

I pulled up one side, exposing her flushed face. "Is it working?"

"Not really. I'm still hot. But then again, your junk is in my face," she pointed out.

I stood beside the bed, naked, and laughed. Hell, I had nothing to be ashamed of. She burrowed her head back under the pillow. Shy and spontaneous, that was Madeline.

"Are you going to fall asleep on me?"

The pillow flew off the bed as she pushed herself up on her hands and knees like a frightened cat. She looked stricken. "No! No, I'm sorry, I won't fall asleep." Her gaze flitted around the room. "In fact, I should get going."

"What? No, that's not what I meant." I picked up the pillow and threw it back on the bed. "Go ahead, fall asleep if you want. You had a *hard* day."

She lifted an eyebrow. "Really? That's terrible, Gage."

"I'm not going to kick you out of bed for eating crackers."

She smiled then clutched her midsection as her stomach audibly gurgled.

"Shit, I forgot to feed you!" I looked at the clock; it was close to nine. I'd lost all sense of time with her. Now I knew how my mother and sister felt every day, and it was unnerving to say the least.

I pulled on a pair of sweatpants and headed down to the kitchen. While I was rooting through the fridge for a makeshift dinner, she sauntered in wearing the shirt I'd discarded earlier—and only the shirt.

"Madeline," I groaned. She was going to kill me. It was a well-known fact that wearing his rumpled button-down shirt was Kryptonite for any man—even a paper billionaire.

"What?" The little vixen tried to blink innocently. In one hand she was holding my phone. "Your pants were vibrating."

"That's what she said."

She rolled her eyes as she passed me the phone. Seven missed calls? The screen was full of text messages from Aaron.

Where are you? Call me asap!

"Somefing wrong?" She'd somehow found an actual

box of crackers in a cupboard and was munching happily on them.

"Aaron's blowing up my phone." I frowned, already annoyed. "I asked him to do some mock-ups this weekend but he said he was taking the weekend off. Really, who takes the weekends off? I expect people to commit to their jobs. It's not a fucking internship."

When I looked up, her eyes had narrowed into critical slits and she slammed the cracker box on the marble-topped island. The crumbs on the hardwood floor underneath her made me wince. My fingers itched to get the broom.

"Present company excluded, of course." It was a poor attempt to cover my ass, and I knew it, which made me grumpier.

A man should not feel grumpy ten minutes after an orgasm, but somehow I'd managed to achieve it. *Goddammit.*

Without even bothering to listen to the voice mails—there were four of them—I called Aaron.

"Hey, wha—"

"Dude, where have you been?"

I straightened immediately at the panic in Aaron's voice, my gaze snapping to Madeline. She must have heard his scream, because she too went on alert and moved closer to me.

"I'm home now—"

"Fuck, man, you gotta get here fast. There's blood everywhere, and I don't know what's going on. They won't tell me because I'm not family, and I can't reach your mom."

"Blood?" Mine ran cold at Aaron's words. "Where are you? What are you talking about?"

I grabbed Madeline's hand. She looked up at me with alarm. "What blood?"

"I brought Bobbie to the ER. There was so much blood and she passed out. But they won't let me go back with her and they won't tell me anything."

My friend sounded like he was losing it. And god only knew what was wrong with my sister. I felt clammy and spacy, flashing on memories of losing our father. I fucking hated hospitals.

Madeline squeezed my hand then let go to fly up the stairs like a pale ghost. I followed behind her as she gathered her clothes. Partly in shock myself and with a hell of a lot more questions, I tried to focus on what needed to be done in that moment. Lists flew through my head, shuffling into mental files and put in order.

"Okay, calm down. We're coming. What hospital?"

20

MADDIE

S ince Gage had abandoned his car at the office, we had to call a cab to take us to the hospital. It was drizzling again, and that added to the demand of a Friday night made our taxi later than we'd wanted it. Then again, he'd wanted it to appear instantaneously, with the click of his fingers. But even Uber wasn't working that quickly.

The best I could do was to hold his hand in the back seat as he made phone call after phone call. Unfortunately, sitting at his right side meant that he had to let go in order to punch out numerous texts. So I smoothed my hand over his thigh instead in a vain attempt to calm him. He flashed me a tight but grateful smile, his square jaw clenching in the shadows.

He was still on the phone when we pulled up at the Emergency Room entrance. In his distraction he merely got his wallet out of his pocket and pushed it into my hand before bolting from the car. With a shrug, I pulled out some money and handed it to the driver, wishing him a good night.

It seemed pretty obvious that the good part of my evening was over.

Aaron was pacing in front of Gage when I walked into the triage area. His thick black hair was puffed out like a French poodle's, and his light pink polo shirt had streaks of blood on it that looked almost like fingerprints. His dark skin was almost ashen gray, his deep chocolate eyes glittering.

What the hell had happened? Had they been in a car crash?

I was startled when Gage grabbed him and forced him down into a chair, but also relieved that he'd stopped the back and forth motion that was already making me dizzy.

"What. *Happened*?" Gage demanded.

"We were having dinner at home. She didn't eat very much, said she had a stomachache. All of a sudden she said she felt sick. So we got up to clear the table, and she b-bent over." His gaze flickered between us like a firefly —bright and unsteady. "She bent over. She bent over and I saw blood on her jeans. It was on the seat of the chair. And it kept spreading."

"She was fine when I saw her this afternoon," I murmured, mostly to myself until Gage whipped his narrowed gaze to me. I would have to explain that to him later.

Aaron threw his hands up, the whites of his eyes bright in his face. "I mean, what the fuck, Gage!" It was a plea, an accusation, and an unanswered question all rolled into one. He looked like he was about to throw up, and I was close to shoving his head between his legs when Gage palmed the back of his friend's head and beat me to it.

"I didn't even know she was coming this weekend. Is that why you bailed on the work I asked you to do?"

I put my hand on Gage's back. "Really not the time."

He took a deep breath in his through his nose and out through his mouth. "Okay. You're right. I'm sorry, you're right."

One day I would get a recording of him saying that.

He turned to me with a grim look. "Can you get him some water? I'm going to talk to the nurse and see if I can get back there to find out *what the hell is going on!*" His voice rose sharply at the end, getting the desk clerk's attention. I already felt sorry for her.

Aaron's torso rebounded a little as Gage let go to stalk to the desk. Then he sagged again, his giant hands twisted together like pretzels before him and his elbows braced on his knees. With a jolt I realized there was dried blood around his fingernails.

"Let's go wash your hands and get a drink, okay Aaron?"

He glanced up at me, the whites of his eyes pink but no tears spilling from them yet. I felt awful just looking at him, my stomach twisting. "What? Maddie?" He frowned, as though surprised to see me. I would have been surprised too, sort of.

I touched his shoulder gently. "Let's go clean up a little." As I helped him stand, which frankly was like moving a refrigerator, I saw Gage throw me a mysterious hand signal before disappearing behind some double doors that needed a keycard for access.

We shuffled to the nearest restroom, where Aaron disappeared behind the door and I waited close by to make sure I didn't hear the thump of him fainting or something himself. When he reappeared his hands were clean and water droplets clung to his hair around his face, as though he'd splashed himself.

"Better?" I asked.

With his legs a little steadier and his nod a little firmer, he croaked, "Water would be good." But all his energy was focused on the locked doors that Gage had gone through.

Looking around, I saw a water fountain but no paper cups. An alcove by the front door housed a small array of vending machines, though. "Okay, go sit down again. I'll get you a bottle."

I didn't have any cash on me, but Gage's wallet still burned a hole in my jacket pocket. With a mental note to repay him, I borrowed a few bucks to pay for the resounding clunk of a full water bottle falling down the inside of the machine. After the briefest of inner debates, I decided to splurge for another. He was a billio —*millionaire*, and he wouldn't care.

As I passed a bottle to Aaron, the silence between us was broken by an older dark-haired woman calling out his name.

"Where is she?"

"Mother?" I confirmed with Aaron under my breath. He nodded slightly.

"She's back there." His hand still shook a little as he pointed to the doors. "Brian's with her. They wouldn't let me go because I'm not family." He sounded like he was ready to cry.

Without another word the woman flew to the desk. She was barely five feet tall but gave off the impression of a Tasmanian devil. That poor clerk was getting her fill of Gages tonight. And I still didn't know what was wrong with Bobbie. The way Aaron described it sounded like a girly kind of problem, and possibly one of the worst kind. My insides crumpled in sympathy at the thought.

"Okay, the nurse is going to get a doctor to come out and take us back," Gage's mother announced. She raked a hand through her thick dark hair in a gesture eerily similar to her children. "Both of us."

"Thanks." Aaron let out a long sigh, like someone had untied a balloon in his chest. He cracked open the water bottle and sipped it, which reminded me that I had one in my other hand.

I offered it to Mrs. Gage. "Um, here."

She turned to me with a confused look in her bright blue eyes. Clearly I hadn't been noticed in the commotion of her dramatic entrance. "Thank you, uh…"

"Maddie. This is Maddie." As an introduction, Aaron's left something to be desired. Not that I could blame him; I was lucky he remembered my name in his current state.

"I work with your son," I said lamely, willing myself not to blush. *With, under, over, around.*

The lines around her eyes deepened with her puzzled look. "I don't understand. Why are you here?"

That was a damn good question. I was beginning to wonder that myself. What was I to Gage? What was I to Bobbie? I felt awkward and in the way, and adrift without Gage's hand to tether me.

"She's cool, Mrs. G."

Aaron's eloquence was just blowing me away.

I shuffled my feet, acutely aware of my bare legs under my skirt—not to mention the still damp panties that I'd dragged back on at Gage's house. Only then did

I realize that I'd left my laptop bag at his house and did a mental facepalm. At least I had my phone and purse, but I couldn't go back for my bag without him—and I had no idea when he would be coming out.

Just then an orderly came out and said he could take Mrs. Gage and Aaron back. With a determined expression Aaron popped up from the chair so fast that he scared the shit out of the orderly, who was about a foot shorter than him. As they scurried to the big doors, I remembered something.

"Here!" I shoved Gage's wallet into Aaron's hand. "Give this back to him."

He just nodded absently, his mind already twenty feet down the hall ahead of him. It didn't occur to him to invite me back with them, and I wouldn't have gone if he'd asked. It wasn't my place.

I was still wondering where exactly my place was when I got a cab home.

21

MADDIE

I fell asleep in my work clothes, just dragging the covers over me in my old bedroom. I dreamed crazy dreams about Bobbie and Aaron playing in Gage's game room and Gage building a dollhouse out of hospital supplies. When I woke, it was to find my adoptive mother was sneaking through my dresser at nine on a Saturday morning.

"What are you doing?"

She whirled around, her stick-straight blonde pageboy swinging like a circle skirt. "Nothing! Putting away your laundry?"

Yeah, it was definitely time to do my own laundry again. Ignoring her strange look at my rumpled clothes, I dragged myself out of bed and joined her at my dresser.

"Uh huh." I looked down into the open, and mostly empty, drawer.

At least she had the decency to blush. I rolled my eyes and fished in a lower drawer for some sweats to change into. Without even the prop of a laundry basket —really, she had to step up her game—she sat on the end of my bed.

"How's the new job going?"

"Um, okay. I think I'm doing a good job so far." After I pulled on a soft sweatshirt, I headed for the closet to hang up my wrinkled sweater. In fact, it probably just needed to go to the drycleaner.

"You sound surprised."

"I guess I am. You know I'm not that great at keeping jobs."

"You can keep a job, Maddie. You just have a tendency to choose not to."

It was lecture time, and the theme was familiar. Hiding as much as possible behind the closet door, I shimmied out of my skirt.

"Here we go." I rolled my eyes. "Maddie, quitters never win and winners never quit!" I parroted back the saying I'd been hearing for a few years now.

I stalked back to the bed to retrieve my leggings. Her silence made me wonder if I'd hurt her feelings. Her expression made me certain of it. *Shit.*

Sitting beside her on the edge of the bed, I lay my head on her shoulder briefly in apology. I wasn't a hugger, and she knew that. She froze as my head cradled into her neck, but we breathed quietly in tandem. That was enough.

Only a moment later I straightened and began pulling on the rest of my "not at work" clothes. That was the one thing I hated about being a grown-up— wearing grown-up clothes. I'd never been one of those little girls that dressed up in my mother's clothes. If I could, I'd live in pajamas, just changing into fresh ones twice a day.

"I'm sorry, Maddie. We just want—"

"What's best for me, I know." I sighed. "I appreciate it. You know I do. I just..." I trailed off, not quite knowing how to articulate what I was feeling. "I, um, started looking for her, you know."

She went rigid and remained silent, probably not sure what to say. The thought of me finding my "real" mother threatened her, if I'd applied my intro psychology course knowledge properly.

I knew I was adopted. It was hard to miss, since it didn't happen until I was a teenager. But as I'd told Gage, until a year ago I'd thought my biological parents were dead. It turned out I was half-right. The year before, I'd re-opened my adoption paperwork in Dad's office while filling out my passport application, and discovered that the woman from whom I'd been separated when I was young had been on her way to prison, not the cemetery.

Yeah, that little bombshell sent me into a summer of spiraling regrets. I wasn't dumb enough to drink too much or act out—after all, I'd spent ten years surviving the system by flying under everyone's radar. My "parents" stoically put up with my confused, sullen state, constantly reminding me that they loved me and wanted me. But after two months of getting the silent treatment, they were ready to duct tape me to a therapist's chair.

I got over it. Mostly. And I should be happy and proud that I wasn't just working retail like some of my friends, despite still living at home. In fact, I counted my lucky stars every day that I had a home to live in. After way too many years in the foster care system, other kids would have been bitter troublemakers. I'd always tried to stay above my emotions, floating above the tension and insecurity, but I was also damn grateful.

The truth was that my hit and miss track record with jobs wasn't just because of the economy. I used to joke that I had ADHD, but I'd grown up feeling like everything was temporary, and still approached life that way. I'd never kept a hobby or a pet or a boyfriend. Maybe if I tried to raise pet boyfriends as a hobby…

I'd survived childhood and adolescence, which was saying something in my case. I'd even gone to college, damn it! I had a relatively useless degree, a regretfully popped cherry from an ill-advised party, and a student loan to prove it.

Now that I was—in theory—an adult, I was supposed to have goals, but I was used to flying by the seat of my pants and it was a hard habit to break. Gage was the first person I'd spent time with who made me want to focus a little more.

"Can you see yourself staying in this job?" she asked gently. It wasn't an unfair question.

I considered it. I liked the work so far. It beat answering phones at a car dealership or transcribing insurance reports from screwy dictations. It was a novelty to be considered almost an expert in something, and I couldn't deny that it felt pretty great to impress somebody for once. Brian Gage's icy eyes and sharp jaw flashed before me, his lips curving into the smirk that I was starting to strategize about eliciting from him. I shook the image out of my head, wondering where he was and how he was doing today.

"No?" She sounded disappointed.

"What?" I realized she had misinterpreted my gesture. "No, I like it. I, uh, like the people I work with —mostly." One of them I liked a hell of a lot, in fact.

I looked around my room, comparing it to Gage's house and finding it sincerely lacking. My mom followed my gaze, pausing on the blank walls and almost empty dresser top.

"You never did decorate in here," she chided me.

I shrugged and sat beside her again with a sigh. My dorm room at school had looked eerily similar—just a narrow bed, a dresser and a desk. The only difference was that I had a TV in my room there and here I just watched stuff on my laptop. "I just haven't gotten around to it. I haven't been back long enough."

"Mad, this has been your room for nine years."

"What can I say? I have no personality," I joked.

She twirled one of my long auburn curls around her index finger and tugged. "Now *that* is not true."

But she didn't push it, for which I was grateful. I was grateful to her for a lot of things, and the reminder prompted me to put my arm around her waist and squeeze affectionately. It was a rare enough thing for me to do that after a shocked pause, she looped her arm around my shoulder and gave me a hard sideways hug.

"Thanks… Mom. Maybe next week we could, um, shop for some curtains or something together. If I don't have to work late…" I trailed off, wondering what qualified as "working late" with Brian Gage. Naked time probably didn't count.

"But you like the job, right?"

My nod reassured her, until I added, "When I stop

liking it, I'll just quit." I was kidding—almost. It was more like I was waiting for the other shoe to drop. This was the first time that I felt really *good* at something, so the clock was ticking as to when I would screw it up.

I had a history of getting out before getting kicked out, but it was time to change that pattern.

22

GAGE

I hadn't known that you could sleep standing up until the doctor's voice woke me and my back was against the wall.

"I'm sorry for the delay, Miss Gage." He was tall man with an East Indian lilt in his voice. He looked around the room and took us all in at the same time as double-checking Bobbie's identification on her wristband.

My mother sat on a chair beside Bobbie's bed, a vague mesh pattern from the blanket tattooed on her forehead from where she'd been resting. The plastic-covered reclining chair in the corner looked like it came from Barbie's Dream House with Aaron's giant frame wedged into it. I squeezed my eyes shut and opened them again, willing the burning in them to subside.

"Would you like me to speak with you alone?" the doc asked my sister.

"No, it's okay." Her voice was tired and her face wan, but we needed news. "This is my family." Aaron cleared his throat. "And my boyfriend," she added, making me wince.

Their relationship was still weird for me. I'd walked in on some sorority type going down on Aaron once in his football days, so there was precedent in my memory for awful, bleach-requiring imaginings involving my little sister. *Blech.*

"Ah." The doctor nodded at Aaron. "Okay, then. Well, first off, I think the baby is okay."

"Baby?" my mother squeaked. If it were possible, Bobbie's complexion paled from wan to paper white.

"Yes. I want to do an ultrasound shortly to confirm dates, but your HCG levels indicate that you're pregnant."

Bobbie and Aaron just stared at each other, neither of them paying attention to the laser beams that were probably shooting out of my eyes at the two of them. How could they be so fucking stupid? I shook my head.

"The bleeding? There was so much blood," Aaron said.

"Sometimes it happens in the first trimester. It could be from implantation, although I think we're a little late for that. It could be a progesterone drop, which can result in the uterus sloughing off some lining. Sometimes it's indicative of a molar or ectopic pregnancy—both of which can be very dangerous, which is why we have to do an ultrasound to rule them out. I take it this was unplanned?"

I barked out a laugh. "I sure hope so."

"Brian!" My mother's reprimand bounced off me. She wasn't the one who was invariably going to have to pick up all the pieces.

Pinching the bridge of my nose, I asked the doctor,

"What do we do now?""

He narrowed his eyes at me. "An ultrasound, then I will talk to *Roberta* about what to expect."

What to expect when you're expecting. That was just fucking great. I wanted to kick something. I wanted to punch Aaron in the face. Instead, I slammed the door on my way out and headed for the cafeteria. With any luck it would sell booze.

It didn't. Two cups of sub-par coffee made me even more edgy by the time I returned to the room half an hour later. I opened the door quietly this time, noticing that the room was dim. Aaron was asleep on the reclining chair by the window, but Mom was gone.

"Where's Mom?"

"I sent her out to get me some fresh clothes," Bobbie said quietly, reminding me that hers were headed for the incinerator. "You know how she is with hospitals since Dad died. She was driving me crazy with baby names."

A snort escaped me. "Yeah, she did a bang up job with ours." Mom had claimed over the years that Brian and Roberta were family names, but I'd yet to find out what branch of the family tree that fruit had fallen from.

I'm sorry, Brain."

My eyes burned, making me blink rapidly. When I pulled my phone out of my pocket, I saw it was almost five in the morning and still dark outside.

"Sorry for what, Pinky?" I said, fighting bone deep exhaustion despite the vertical nap earlier.

She glanced over at Aaron, her face crumpling. "For disappointing you."

I sighed, not sure what to say. I was angry with her for not using protection and getting pregnant, angry with her for getting involved with *my* friend in the first place, and now all that anger warred with the pity I felt over her situation and guilt over being angry in the first place. I was officially fucked up, emotionally.

A few months ago people called me a robot. Okay, more like an asshole, but the point was that I didn't always play well with others. My patience was limited, and so was my capacity for sympathy.

"How could you be so careless?" *What about taking over the world?*

The look on her face made me want to take back my words, and if Madeline had been there she would have thumped me.

Oh shit, Madeline!

A quick look at my phone confirmed that she'd left a couple of text messages and one voice mail at around midnight. My fingers tightened on the phone as I itched to call her back and hear her voice, but at five in the morning I didn't think it was the best idea.

Instead I hovered over a text box, but couldn't figure out what to say. In the end I settled for *"I'm okay. Will call you later."*

Straightening up didn't help my aching back, and I stretched my neck by methodically bending my head from side to side. I shoved the phone back in my pocket, then looked up to see my sister's face wet with tears. *Fuck.*

"Shit, I'm sorry." I moved stiffly to her side and patted the lump of her leg under the hospital blanket.

Her shoulders shook as she tried to cry as quietly as possible, presumably so she didn't wake up Aaron. If anything her attempt to stifle it made it worse, but at least her face was showing some color now.

"I'm such an i-i-idiot," she whispered harshly in

between sobs.

If I'd felt bad for my thoughtless words, it was nothing compared to how shitty I felt for internally agreeing with her. But she'd made so many mistakes in her life—avoidable, dumb mistakes. Bad decisions leading to bad outcomes. She lived her life like she was playing Minecraft in survival mode—just digging holes and building walls and waiting for random animals to wander through and screw up her environment.

"No, you're not," I said haltingly as she sniffled. She raised her swollen, watery gaze to me and burst into tears again.

Aaron groaned as he shifted in his chair. We both stilled and looked over at him. Part of me wanted him to wake up so he could comfort her—which surely he could do better than I could. Another part of me wanted to punch him in the face for putting everyone in this situation, but I knew it wasn't really his fault.

Too many emotions had built up in me—anxiety, irritation, jealousy, helplessness. By midnight I felt like a pressure cooker and it only took the tears of my mother to blow my valve.

"I should have known," Bobbie castigated herself in a low voice. "I should have known I was pregnant." She looked up at me with wide eyes. "But I swear I didn't. My periods are always so irregu—"

I held up a hand to stop her, not needing that much information. "It's okay."

"It's probably best that this—" She broke off, her voice quavering. "I can't take care of a baby! I can barely take care of myself."

I couldn't argue with that, mostly. "But you've been trying really hard," I reminded her. She'd shown a lot of professionalism and initiative at the resort. And she seemed, well, happy. In her element, with more confidence and self-awareness than I'd seen in her in years. "I'm actually pretty proud of you," I told her gruffly.

Her eyes narrowed in suspicion. I'd probably never said those words to her before, or if I had the last time had been when she graduated high school. "Really?" She sniffled again, and I reached for the scrap of paper they called tissues there.

"Yeah. You've been doing okay."

She seemed far too pleased with my damnation with faint praise, which made me feel like even more of a jerk. In between blowing her nose, she asked where our mother was. I'd sent her home to get some sleep about an hour before. I'd told Aaron to do the same, but he flatly refused.

"Is he good to you?" I asked her.

Bobbie nodded. "He's better than I deserve. I'm such a screw-up."

"Stop it. You're not. Okay, maybe you haven't always made the best decisions, but you're changing things now, right? Give yourself a break—literally. Sleep. Let yourself heal." I patted her leg again. "Then you can get back to work and accomplish something, right? Get back on that horse, so to speak."

She gave me another nod, her chin scrunched tight and her lips pressed together in a thin line.

Just then a woman peeked through a crack in the door, spotted us, then opened the door to push through a monitor on a cart.

"Miss Gage?" Her smile was much too bright for someone at work at dawn. "I'm here to do an ultrasound. Are you ready to take a look at your baby?"

23

GAGE

I got home later that morning, feeling numb and cold. After peeling off all my clothes and standing under a hot, cleansing shower for what seemed like hours, I fell into bed for what ended up being the whole day.

Then I fell into a funk for all of Sunday. Bobbie was still pregnant, and I didn't know what to do. The fact that there was nothing for *me* to do about it didn't totally register.

I'd had the decency to leave the room while Bobbie and Aaron stared at the ultrasound screen in shock, but the acrid coffee I found didn't wake me from the surreal dream. If Bobbie wasn't ready to be a mother, then I wasn't ready for her to be a mother. I was terrified that she would change her mind, like she had about boyfriends and jobs, and I would be stuck bailing her out—only this time with a helpless little baby.

Nightmare scenarios kept going through my head. Bobbie and Aaron dying in a car crash and me having to take the baby, since my mother would probably be too scattered to deal with it. Aaron bringing the baby to the office in a carrier on his chest, ridiculously proud yet unproductive. Madeline swaying the baby in her arms to soothe it—okay, that last one wasn't a total nightmare, but it was still weird to me.

Needing distraction from my thoughts, I retreated to my playroom. I was about to beat my own high score in Mortal Kombat on Sunday evening when my doorbell rang. Needless to say, I pooched the game and was in a foul mood when I stomped down the stairs.

When I opened the door to Madeline, I was speechless. Just the sight of her windswept hair and rosy cheeks blunted some of the fury and fear I felt. She worried her bottom lip with relentlessly, and I stood there like a statue until she had to ask if she could come in.

"Yeah. Oh yeah, of course." I snapped to attention and stepped back so she could enter. Then I crossed the cold floor of the foyer in my bare feet and sat on the second rise of the oak stairs.

She stared at me, not making a move to take off her shoes or coat. *Okaaaay*, I thought. If she didn't want to stay, that was probably best, since I was in a precarious mood.

"How are you?"

"Fine," I answered automatically. "How are you?"

"Uh, I thought you'd call me back."

"Sorry. I got… caught up." I put my head in my hands, combing my fingers through my hair. *Had I showered today?*

"How's Bobbie?"

"I'm not sure," I said slowly.

"Where is she now?"

"At Aaron's."

With a sigh she sat down on the step beside me.

The warmth of her palm bled through my T-shirt when she gingerly placed her hand on my back. It permeated through to my heart like she was holding it in fist.

"What happened?"

"She was—*is*—pregnant."

She began to nod then cocked her head. "I wondered if maybe she had a miscarriage?"

I snorted. "That's what I thought."

Madeline recoiled a little at the disdain in my voice. I cringed myself when I heard it, but couldn't seem to stop it from spilling out of my mouth. It was like I was projectile vomiting all my shitty emotions.

"What do you mean?"

"It looked worse than it was. They said something about breakthrough bleeding; I wasn't in the room when the doctor was there. But apparently she's still pregnant."

Her hand moved off my back. "And that's a problem?"

"I just don't know." I raised my head to meet her curious gaze then averted my eyes. "I hate to say this about my own sister, but I'm not sure if she should have kids."

She gasped. "Why would you say that? My god, that's pretty cold, Gage." Silence stretched between us despite how close we were sitting. "What is she going to do?" she finally asked.

"I don't know. It's her decision, I guess. And Aaron's, if she wants to include him." I shrugged, but I truly hoped that she would involve Aaron. He didn't deserve to be left out of it, even if I preferred he wasn't *in* it in the first place.

"But you have an opinion." It was a statement, not a question.

"She hasn't had the greatest track record with her decisions. But it's her body," I said. "Her life. I just don't want her to ruin someone else's."

She eyed me so closely that I felt like getting up and walking away. Hell, I was already uncomfortable. "You don't want her to ruin *your* life," she said flatly.

"I never said that."

Madeline was quiet for a moment. "There are options, Gage. I was adopted, remember?"

"Yeah, eventually! You really think that those, what —ten years in foster care were the best of your life?"

She gasped and jumped to her feet as though I'd just slapped her. "What?"

Shit. I couldn't say or do anything right. "I mean, weren't you unhappy, Maddie? Would you honestly want that for another kid?"

"I can't say that I would recommend it, but are you saying that you think it would be better if I were *dead*? Or to be with a neglectful or even abusive parent?"

"No, of course not!" I shouted, tugging at my hair again in frustration. "*Fuck*! I just hate everything about this goddamn situation."

"Because you can't control it."

I grimaced at the truth that was so obvious to both of us.

"I hate to break it to you, Mister 'No Excuses'—" She raised her fingers in air quotes as she rolled her eyes at me. "But there are things in life beyond your control. And I think Bobbie deserves your support, no matter what."

"Why, just because she's my sister?"

"Some people don't get to have a family," she said pointedly. "You're lucky."

"You have a family—the parents who adopted you, right?"

"Sure, but every day I have to live with the fact that my mother didn't want to come back to me, didn't *want me.*"

"And you also have two people who *did* choose you."

She opened her mouth to respond then closed it again.

"I thought you of all people would be on my side, Maddie. You hate commitment," I scoffed. "You want to quit everything."

With an angry huff she stalked across the foyer to where her computer bag was resting against the wall. After she yanked it up and slung it over her shoulder, she whirled back on me with shiny eyes and a tight mouth. "You don't get to have a side on this. And I was *trying* to change. I didn't want to quit *you.*"

Something unspoken hovered in the air between us. A snort escaped me. "Don't change for me."

"Oh, don't worry—I won't."

Her voice was sad and angry at the same time, much like mine probably was with Bobbie. I'd really fucked this up now. Of all the things that I could control right at that moment, the number one priority should have been my own mouth.

"Madel—"

"I just stopped by to get my laptop," she interrupted. "I'm sorry to bother you." She looked over at me, then up the stairs. Her face softened a little. "Thank you for showing me your house the other night. It was —it's really, um… amazing." She reddened a little, maybe at the memory of what happened the other night.

With my knees cracking from fatigue, I rose from the stairs and reached for her, but she neatly sidestepped me. I wanted so badly to take her in my arms, to kiss her until we were both dizzy and our brains foggy.

"Maddie, I'm so—"

"Gage, what do you want from me? I'm trying. Bobbie's trying." She sounded like she was about to cry. If Bobbie's tears had dented me, then Madeline's had the power to break through me like a bullet leaving a ragged hole behind in my chest.

"*Shit.* I'm an asshole."

She nodded, the glassiness in her eyes finally breaking. Maybe she couldn't see me properly through her tears, but she didn't evade when I approached her. When I tugged her against me, her fist came up to drum on my sternum. A shiver went through me as her palm splayed out and her fingers touched my skin above the collar of my worn t-shirt.

"You're an asshole, Gage," she said shakily, staring at my chest as my arms went around her.

"I know."

"You want everyone around you to *commit*," she spit out. "To go whole hog with no regrets, no hesitation, no do-overs. Some people can do that. Some people can't. I don't know, maybe there's something to be said for looking before you leap."

She leaned forward and wiped her eyes on my shirt. I didn't really mind. At least she didn't blow her nose on me.

"I guess."

"But now," she continued, "when your sister is

thinking about truly committing to something in the biggest way you *can* commit to something, you're condemning her for it. Isn't that a little hypocritical?"

Maybe it was. It probably was. My body sagged a little as she leaned her forehead against me. Her breath was hot through the thin cotton of my t-shirt. She sniffled once, twice, her back shuddering with a heavy sigh.

"I'm sorry," I said hoarsely.

Needing to see those cinnamon eyes, even if they were red and puffy, I tilted her chin up. Her expression was sad but defiant. I grudgingly had to admire the way she called me on my bullshit, even if I didn't agree.

I could see that I'd hurt her—really hurt her. What twisted in my gut worse than the fact that she was probably right was that she doubted me, and maybe even mistrusted me. My throat felt like it was squeezing shut.

"I'm scared," I admitted. Everything was spinning away from me and I couldn't grab it.

"I know."

Without another word, she stretched up and kissed me softly—and with more compassion than I'd earned. Her lips were swollen from her biting it and salty with tears, but they bound me tighter than any rope ever had.

God, I was falling for her. The realization startled me.

Even before the retreat, I'd sneered at the idea of trust exercises. Honestly, I'd joked with Aaron that if anyone thought I was falling backwards and trusting my staff would catch me, they clearly had never worked at my level. Now I was falling backwards and I wanted—maybe even *needed*—her to catch me.

And I'd just given her a bunch of excuses to jerk her hands back.

She kissed me again lightly. The casual brush of her lips, like an afterthought of pity, stabbed me. I tried to tighten my hold on her waist, but she drifted away.

"I think you need some time alone," she said flatly, turning to open the door. I wanted to scream at her *"No! I've had enough time alone! I need you!"* but it got stuck in my throat. She was running away, just like I'd feared. Just like I'd predicted she would. I had to be honest with her.

"I'll see you at work tomorrow, sir."

"Madeline, I can't help thinking. It keeps going through my head on a loop, like a song you can't get rid of."

"What?" She wearily hitched the bag higher on her shoulder, looking like it weighed a hundred pounds.

"The baby. What would you do if it was you?"

24

MADDIE

W hat *would* I do if I got pregnant? It was a good question, and it plagued me all night. I'd always been obsessively careful, terrified at the thought of being responsible for another human. It was more than a little ironic that I was cheerleading Bobbie when I didn't think I could handle it myself. To be honest, that was probably why most of my sexual experience was primarily with my vibrator.

When I woke up for work the next morning, I felt like I'd barely slept at all. It took a lot more makeup than usual to cover the dark circles under my eyes, and the freckles on my nose stuck out like a connect-the-dot picture against my pale face.

"Don't you want breakfast?" my mother asked as I zipped up some knee-high boots. My wool plaid skirt twirled around my calves, the green in it matching my blouse. I looked in the mirror by the front door, and was happy to note that I looked way more put together than I felt.

"No, it's okay. I'm not really hungry."

She leaned against the archway to the kitchen, her concern radiating so strongly I was afraid it would burn me. I was lucky that she worried about me—but like I'd told Gage the night before it didn't erase the fact that my biological mother had essentially thrown me away.

"What's going on, Maddie? Did you, um, find your birth mom? Is that why you're upset? You can tell me, you know." Unable to look me in the eyes suddenly, she turned back into the kitchen and started fussing with putting away the breakfast food she'd gotten out for me.

I sighed and walked back into the kitchen, the heels of my boots clacking on the tile.

Cereal boxes back in the cupboard, milk back in the fridge. She tidied up methodically and efficiently, like she'd done for the last ten years I'd known her. I knew she had to get ready for work soon herself; she was lingering just for me.

"I know I haven't always been supportive of your desire to find her," she said as she faced the fridge. "But I just don't want to see you get hurt."

"It's not that. I mean, I appreciate it, but that's not why I'm upset."

Her posture eased a little as she turned back to me. "Oh."

"A friend of mine is pregnant and she doesn't know what to do," I explained.

My mother's eyes popped out.

Uh oh. "No! Not *that* kind of *friend*. It's not me; Jesus, calm down."

"Sorry."

"It's my, uh, boss's sister. He's freaked out."

"Why? Is she a teenager or something?"

"He just doesn't know if she should have it." It

sounded ridiculous even as I said it, and my mother agreed.

She frowned. "Why is it even up to him?"

"It's not. I think he's just, I don't know, worried that she can't handle it."

"I see. Well, like you said, it's not up to him. You know that saying that God doesn't throw anything at you that he doesn't think you can handle? Maybe he should think about that."

I rolled my eyes. "I don't think Gage is a particularly spiritual person." Unless he'd taken me too seriously when I called out blasphemies when in the throes of passion.

"Maddie, she's a grown up, right? He has to let her make her own decisions. And she has to stand by them herself." She walked to the front door, got my coat out of the closet then she handed it to me with some advice. "Be a friend to her, and be a friend to him. But don't get in the middle. It's not your place if he's your boss."

My face burned. "He's not just my bo—"

"Maddie! Is that who you've been seeing? Who you were with Friday night?"

I cursed my fair complexion. It always gave me away. Then again, I reminded myself that I was twenty-four years old and had nothing—okay, not much—to be ashamed of. My V-card had been lost in a dumb decision in my freshman year at college, and I wasn't exactly bragging about my handful of experiences since.

"How long have you been, um, seeing each other?" she asked.

"About a month? Six weeks?"

"That's a long time for you."

The sad part is that she wasn't being facetious. I

rarely went out more than a couple of times with the same person. I hated commitment, and that included dating. I couldn't even buy the same shampoo twice.

Brian Gage was probably the closest I had come so far to having a boyfriend. Considering that he was wealthy, demanding and my boss, it was probably not the best precedent to set.

My mother looked like she was not only biting her tongue, but swallowing it as well. "Maddie, do you know what you're doing?" she finally asked.

Not a clue, Mom.

"More or less?" I said with a bright smile. I considered it a minor miracle that she didn't ask me about the recent increase in underwear in my laundry pile.

"We will talk about this later," she threatened. "You'd better go or you'll miss your bus."

※

O f course, I did miss my bus. *Damn it.* I'd decided after graduating against getting a car in order to save money, but it meant that I was at the whim of public transit or the kindness of others. And today, it meant that I walked into work almost an hour late.

Susan stuck her head out of her office to make a point of my tardiness when I walked past.

"Maddie, Brian has been looking for you. I tried to help him myself..." She trailed off with a coy smirk on her face, no doubt wanting me to wonder just how she'd tried to help him.

"Thanks, Susan."

I gave her a smile that didn't reach my eyes, and only the fact that I knew she was watching me walk down the hall to my desk kept me from turning back and giving her the finger. I had remarkable self-restraint —perhaps it was the recent rope training.

Gage's door was closed. I put my bag under my desk and hung up my coat. Then I sat in my chair and rearranged my desktop. Stared at the door. Nervously rubbed my leather-covered calves together like a cricket. Stared at the door. I didn't hear any noise from inside; for all I knew he wasn't even in there.

I wasn't afraid to see him. I longed to see him, in fact. I spent much of the night recalling the smell of his skin, the sardonic arch of his eyebrows, his thoughtful gestures and geeky jokes. He was frightened, a state so foreign that it produced new and strange emotions within me as well.

I'd never really wanted to comfort anyone before—I think probably because the compassion of others made me too uncomfortable when I was younger. But something about Gage made me yearn to submit to him and take care of him at the same time. For a girl who'd spent twenty years building walls around her heart, it was terrifying to suddenly find a door there. It was tempting to barricade it.

So lost was I in my head that I jumped when I heard my name.

"Madeline!"

Gage stood in the doorway to his office, looking freshly pressed but the lines around his eyes were tight and a groove seemed permanently etched in his forehead.

I took a deep breath in, lacing my fingers together in my lap. "Gage, I'm sorry about yesterday. I shouldn't have—"

"We have a problem."

What? "Is Bobbie okay?"

He shook his head. "A work problem."

Any problems with work concerned me, of course, but I hated that he didn't answer my question about Bobbie. "What is it?"

"Come in here."

He pivoted on one heel and marched back to his desk, clearly expecting me to follow. I scrambled off my chair and chased behind him.

"Close the door," he ordered.

Standing in front of his desk, he slumped down a little to rest on the edge. The cracks spreading through his immaculate façade made him more real, more human. I remembered from somewhere that on old paintings and porcelain they called that "crazing," which suddenly made perfect sense. He was crazing.

"What is it?"

He stretched his right arm out, his palm facing up. It was the international symbol for "come here… give me something… take my hand… I need you."

I went to him.

When I was close enough to touch, he pulled me into his arms and hugged me tighter than anyone ever had before, even my parents. My eyes filled with tears, and not just because I could barely breathe.

"Forgive me." His voice was hot and broken in my ear.

I couldn't trust my own voice, so I just wrapped my arms around him to hold all the pieces of him together. Seconds felt like minutes and minutes like hours as we clung to each other. He leaned back against the front of his desk, his legs spread and me nestled between them.

A perfunctory knock rattled the door before it swung open. "Brian? I brought those—*oh!*"

I just about tripped over Gage's long legs on either side of me as I extricated myself and spun around. Susan stood there, a sheaf of papers in her hand and her mouth twisted in an ugly sneer.

"Well, I guess we know why he brought *you* on the retreat now."

I was burning and speechless with humiliation. It would be all over the office in an hour that I was sleeping with the boss.

I wasn't stupid. This was not a career move recommended by any guidance counselor, and we had been playing with fire. But to be caught in an embrace by the jealous vamp in Human Resources was the worst possible scenario. On the other hand, at least we had all our clothes on.

Gage simply sighed. "What do you need, Susan?"

Stumbling to a safer distance at the side of his desk, I gaped at his nonchalance. Of course *he* didn't care— he wasn't the one going to be fired. Wait, would I really be fired? Could Susan do that? Wouldn't that be up to Gage himself?

"I suppose I need to update the fraternization policy with you, Mister Gage. But for now, I brought you the files we discussed first thing this morning." She threw me another arch look to remind me of my late arrival. I hadn't been using the *Happit* lately.

Gage straightened and took the small stack of manila folders from her. "Thank you. Anything else?"

"Only for Miss Jones to join me in my office after your, er, meeting is finished here. I have a few other policies to review with her."

Oh shit. Maybe she *could* fire me.

After shooting me a smug look, she sauntered out the door, leaving it wide open. Gage did not suggest I close it, instead he was busy spreading open the manila folders on his desk.

"This is the problem I mentioned earlier," he said absently, poring over some papers. He'd circled back to his throne and was sitting while I still stood at the side of the desk.

It took me a moment to remember anything that happened before he took me in his arms. "What?"

He drummed his fingers on the glass top of his desk, looking up at me. "Madeline, before we get into this I need to make something very clear."

I swallowed. "Okay?"

"It is critical that I compartmentalize better. It got away from me, but this—" He gestured between the two of us. "—can't happen at work anymore."

"I understand, sir." I didn't like it, but I understood. But if he wanted me to work twelve-hour days with him and not touch him, not share secret smiles or little jokes, then that didn't leave much other time to explore our relationship.

His gaze searched me. He looked almost disappointed at my ready agreement. Was I supposed to straddle him in his chair and demand that he go down on me during lunch breaks or something? Although the idea had potential…

I liked working for Gage, with Gage. But I also just plain liked him. It was hard to separate the two—my boss and my boyfriend—but he was the first man I'd met who cared more about my successes than I did.

Unfortunately, that also meant that he would feel my failures more keenly.

"Now, this is last year's application for a grant from the National Science Foundation. Needless to say, it was unsuccessful." He frowned at the file. "You'll be glad to know that I even said please, for all the good that it did. I want you to work on this year's application."

I scanned through the information lying on the desk. "It's not for very much money," I pointed out with surprise. "Why go to the trouble?"

"A few reasons. One, the prestige and visibility." He ticked the reasons off on his fingers. "Two, it puts us in the pipeline to apply for other funding for R&D, stuff like NIH if we're going to expand our biometrics. And three, it looks good to other VC firms who are thinking about taking a chance on us."

Should I remind him of all the other tasks he dumped on me last week? I wondered. Given the weekend he'd had, I doubted that my complaining about my workload would help anything. Shuffling the papers back into some semblance of order, I nodded. "Okay, I'll give it a shot."

"You'll do your best." He raised an eyebrow.

"Yeah, yeah." I waved my hand at him then rapped the folder on his desk to line up the papers inside.

"As your boss, I have full confidence in your abilities."

"Thanks, boss." My salute was lopsided, but then again so were my abilities.

"As your boyfriend—" He looked a little like his tie was strangling him as he said it; I figured it wasn't a term he'd used on himself too often. In contrast, my inner girlfriend was ready to jump on his glass and steel desk and tap dance. "As your boyfriend, I would like to have you for dinner tonight."

I wasn't sure if he meant have me over to his house, or literally have me for his main course. Either way, I was hungry. My attempt at a wink made him smile, at least.

"I guess I'll take care of dessert," I said.

25

MADDIE

G age and I decided not to leave the office together, for appearance's sake. Not that it really mattered —my ears were burning all afternoon, even though we'd barely spoken since I left his office. The grapevine had been very effective, but what else would you expect from an app development company? The whole point of the business was making people feel like something they'd never needed before was crucial to their everyday life.

By the time I trudged up to his doorstep, it was dark and my legs felt like sausages after being encased in tall leather boots all day. Sexy? Yes. Comfortable? Not exactly. The two rooms on either side of his front door were lit up like happy eyes to welcome me, and my mood lifted a little as I saw he'd lit a fire in one of the fireplaces.

My hand rose to the bell when he swung the door open. I almost stumbled into his arms from the surprise before stumbling into his arms on purpose anyhow.

"Hi." He kissed my ear, his hands steadying me.

"Hi," I sighed. It had been a long, annoying day, but I'd finally gotten to the best part.

All too soon he pushed me back and helped me off with my coat. My bag got shoved under the console table while I sat on the bottom stair to peel off my boots. I let out an audible sigh of relief at the same time that Gage disappeared to the back of the house where the kitchen was.

It seemed like a week since he'd sat right there and ranted about Bobbie's pregnancy, but it had only been twenty-four hours. I made a mental note to call her the next day.

I flexed my stocking-covered toes against the hardwood, trying to stretch out my cramped feet. *Ah, to hell with it.* My tights also came off and got wadded into one boot. I wandered over to the fireplace, bunching up my skirt to feel the warmth on the backs of my bare legs.

Gage reappeared with a glass of red wine in each hand. "Better?" he asked.

"If I sigh in relief any more, I might start hyperventilating," I joked, letting go of my skirt to take the offered glass. "God, I love fires. I mean, fireplace ones, not like arson."

"And here I thought you were a closet pyromaniac." He sipped his wine.

"Ha ha. I never went camping as a kid, never lived anywhere with a fireplace. I always wanted one. I thought they were so romantic. I love that nothing is ever the same with a fire—it's always changing, unpredictable."

"You do know you can watch it on TV at Christmastime, right?"

"Yeah, but I always get jerked out of my little fantasy when the guy in the flannel shirt comes to poke at it."

With my long wool skirt now down and absorbing the heat, I was getting a little too warm. I padded over to a very plain, very beige couch and sat down, careful not to spill any wine.

"What happened with Susan?" he asked, walking over to lean on the armrest beside me.

I was a little surprised to see that he'd changed into his worn jeans when he got home. But his light blue shirt was still on, the sleeves rolled up and the top few buttons undone. It matched his eyes.

"I'm sure she emailed you a report." I rolled my eyes, tasting the wine. "Mmm. Anyhow, she basically advised me to keep my personal life and work life separate."

Actually, she had said something nasty about keeping my legs together in the office, but I didn't want to tell him that. And she was right, regardless. That's what irked me so much—the fact that she was justified in her sanctimonious attitude. Gage hummed in response, examining his wine glass.

"I, uh, texted Bobbie today," I told him. "I went to ask Aaron how she was doing but he wasn't in the office today."

Gage's gaze moved from his wine to the fire. "Yeah, he stayed home with her," he said absently. "He'd better come in tomorrow, though. He's getting behind."

I couldn't tell if he was joking, and suspected that he wasn't. "She asked me to come by tomorrow after work." His frown made my heart hurt. "Um, do you want to come with me?"

"No, that's okay."

Clearly whatever was happening in Gage's head was still happening, and he needed more time to deal with it. Extracting it from his ass would be a good start, though. I decided to change the subject as he swigged the rest of his wine.

"What's for dinner?" The scent of rosemary and garlic drifted from the kitchen.

"Lamb chops."

"Yummy. Will it be ready soon?"

"We've got time."

"For what?"

Rising from his perch, he plucked my wine glass out of my hand, still half-full. He looked thoughtful as he placed it and his empty glass on a side table. "You know, Madeline, it occurs to me that we've gone about this a little backwards."

This? I cocked my head. "How so?"

"I had you blindfolded and you tied me up even before we kissed."

I shifted on the couch, feeling a little too close to the fire. "Hmmm." That was true, but I hadn't minded at the time.

"Then I made you come before our first date."

Also true. The memory of it made me a little breathless, in fact. He sat beside me on the couch, carefully turning me to put my legs over his lap and my back against the armrest. He slipped one hand under my long skirt, smoothing his palm along my shin. I cringed, mentally smacking myself for not shaving my legs that morning.

Gage didn't seem to care, though. His hand wandered higher up my leg, over my knee and squeezing my thigh gently. Part of me wanted to withdraw my legs and run away, embarrassed that my thigh could so easily be squeezed like putty. Argh! Why didn't I have shapely, rock hard legs with a thigh gap a small child could pass through?

Then his fingers slipped over my inner thigh, tickling me just below where my legs met.

"Gage…" Biting back a gasp, I tried to look at him sternly. Yeah, it didn't work.

"Maddie…" He didn't even bother trying to hide his glee as the tips of his fingers brushed across the crotch of my panties. "You naughty girl, have you been this wet all day?"

"Not *all* day." He didn't need to know about the extra underwear stashed in my desk drawer on a regular basis now.

His smile was smug and delighted, like an adolescent boy who'd snapped a bra strap that then came undone. "Do you think about me when you're at the office?"

I gave him a "well, duh!" look. At the office, at home, on the bus. I didn't want to inflate his ego anymore—if that was even possible—but it would be fair to say that I thought about him way more than was smart. But Brian Gage had a way of bringing out my inner stupid.

"I think about you," he said. "I think about you all fucking day. I get hard and have to stay at my desk until I make it go away so I can get up. You're the reason I've been having meetings in my office instead in other people's."

Oh. "Sorry?"

He made a growling sound deep in his throat that went straight to my clit. "No, you're not."

I grinned. "No, I'm not." The image of a strained

Gage trying to hide his hard-on under his desk made me want to giggle. "Uh, you do know that your desk is clear glass, right? Everyone can probably see you anyways."

His eyes widened in shock; clearly he hadn't thought of that.

With the dexterity of a Cirque de Soleil artist, he lifted my legs off his lap, pulled me so that I was lying on the couch, my hair flowing over the armrest, and twisted around until he was prone on top of me. His knees held him up, one on either side of my leg over my skirt, effectively pinning me down. I was at his mercy—and so far he'd shown me little.

26

MADDIE

He lowered his head to mine, kissing me sweetly at first. His lips were soft against mine, but when they parted a little I could taste the rich wine we'd had. When I whimpered a little, needing more, he deepened the kiss until I felt like I'd drunk the whole bottle myself.

My arms went around him, my hands almost clawing at his back through his shirt. Kissing Gage was quickly becoming my favorite pastime. His mouth slanted over mine, drawing out the deepest, darkest response from me. He dragged desire out of me that I didn't know I had in me. My hands went to his head, his silky hair between my fingers and his jaw clenching under the heels of my hands.

"Gage, I need you."

"Oh god, I need you too."

I looked in his eyes and saw him struggling to reconcile the pressure of his passion with his need for control. I kissed him tenderly then nipped his bottom lip to surprise him. He moaned, his pupils dilating with arousal.

"Let go for me," I begged him. "I want all of you, not just the parts that you think are appropriate or safe. I want you to let go of all that self-restraint and give me everything. You want everything from me? Well then, you have to give it up too."

He looked thoughtful, even a little frightened at the idea of losing his grip on the reins. "You want my best and my worst," he mused.

For better or worse, in sickness and in health… I couldn't ignore the familiar words that his own triggered in my head. Even the fleeting idea of commitment like that should have scared me, but there, in his arms, the fire spitting behind us, I felt safer than I had since my Gotcha Day.

"Well, maybe not your worst," I warned him. "You can be a bit of an, uh…"

"Asshole?"

"I was going to say know-it-all, but that works too."

He slowly licked up the side of my neck like I was an ice cream cone, making me hitch a breath in my straining lungs. "Are you sure you want my best?" he whispered.

"I want you—the real you, the scary, ugly you. Not the CEO or the optimized iteration." I couldn't help scoffing at the jargon he sometimes dictated.

"I'm trying to communicate plainly with you here, so strip all that crap away and gimme gimme gimme. I'm not saying I have to be on top or anything." My face heated at his raised eyebrow. Maybe his words of confidence and trust had seeped into me. "Or that I want to be in charge, but I want to be on the same level."

Slowly he nodded. "That seems… fair."

Despite my bold words, I was trembling with nerves as well as lust. I'd never asked so much of him before. And if I were being honest, I was a little afraid of getting it. But I was putting myself out there, climbing that pole and leaping. The least he could do was jump as well.

"Forget 'fair', Gage. You're measuring, analyzing again. Just *feel* me."

His hands roamed over me, his gaze following closely behind. His knuckles nudged the curves at the bottom of my breasts and pressed gently to feel the bumps of my ribcage. He tugged my blouse out of the waistband of my skirt so he could slide his hands across my warm, tingling skin.

"Ahhhh!" A gasp escaped me as I reminded myself to let go as well.

With surprising grace, he rolled me to the floor in front of the fireplace and undid the buttons on my blouse. I pulled it off while he took off his own shirt, and my hands went to the fastening on my skirt. Gage bent over to slide my skirt down my legs. He tossed it on the couch while he slowly undid his pants.

"Are you sure?" he asked, his hands paused at his waist.

My answer was to wriggle out of my bra and panties and lie there, letting the heat from both his gaze and the fire lick my naked body.

With a pained grunt, he shoved his jeans and briefs down and kicked them off. He stood above me, his erection in his hand. He was strong, lithe, and all man. Idly he stroked himself, watching me watch him. Inside I was loosening, lengthening in anticipation of him, my body reacting in pure, primal ways.

I stretched out my arms and spread my legs, beckoning him. "No games, no expectations. Just us."

His hand moved over his cock as he bit his lower lip. "What about—"

"*Just us*. I trust you, Gage." Did he have any idea what that meant to me? It was not something I doled out lightly.

He knelt before me, his shaft bobbing between us. Despite being on display for him, his gaze was completely focused on my face. The crown of my head was hot from the fire, but the way he looked at me made me shiver.

With a tentative touch, he tested my readiness. The second he touched me I wanted to yelp and moan. But I forced myself to be still and quiet, to let him feel me. He bent over me, the hot, hard tip of his cock nudging at my entrance. He offered each of my nipples a soft, wet kiss then rested his ear on my left breast.

"I can hear your heart," he said quietly, his head rising and falling with each breath I took.

"I'm impressed you slowed down long enough to listen."

He lifted his head to look at me. Other than a faint line across his forehead, his face was smooth, washed clean of worry or fierce ambition. "Jesus, Maddie. You will be the death of me."

"No." I smiled. "I will be the life of you. I promise. But I have health insurance through work, just in case. Now fuck me."

He let out a sharp laugh then sighed, averting his eyes. "No, Madeline. I'm not going to fuck you."

I stilled in shock and shame. *Oh god*. This is why I

shouldn't commit. It was too risky, too easy to look foolish and vulnerable and oh my god why did I—

"I want to make love to you," he said, interrupting my inner tailspin.

My heart stretched like an overinflated balloon, threatening to pop.

A cracked noise burst from my throat as I reached for him. With determined deliberation, he lined himself up at my entrance before cocking an eyebrow at me. I nodded, swallowing hard. My hips tilted in anticipation.

He entered me slowly—too slowly—getting about halfway inside when I groaned. Already I felt full, my whole body swollen with my need for him. Then he stopped.

"Please, Gage. I need all of you," I repeated.

His forehead, neck and chest were getting damp from heat and the strain of subduing his desire for domination.

"Meet me in the middle," he demanded in a hoarse voice.

So I ran my hands over the muscles of his shoulders and back, down to the flexing perfection of his ass. Clutching him and with my legs wound around his thighs, I enveloped him. We both exhaled as he bottomed out inside me. I'd never felt so close to anyone, had never even wanted to. It was intimate and genuine and terrifying.

"God, Madeline. You take my breath away." He rested his forehead on mine. His breath was hot on my face, caressing my lips like a ghostly kiss.

I felt the same way. Then again, he was lying on top of me and probably outweighed me by at least sixty pounds.

We began rocking together slowly, instinctively knowing to work together as a team. Maybe we were finally mastering effective interpersonal communication. Every stroke he made, I rose to meet. Every time my lips met his skin, we branded each other.

"Fuck, you feel amazing," he grunted harshly as he slid home inside me.

"I know, I know!" A familiar tension was building in me, making me want to cling to him so it didn't slip away. He kissed me, his tongue darting into my mouth with every drive of his hard body against mine. It still wasn't enough.

He thrust again and again, making my head tilt back in dizzy rapture. "Oh my god, I feel like you're touching my heart from the inside!"

"Madeline, I'm so close," he ground out in warning. The lines around his mouth and eyes tightened.

I ran my hands up and down his back, memorizing the line of his spine. "It's okay. Let go. I'm there too," I panted. My climax was bubbling deep within me, promising to burst up and flood me.

Then it did, spilling forth and drowning me with pleasure. "Gage, oh so good!"

He arched back a little, the tanned line of his neck taut. A harsh shout burst from his mouth, and when he looked down at me it was with a shocked expression. He'd truly lost control with me.

"Take me, Maddie. Take it all." His blue eyes were wide and wild. He tried to hold the rest of his body straight and strong, but his hips jerked against me help- lessly, as though disconnected from his brain.

Watching him ride out the orgasm that I gave him was the hottest, heaviest thing I'd ever seen.

"Holy shit," he breathed, collapsing on me. He burrowed his burning face into my neck, his body trembling as he tried to regain control of his senses.

I fondled the smooth dark hair at the back of his head, my own body still pulsing as it tried to keep him inside. It took me a moment of feeling his weight on me to recognize all the emotions competing for attention in me—I'd spent so many years trying to push them down.

I felt sated, relieved, happy, shy, and safe. Mostly I was proud—but for him. I was so happy that he could feel the joy of being spontaneous, of letting go of his expectations and fears and just living in the moment, in me. My eyes burned and watered at the wave of emotion that came over me. Gage had really given himself to me, and it was the most valuable gift he could ever bestow.

With a reluctant groan, he rolled off me but still pulled me with him so we were lying on our sides facing each other. The heat of the fire was probably singing my hair, but I didn't care. He trailed his hand over the curve of my shoulder, the dip of my waist and the swell of my hip, with rapt focus and reverence.

"Yours," I whispered.

"All mine?"

I pressed my hand to his heart, feeling it beat under his hot skin. "All *mine*." Then I gathered my courage to do what I had to do. "Gage?"

"Hmmm?" He was completely distracted by my skin in the firelight.

"I quit."

"*You what?*" I snatched my hand back as though sparks from the fireplace had ignited her skin.

"I quit. My job," she added.

That's what I thought she'd said. I'd lost swimmers, not brain cells. What was she talking about?

I examined her closely. She'd rolled onto her belly, her chin resting on her crossed arms. A dreamy smile masked her face and her eyes closed against the glow of the fire, which needed stoking.

"Madeline, what are you talking about?"

For someone without that much experience with men, she sure knew how to kill the mood. Then again, that could explain her lack of experience.

She turned her head, resting the side of it on her forearms to look at me. "Do you want me?"

My gaze swept over her pink ear, the bright hair swept around her neck like a scarf, the valley of her spine sweeping down to the creamy hills of her ass. With her arms raised, the sides of her luscious tits bubbled out from beneath her body.

Oh, right. She'd asked me a question. "Of course I fucking want you." *There. That was pretty effective communication, right?*

Her smile was like a shooting star. "Do you want me to be your, uh, girlfriend?" She glanced at the fire, trying to hide her shyness and the glow in her cheeks.

At times I forgot how much younger she was than me. This was not one of those times. "Yes, Maddie. I'm all in. God help me, you're mine."

"Then I have to stop working for you." A divot appeared between her arched eyebrows as she frowned. "*Why?*"

"I can't be your girlfriend and your assistant, Gage. It's exactly why I didn't want to share a suite with you in the mountains. Everybody will think that I slept my way into my job."

Was she crazy? "But you started months ago. They know we weren't together then." *Didn't they?*

She pushed herself up onto her knees, placing her palms on her thighs. I tried not to look at the shadowy crease at her center. Clearly I was unsuccessful; with a huff, she reached for her clothes.

"Focus, Gage. I know you're good at that."

I sat up as she threw my jeans at me. She had no idea how hard it was for a man to focus while watching a gorgeous woman put on a bra. "We're not sharing a suite now. The next retreat we go on, I'll get you a room at the other end of the hotel." *Like hell I would—book another retreat, that was.*

"I can't do both jobs at once, not well anyway. I'm trying to commit here, but I recognize my limitations. Remember, Susan said I needed to keep my personal life and my job separate." She looked down at the panties she'd discarded earlier then shrugged casually as she pulled on her skirt without them.

"So, compartmentalize!" I shouted, trying not to stumble as I shoved one leg at a time into my jeans. Apparently we were both going commando.

"Compartmentalize?"

"That's what I do! It works—mostly." Well, except for the painful hard-ons I got at the office. I ignored her knowing smirk. "Shit, Maddie, you can't quit. I need you."

In just her bra and skirt, she stepped into my shadow and put her hand on my cheek. "I need you too." Dropping her hand, she wrapped her arms around my waist and pressed her cheek to my bare chest.

"But work—"

"If I don't quit, Susan will fire me," she reminded me. "We're not great at being on the down low."

I took a halting step back, propping my hands on my hips. "You know, some women would love to have a man like me worship at their fucking feet."

She sighed. "That's not the point, Gage."

"I won't let her fire you. Executive veto. I'm the boss, remember?"

"Which would just prove her point!" She found her blouse on the floor and turned away to put it on. She was replacing her armor as she spoke. "This isn't easy for me either, you know."

"I hate quitters," I couldn't help saying. "You're not a quitter."

She froze, her head bent and her fingers on her buttons. After a few seconds of silence, she finished doing them up and pivoted to face me. "Yes, I am, Gage. I know that about myself, but I'm trying to change. You make me want to try, want to stick to something."

"So stick to me!"

"I want to. As your girlfriend." Her chin was stubbornly set, but there was doubt in her eyes.

"But—"

"Would you rather keep me as your lover or your assistant? Because I can't be both; you have to pick."

Even in the flickering light from the fire, I could see the hurt and disappointed expression on her face as she handed me my shirt. I tossed it aside, glaring at her. *Ah shit.* No man should have to be in this situation. I scrubbed my face with my hands, my stomach in knots.

"I said I was all in. That meant *everything.*" *I gave her all of myself. I let go for her, and now she wanted to let go of me?*

"I'm sorry. I want you too. I just can't do both. It's too hard."

Her shoulders sagged, and she looked pitiful—but determined. For once, she'd made a decision. If it wasn't the *wrong* decision, I would have been proud. Instead, although it wasn't my fault, it was going to be my problem.

For a wealthy, successful man, this was like *Sophie's Choice*—the horrible choice between an amazing woman in your arms and a fantastic employee in your office. *Fuck.* I bet Bill Gates never had this problem. Wait a second, didn't he marry somebody who worked for him?

"Gage?"

I shook my head. "This isn't fair."

"I'm sorry," she repeated. "Life isn't fair. Believe me, I know."

"Argh!" *I couldn't decide!* I took a few deep breaths,

frowning. "Maddie, the lamb chops need to come out of the oven."

"Is that code or something?" She looked puzzled.

"No, dinner! It's probably overcooked by now."

"Oh!" She hustled out of the room, leaving me to my existential crisis. I heard a clunk and a curse come from the kitchen, and when she returned her face was red.

"I guess the question, Gage, is whether you want me for me."

Her simple words and sober expression took me straight to our car ride back from the retreat. Then she told me she wanted to be wanted for *her*, just her—the way she hadn't been wanted by her mother. I felt sick.

Of course I wanted her for her, what was I thinking? Assistants could be hired; girlfriends couldn't. Well, okay, they could, but no man really wanted *that* kind of girlfriend. I had to let her make her own decisions. If she wanted to be with me, how could I say no?

28

GAGE

"Where's Maddie?"

I looked up from where I was staring at my desk. She was right—you could totally see my crotch through the tempered glass top.

"She's at lunch," I told Bobbie.

"Why so glum, chum?"

My sister stepped inside and slowly sat down on the leather couch in the corner. So many memories of Madeline on that couch... And now she'd given her two-week notice.

My fingers combed through my hair, and I tried to tug the despondence out of my head. It didn't work. The wrong woman was still sitting on that couch, and Maddie was probably out doing job interviews during her lunch hour.

"What are you doing here?" I asked.

"Having lunch with my big brother?"

I waited silently.

"Okay, I was supposed to have lunch with Aaron but

he's still stuck in some sponsorship meeting. So I thought I'd try Maddie instead."

I was the consolation prize. *Great.* I gave her a noncommittal grunt, but at least the tightness in my chest eased a bit when she stood up to approach my desk.

"You're looking better," I said as she sat down in the visitor's chair. "You've got some color again."

"Yeah, now I'm green." My blank stare made her roll her eyes. "Morning sickness, Brainiac." She clutched her belly, bent over and faked a retching sound.

"Charming."

"Isn't it? One of the fun things about pregnancy." Her tone was sarcastic but her demeanor made me wonder if she was gestating a unicorn—she was so damn chipper.

"You mean there *are* fun things about pregnancy?"

"Sure." But then my sister pressed her lips together tightly. Either she was going to hurl, or she'd decided not to talk about it anymore—at least not with me.

I grabbed a file folder from a fan-shaped array of them on the left side of my desk. "I don't have time for lunch, sorry."

The truth was that I was still uncomfortable around a pregnant Bobbie. It was hard enough for me to accept the fact that I had no control over the situation, but now Madeline was pressing me to accept the fact that it shouldn't be a "situation" for me in the first place. Which reminded me…

"Don't you have a job to get back to?"

Bobbie's mouth turned down. I hadn't meant for my words to come out sounding so, well, snarky. But really, was she still working at the lodge? Or had she quit that job now too?

"I talked to them, and they were really understanding." '*More understanding than you,*' was the unsaid implication. "It's kind of shoulder season now, so things are slower. It's getting too late for hikers but too early for skiers." She shrugged. "I'm taking my vacation time now to figure it out."

"Are you going to quit?" My stomach soured at the thought of another abandoned career.

She shook her head emphatically. "No. I really love that job, and I'm good at it. I'm just trying to, well, you know."

No, I didn't.

"Are you still staying with Aaron?" Our mother had downsized to a one-bedroom condo a few years ago, not that it had stopped Bobbie from crashing there before in between jobs and apartments and boyfriends.

"Yup. He's been really… amazing." She sighed, and despite the bit of pallor lingering on her skin she looked happy. Birds-chirping-around-her-head kind of happy, in fact. I had to grudgingly admit that it looked good on her.

"How does he feel about the baby?"

She frowned. "He's okay."

"Okay?" My eyebrows rose. "Well, that's a ringing endorsement."

"I don't know. We've kind of been avoiding talking about it too much. We just started dating, and we're not quite sure what we're doing yet."

She made a vague gesture to her lap, which disconcerted me. It was a bit late to have the birds and the bees talk with her.

"You mean with dating?"

"I mean with the baby." She folded her arms protectively over her stomach, looking worried. The imaginary birds around her head fell silent, one of them metaphorically plummeting to the ground.

"How can you not know?"

It boggled my mind. If it were me, I would have already had several conversations and set agendas and goals and made a list of pros and cons and—*oh*. This was probably exactly the kind of thing that Madeline was talking about.

"We're just not sure what to do. I still don't know if I'm ready for this."

Bobbie looked at her lap, then up at me, then down to her lap again. It felt like she was silently asking me for advice, and for once I had none to offer. Madeline had told me to back off, and I was trying my best. I didn't know if Bobbie was ready for this either, but I knew I couldn't actually tell her that.

"I don't think anyone is ever *really* ready to be a parent," I said lamely, opening a folder and staring blankly at the contents. "It's kind of a learn as you go along thing, right?"

She nodded. "You know what I keep thinking, and I feel so guilty about it?"

"What?"

"I keep wondering if I'd be a better mother than Mom was."

Wow. I shoved the folders aside. She pretended to be staring at her hands, but she was peeking up at me every few seconds—probably to gauge my reaction. My initial reaction was one of a complete loss for words, though.

She probably hadn't expected that—I usually had an opinion about everything she did.

"Say something, Brain!"

Shaking my head, I leaned back in my chair, trying to approach this conversation systematically. "Do you think Mom did a bad job?"

"No! Not really."

If she was waiting for me to put words in her mouth, she'd better get comfortable. I bobbed back and forth in my chair as it reclined, flipping a pen between my fingers.

"It's just that… well, I think it was harder after Dad died, right?" she said. "It's not like she *lost* it, but she didn't really have her shit together either."

Pot. Kettle. Madeline would have been proud of me for keeping my mouth shut. I merely hummed instead. Of course I agreed with her, but I didn't trust my opinion not to run away from me without letting my brain catch up.

I cleared my throat before coming up with, "It was hard at times for all of us."

Holy shit. If I came up with any more of these mind-blowingly erudite observations, I would have to record them and write a fucking motivational book.

My sister looked at me as though an alien had replaced me. I threw the pen down on the desk.

"Okay, fuck. I don't know, Bob. Yeah, there were times when I worried Mom might burn down the house, but that didn't mean she didn't love us. Hell, she was almost *beside herself* with her love for us. Nobody's perfect." *Well, except me, right?* It was a good thing that Madeline wasn't there, or she'd give me a withering look.

"Remember the time she forgot to pick me up from camp? She thought it ended the next week?" She snorted, but I still remembered the tears mottling her face when an irritated senior counselor dropped her off.

Of course, it hadn't helped that it was the beginning of my entrepreneurial programming phase, and I'd managed to convince her that Mom had sold her to Camp Iwanna to finance my new computer.

"You always got along better with her than I did," I pointed out. "You guys are a lot alike."

"That's what I'm afraid of!"

When I looked at her more closely, I saw new lines of worry etched in her face. This baby thing was really freaking her out. Hell, it was freaking me out too.

"You can't live your life in fear," I said.

I knew Aaron would step up—that was just the kind of guy he was. He also knew that I would string him up by his life-giving balls if he didn't. And to whatever extent she could, I knew that our mother would enjoy being a grandma. Bobbie just needed more confidence. It was sobering to realize that I was probably a big part of the reason she doubted herself.

"Ha! That's easy for you to say! You've never been scared by anything."

I swiveled in my chair to look out the enormous window behind me. *Shit, she was so wrong.* I was scared of lots of things, which is why I had a low tolerance for excuse making. It would be too easy to do it myself.

"Brain?"

"Everybody's scared of something," I muttered, looking out over downtown. Busy people, busy lives, failure, success, family, solitude—it was all out there. Some people worked their asses off for it, and for others it fell into their laps.

If I were going to be honest, I would tell Bobbie that I was afraid that I would lose Madeline, or at least fuck it up somehow. I was afraid that my ideas and applications were one-hit wonders and that I would crash and burn like so many start-ups before me.

With a jolt I realized that I already lived in fear; it was what drove me to succeed. I kept pushing Madeline to take a chance, but all the chances that I'd taken weren't risks so much as they were tunnel vision. The real leap of faith would be to let go of the reins a bit.

"Honestly, Bobbie, I think that having that fear might help you as a parent. If you're aware of what you'll fuck up, you'll try harder."

"Gee, thanks."

"Seriously, it's the clueless, arrogant assholes who screw up their kids." *Like me?* Again, I imagined Madeline and myself in this situation. For the first time, the idea didn't make me want to puke.

A strange noise behind me made me turn back around. Bobbie's face was pink, and she pressed her fist into her stomach.

"Sorry. I'm hungry. But thanks for the, uh, pep talk."

I exhaled heavily as I stood up. She rose as well, then paused as I slipped my phone into my pocket. "Okay, let's go feed the parasite," I grumbled, but my sister's surprised smile was contagious. Maybe there was hope for me yet.

29

MADDIE

The things that I'd collected over a few months of working at Apptitude didn't even need a banker's box to carry out. It all fit in my laptop bag.

Every day that I worked after giving Gage and Susan my two-week notice was harder than the one before. Every day I went back and forth over my decision to leave so I could commit myself to trying a real relationship with Gage. Every day his expression was a little more hangdog, a little more mournful. The look on his face tied my stomach in knots, but for once I decided not to let myself be wishy-washy.

In the end I didn't even have to work the whole two weeks. Susan let me know that they would manage without me but I would still get two weeks of pay, and I got the bum's rush out of the office.

Before I left on my last day, I allowed myself one solid hour of necking with Gage on the black leather couch in his office.

"Are you sure about this, Madeline?" he drawled in my ear. We were curled up like baby cats on the couch, my back against the armrest and my former employer deliciously crowding me into the corner.

Even someone whose decision was carved in stone would wobble a little with Brian Gage's five o'clock shadow brushing over their earlobe. I fought a shiver, not wanting to show any hesitation. I wasn't strong enough to withstand a full-on siege, and we both knew it.

"Yes? Oh god, right *there*."

His lips curved into a smile against the side of my neck as his fingers deftly undid the buttons of my tailored white shirt. "Really sure? You won't be able to do this every day," he reminded me.

"I'm sure I'll survive." *I might self-combust, though.*

My tongue ventured out to taste the divot at the base of his throat. His skin had that end of the day smell—the pure masculine scent left on him after the veneer of shampoo and soap had worn off. It was intoxicating to me. Maybe all this attraction was just pheromones. "I'll live." *Probably.*

"But I won't," he groaned as I untucked his shirt. "Really, Maddie? A black lace bra under this shirt that just screams *businesswoman?*"

My fingers were practically itching to undo his zipper and… no! I was an adult, and I had more self-control than that. "There's always after work."

"The first time she makes a decision, and it takes her away from me," he complained under his breath. Of course, I heard him since his breath was practically on my own lips.

My mouth sought his in a passionate attempt to stop him from making me doubt myself. His tongue helped, but it was his hands on my breasts that really bolstered my self-confidence. I had to stop making out with him at work, so that I could get naked with him outside of the office.

"What else does my shirt scream?"

He tilted his head. "I can't hear it very well, since it's all the way over there on the floor now."

So it was. My nipples hardened in the cool air of the office, rising to meet his urgent touch.

"You sure you don't want me to try to train the temp?" I hadn't heard much about my replacement, but assumed that he was getting somebody from the temp agency through which he'd found me.

"Hmmm?" He was twisting a lock of my hair with one hand and teasing a circle around my bellybutton with the other. Heat built in my core, but all my spare underwear was packed, so I reluctantly stilled his fingers before they ventured lower.

"Training?" I repeated.

"Right. Unneeded for now." With a frown, he flopped back against the couch beside me. His erection was on full display, but he showed not one iota of shame or embarrassment—just a whole lot of tenting. "Susan's going to help me out for a while."

Pretty man say what? "Explain?"

"She took a course in business communication and wants to work on her skills, so she offered to work with me until we find your replacement." He grabbed my hand and kissed my palm. "You're a hard act to follow."

"She wants to follow *your* 'hard act'," I muttered. Susan was probably already imagining late nights on this very couch. She was a relatively nice person, but a little too flirty with my man.

I traced an outline of the bulge in his trousers with

my fingernail, making him hiss in pleasure. There was a sexy tendon in his neck that was calling my name as well. *Decisions, decisions.*

"So what are you going to do with your time now? Other than me, of course."

Gage waggled his dark eyebrows in a manner I'm sure he thought was seductive. On anyone else it would look ridiculous, but I found pretty much everything about him irresistible. I rolled my eyes and tried to escape my little corner of the couch, but he pulled me across his lap instead—ass end up.

"Hey!" I twisted around to glare at him.

His hands splayed across my backside, exploring the center seam on my leggings. "I believe I owe you a spanking."

"That was just playing. Goofing off."

"I never just 'goof off,' Madeline. Now it's time for you to get off."

Party pooper. "Okay," I sighed. I squirmed to move off his lap, but let out a delighted yelp as his palm stung my skin. My neck tweaked as I jerked my head around, but he just smirked at me.

"Different kind of 'get off.'"

Oh. In that case... I wriggled to get more comfortable, but there was a good chance that my sudden breathlessness had more to do with his intentions than my ribcage pressing into his thighs.

"Isn't it time we had a safe word?" I asked.

"Do you feel unsafe?"

"Not exactly." Nervous, maybe? I'd never been spanked before, and I was surprised at how damp the idea made me.

I was spread over his lap like a napkin at a nice

restaurant, my knees and arms on the couch on either side of him. My back was arched due to the angle that my hips were pressing against his thighs, pushing my ass further up. The leather of the couch cooled my heated face.

Gage walked his fingers up the back of my thigh and over my ass to hook them in the waistband of my leggings.

"Can't you be spanked through clothes?" I asked him.

"Of course."

Without hesitation he peeled my leggings down to expose my cheeks. Then Gage snapped the top of the thong I wore to avoid a visible panty line.

"Hey!" I gasped, resting my face on my hands to look back at him. His expression was intense and amused at the same time. With one hand he massaged me and with the other he reached over to touch my face.

"I can't wait to make these cheeks as pink and warm as this one."

Oh god. I was going to die of embarrassment and arousal while sporting a raspberry-lace whale tail. "Gage, you can't *say* things like that to me."

He gave me a raised eyebrow, as though to say "Have you met me?" I was pinned by his disbelieving stare. And then he smacked my ass.

"Ow!"

The sudden flick of his fingertips startled me, even though I knew it was coming. He didn't even use his whole hand—just stunned me with the whiplash of his first three fingers. It was the kind of slap you'd give a child on the hand for trying to sneak cookies before dinner—or at least the kind I got in one foster home.

"Am I supposed to be counting these or something?" I asked him.

The lascivious gleam in his eyes filled my heart and broke my courage at the same time. God help me, but I was up for anything with this man.

He frowned. "Do you think I'm punishing you?"

It was a good question. "You're still mad that I quit," I pointed out.

"Disappointed, not mad."

It was my turn to raise an eyebrow.

"Okay, I'm a little mad."

"But you get why, right?" It was important to me that he understood why I couldn't work for him anymore if we were going to pursue a real relationship. I was ready to take that leap of faith and commit my heart to him, which was a hell of a lot scarier than committing my working day to him.

He was silent, one hand on the small of my arched back and the other slowly petting me.

"Gage? Look at me." His head tilted. If I craned my neck anymore around, I would look like I was possessed. "I want you."

"You're half naked and bent over my knee. I should hope you do."

"Smart ass."

Once again his hand came down, lighter this time but with no less of a sting. My ass actually smarted, which I supposed I had asked for. My whole body was heating up, and I was glad that my leggings hobbled me at the knees, because it made it a lot easier to squeeze my thighs together.

"Uh uh uh," he scolded me. "I see what you're doing, Madeline." He dipped between my legs, making me gasp as he traced along my crack to the moist darkness below. He spread his fingers, preventing me from clenching my upper thighs together for relief.

"Gage…" It was a plea for mercy, a request for more, and a warning not to destroy me, all rolled into one simple utterance of his name. But as he circled my entrance, I barely remembered my own name. "*Ohhh*."

My shiver turned into a pained hiccup when he brought his palm down this time, fully spanking me across both cheeks. *Holy fuck*.

"You're dripping, Madeline."

"Brilliant observation, sir."

I turned my face back to the smooth surface of the couch. I couldn't watch him anymore, couldn't handle the lust in his eyes without exploding myself. "Am I a-allowed to come?" I asked with a tremor in my voice. Considering what I had done to him on this very couch, I definitely needed to ask.

"What do you think?"

I *hated* when he did that—turned my questions around on me. If I knew, I wouldn't have asked him! Either I was right and looked like an idiot for asking him in the first place, or I was wrong and potentially made him angry. No matter what I did, it was hard to win. Speaking of which, I felt the length of him harden under my stomach where I lay on him.

"I think this turns you on a little," I said, arching my back to press my belly into his erection.

"I'm not the only one."

He gently slipped one finger into me at the same time as spanking me again.

"Oh god!"

Then he withdrew his hand and I heard him say,

"You taste like a mimosa, Madeline. Bright and sparkly and dangerously easy to drink."

The low thrumming in me cranked up, until I was squirming on his lap. "Can I come, sir?" I repeated my question, jerking my head up as he rained a small shower of smacks all over me, from my sacrum to the crease at the back of my upper thighs. He'd better freaking say yes, because I was going to lose it anyway.

"Oh Madeline, your skin is all bright and blushing." The reverence in his voice was admiring, not creepy. I was surely blushing all over, but a part of me delighted in pleasing him.

"Do you like it?" I asked shyly.

"I *love* it."

I could tell. I was feeling a little like I was between a rock and a hard place—literally. All of a sudden I felt as though we were too far apart, disconnected despite our position. Bending my elbow, I reached my hand back and he twined our fingers together.

"I want you to come, Maddie."

That was all the permission I needed. Our fingers still locked together, he brought his other hand down on my ass and I flew apart.

"Yes!"

I closed my eyes against the roiling swells of pleasure spreading from my belly. My climax was sharp, swift, and left me boneless over his hard body. I didn't get to enjoy it for very long, as he scooped me up into his arms and cradled me against his chest.

"Ouch!" My ass was a little tender as it rubbed against his pants, and the erection he sported underneath.

With a gentle hand he tilted my chin up and turned

my head to face him. "Good girl," he said succinctly before kissing the breath out of me.

I felt ridiculously proud of myself. I'd taken another chance and it was okay. I felt like I was flying in his arms, and he was holding out my wings for me.

"I'll miss you at work," I admitted, his nose nudging mine in an Eskimo kiss.

"You'll do great. Maybe I'll get more done without your ass distracting me."

Well, there was that as well.

30

GAGE

F rom: Brian Gage (brian.gage@apptitude.com)
To: Madeline Jones (madeline.jones@apptitude.com)

Re: Stockwell VC file

I can't find the last letter we sent to Vik at Stockwell. It's not in my email. I tried your desk drawer, but I only found a pair of black panties. I'm keeping them, btw. But I still need the letter for Susan to use as a template.

F rom: Madeline Jones (madeline.jones@apptitude.com)
To: Brian Gage (Brian.gage@apptitude.com)

Re: Re: Stockwell VC file

Try the filing cabinet in your office on the left, third drawer down, under "Investors-Companies" (not Investors-Indiv.). Also, it probably is in your email. Look harder. Try searching "stockwell" in that little empty bar at the top of the screen.

Which black ones? Lace or stretchy? Please tell me
Susan wasn't with you when you found them.

F**rom:**   **Brian**   **Gage**
(Brian.gage@apptitude.com)
**To: Madeline Jones (madeline.jones@appti-
tude.com)**
Re: Re: Re: Stockwell VC file

No, she wasn't with me when we found them. I don't
know which ones—they're stretchy lace!

I found the folder, but the letter isn't in it. I need a
hard copy. And I know how to search my email, thank
you very much. I'm not a complete n00b.

F**rom:**   **Madeline**   **Jones**
(madeline.jones@apptitude.com)
To: **Brian**   **Gage**
(Brian.gage@apptitude.com)
Re:changing the subject

WTF? *WE* found them?
You are in big trouble.

F**rom:**   **Brian**   **Gage**
(Brian.gage@apptitude.com)
**To: Madeline Jones (madeline.jones@appti-
tude.com)**
Re:Re: changing the subject

I'm not the one who left them there. Most people
keep granola bars in their desk, Madeline.

BTW, I told her they were mine. I think your worries

about her coming on to me are probably over. And they smelled delicious.

From: **Madeline** **Jones** (**madeline.jones@apptitude.com**)
To: Brian Gage (Brian.gage@apptitude.com)
Re: OMFG

You are a total creeper. I expect to see you in that underwear later on, sir.

From: **Brian** **Gage** (**Brian.gage@apptitude.com**)
To: Madeline Jones (madeline.jones@apptitude.com)
Re: Yes, yes I am

You'll have to persuade me.

From: Susan Lee (susan.lee@apptitude.com)
To: Brian Gage (Brian.gage@apptitude.com)
cc: Nikhil Subhash (nikhil.subhash@apptitude.com)
Re: Violation of company email TOS

Mister Gage:

Please be advised that company email accounts, their usage and contents are monitored. In short, you know better.

Madeline Jones's account has been terminated, since she is no longer with the company. If you have an alternate address for her, please feel free to forward this message. I will drop a courier envelope by your office later for you to return her property to her.

Sincerely,
Susan Lee
Director of Human Resources, Apptitude Technologies

I missed her. Somehow, Madeline was spending almost every night at my house, but I still craved her throughout the day. There was absolutely no excuse for it, except for the fact that she wasn't just outside my office door. Or inside my office door. Or pressed *against* my office door.

Her black panties were now stowed in my desk drawer, much to her shock and horror.

"What do you mean, you didn't bring them home?"

We were eating spaghetti at the granite island in my house, without any sensory deprivation. Although, the way she sucked the occasional strand into her mouth made me shift uncomfortably on my stool.

"Exactly what I just said."

"Gage!"

"Possession is nine-tenths of the law." I gave her a smug smile as I twirled my pasta. My pants grew tighter at the memory of those panties.

She stabbed her fork at me. "I want them back. I don't just leave my underwear anywhere, you know."

"Come to the office and get them. They're at the very back of my bottom desk drawer, so you might have to bend waaay ov—*mmph!*" She fed me her forkful to shut me up.

"Perv."

I swallowed, swiping a piece of paper towel across

my mouth. I'd already taken off my dress shirt, but I still didn't relish getting spaghetti sauce on the plain white tee I had on underneath.

"How's the job hunt going?" I hated that she was looking for a job. She *had* a job—with me.

"Meh. I'm back with the temp agency, and they've got me going out on jobs, but they're so…" She trailed off, slurping up more spaghetti.

"What?"

"Boring! It's all just answer phone, stuff envelopes, data entry."

There was a pleading relief in her eyes at being able to tell me just how disappointed she was that not every boss out there was like me. At least, that's how I was interpreting it. She put her fork down.

"Sounds pretty simple," I said.

"That's the problem. Anybody could do these jobs."

I reached across the island and touched her jaw. "But you're not just anybody."

Her cheeks brightened. "Maybe that's the problem," she said quietly. "You made me feel like *somebody*."

"Because you are. Look, I might be a bit overbearing at times—" I chose to ignore her polite snort. "—but I generally know what a person is capable of if they put their minds to it. You have a talent, Madeline. Even Aaron sees it. He said you gave him a lot of really great suggestions for the New Year rollout coming up."

"I'm not sure that counts. His brain stem has been severed by Bobbie's baby news."

Yeah, well, I didn't want to go there right then. "Don't sell yourself short, that's all I'm saying. Keep looking for the right job. Then when you're ready, it will still be here waiting for you."

She narrowed her eyes at me as I blinked innocently. Okay, not that innocently.

"That sounded awfully specific," she said.

My plate made a godawful scraping sound on the granite as I pushed it away from me. "So sue me. I want you back."

"I haven't left you!"

"You quit!"

"You said you understood!" Her sigh was heavy. Our dinner now forgotten, we sat there on our stools, glaring at each other over the island.

"I'm going to kill her," I confessed.

Maddie's eyebrows drew together. "What? Who?"

"Susan."

"Wouldn't it be easier to fire her? It is your company."

I dragged my hand through my hair. "I can't replace her just like that."

"Why not? You replaced me with her!" Bitterness bled through her voice.

I knew she wouldn't understand. This was so embarrassing. "If my Human Resources person is harassing me, who do I report them to?"

She leaned forward, her hands splayed out on the island. "What do you mean?" Her expression was deadly. It was, well, hot.

"What do you think?"

Madeline's mouth fell open, her lips plump and rosy.

"You see my problem," I complained.

I hated to admit it, but she'd been right about Susan. My claim to the lacy lingerie hadn't thrown her off the scent, and with Madeline not there to guard my office door, she'd developed an unwelcome habit of dropping in. I'd considered locking my door, but too many people in the company *were* welcome and even expected throughout the day. I didn't have the time to get up and answer every knock. It was ridiculous and demeaning to even have to consider barricading myself in.

"Doesn't she know that you're—that we—?"

I thought about the panties. "I'm sure she suspects. But you're not there…"

"I'm here now," she said. I blinked at her, not quite understanding. She hopped off her stool and rounded the island to me. "Really, Gage, for a brilliant, wealthy man, you really are dense sometimes." Grabbing my hand, she pulled me off my stool and led me to the staircase. "Looks like I've got some property to mark."

This was not where I had planned to go with this, but I wasn't about to complain. Not when Madeline was peeling off her T-shirt and the clasp of her bra was beckoning me.

By the time we entered my bedroom she was miraculously down to her bra and panties, which did not match in any way but captivated me nonetheless, and I was still fully dressed. I was also hard as a fucking rock from watching her casually shed her clothes in front of me.

Her gaze moved to the bed, and I followed it— straight to the eye hooks screwed into the pallet headboard.

"I promised to tie you up," she said thoughtfully.

I swallowed. "Yes, yes you did. Is that something you want to try?"

With a start, she ripped her gaze from the bed and stepped close to me. Wordlessly, she undid my pants before I helped her tug off my t-shirt. Her breath was hot and hesitant on me, her eyes focused on my chest. I nudged her chin up so I could look in her eyes.

"Madeline?" I couldn't read her expression; it was shuttered to me. The warmth was there, but not the openness I usually saw.

"Do you have some ties?"

I raised an eyebrow. *Did I have some ties?* I was a wealthy businessman. She was kidding, right?

With my erection throbbing against my open fly, I stalked over to the closet. Without even looking at them, I grabbed a handful of neckties from a rack inside the door and threw them on the bed between us like a dare.

"Will these do?"

Her lips curved and her cheeks reddened. "I think so." She picked one up, running it across her palm with a silken swish. "I'm not very good at knots, so you'll have to tell me if I'm doing anything wrong."

I would beg to differ. The knots she'd created in my stomach were pretty damn tight already. But I nodded slowly.

"Take off your clothes," she ordered, absently winding a tie around her wrist like a cuff bracelet.

With relief and trepidation, I stepped out of my pants and briefs, my fist closing around my cock. Never taking her eyes off me, she hooked her thumbs in the waistband of her panties and pushed them down. From tousled head to painted toes, I drank her in. Every curve, every freckle, every little hair—they all fit against me perfectly, even from two feet away. I bit back a groan as I saw a shiny sweep of moisture on her inner thighs.

I was admittedly a little shocked at how easily she'd become necessary to my existence. And if it shocked *me*, then I was sure it was driving her crazy. Then again, when I wanted something I pursued it, and I damn well wanted her. She knew that, but I was about to prove how much.

Naked, I stepped toward the bed. "Do anything." The words almost choked me, but my desire for her was more urgent than my need for control.

She twisted a tie between her two hands, threading it back and forth between her fingers, looking pensive. "Are you sure?"

I nodded, closing my eyes.

"Get on the bed."

Well, that was a pretty basic start. I could do that. I knelt in the middle of the bed. "Now what?"

"Now I blindfold you." She knelt on the bed beside me. The silk tie was cool against my eyelids as she tied it surprisingly tight at the back of my head. "I don't want this sucker moving," she muttered. I startled as she kissed me, then felt the air around me shift as she moved off the bed again.

I remained still, unseeing, and I waited. The little hairs on my arms stood up, my erection flagging a little. What the hell was she doing? Examining me? I heard her breathing, so I knew she hadn't left the room.

"You'd better not be taking pictures right now," I joked.

"Now there's an idea."

"Madeline…"

"Lie down."

I did.

"Raise your arms."

I did, slowly.

Her hand closed over my cock, teasing it until it lay hard and heavy against my belly. She leaned over the bed, the tangy scent of her arousal falling over me like a blanket. Something tickled my thighs, and I shuddered as I realized it was her hair.

"Fuck," I wheezed out.

She hummed in response. "We'll get to that." The bed bounced as she jumped on and straddled me. The heat at her core settled over me, making me groan.

"Hmmm, what to do, what to do."

She bent close to me, the spicy smell of her hair filling my nostrils. The muscles in my abdomen clenched as she licked a line of fire across my chest. It took everything I had in me to stay relatively still. I felt her gaze on me like a branding iron.

My mouth curved but my voice was tight. "I'm starting to feel a little objectified here, Madeline."

"That's Mistress to you," she joked.

I shook my head, automatically lowering my arms. The force with which she pushed my hands back up toward the headboard was a little surprising, but the efficiency with which she tied my wrists to the eyehooks completely overwhelmed me. But it was fuck hot.

"Have you been practicing your knots, naughty girl?"

"Maybe," she said slyly. She ground against me, her damp panties the only barrier against my aching erection. "Are you going to let me take the lead here?"

I wanted to, but it was hard to let go. I'd experienced some of that loss of control the first time I'd made love to her in front of the fireplace, but the memory still unsettled me. Okay, yes, it had also fueled more than one solo morning shower session that left me gasping for breath, but that was fantasy, not reality.

The reality was that I could smell her but not taste

her, feel her but not see her. My senses were straining against each other, instinct against intellect, heart against head. I must have taken too long to think about it, because she began to slide off me.

"I'm sorry, Gage. Maybe this was a bad—"

"No! Wait!" My stomach tightened as I tried to sit up, my shoulders twisting behind me as I forgot about my bound hands.

"Hey, okay, okay. Don't do that," she scolded me, pushing me back down on the bed. "You're going to hurt yourself." She draped herself back over me, kissing my chest and neck. "What's going on in that big brain of yours, huh?"

I sighed a little in relief at feeling her on top of me again. "It's just weird for me, that's all."

"Weird for you? This is all new to me." She began sucking my neck into her mouth in tiny bites. "If I'm home I need to touch myself to get to sleep, but I still dream about you. It's infuriating."

I was glad to have that effect on her, because she certainly had a similar one on me. "Join the club," I chuckled.

"There. Susan should notice that now. It's the best I can do without a self-inking stamp."

"I'll get a tattoo." I was only half-joking. Her hair brushed against my lips as she continued to nip along my jawline.

She rose up to kiss me. Her sigh was heavier than her weight on my chest. "Do you know how wrong I feel at times? You sign my paychecks and I'm practically dripping on your balls right now."

Her little contortions pushed me to the edge, then she until I was ready to bruise the shit out of my wrists in order to wrench my hands free and hold her hips until we both came screaming. Every part of my body was numb but for where her skin met mine. Pinpricks of sensation ran from her lips through my veins, engorging me with need.

"You're my *boss*," she whispered against my mouth. My lips felt dry, and I knew that if I licked them I'd taste her.

"I'm not your boss anymore, Maddie," I said hoarsely.

"Oh Gage. You don't get it." Her voice cracked. "Whether I'm in the office or not, you own me."

Suddenly I understood exactly why she'd quit, and exactly why it didn't matter. She thought I owned her? It was more like the other way around. I belonged to her, and all I was getting was a month-by-month lease in return.

"Madeline, let me see you. Please, baby."

She hesitated, her soft body quivering on top of mine. Then she moved back a little and before I knew it she had her hand around my weeping dick and pulled the crotch of her panties aside to plunge down on me.

"Ungh!"

I almost bit my tongue as I felt the elastic band of her underwear tighten around the base of my cock. I was completely encased in her, trapped beneath her, struggling to control my reactions.

"How does it feel?" She began undulating on me, her hands splayed over my chest. My neck ached as I thrashed my head from side to side. "How does it feel to know that someone else is holding your heart in their hand? That they could just squeeze—" Her walls clamped down on me, making me gasp.

"Madeline, take off this motherfucking blindfold. *Now.*"

Her knees squeezed my hips as she rose up. I felt the fumbling of her fingers at my temples, and I blinked black spots from my vision as she pushed the tie up and over my forehead. It took a few seconds for me to focus on her—the reddish curls hanging over one shoulder, almost touching one distended rosy nipple, her glowing cheeks and hooded eyes. She looked wanton and afraid all at the same time.

And goddammit I wished I could touch her. My hips jerked up, trying to bring her back to me, but she hovered above me, just out of reach. I felt like my heart was about to burst out of my chest.

"Maddie, *please*. I need you. All of you."

With a fierce expression, she drove down on me. The tightness of her entrance combined with the intensity of my emotions was too much for me to bear, and I spluttered helplessly into her. As I rode out the shock of my orgasm, she slid over me to chase her own.

When her motions became choppy and she ground to a halt, her mouth opened and closed in silent words that I couldn't make out. And I was too afraid of spooking her to say anything myself. My eyes closed as she stretched out over me, her hands clinging to my wrists as they dangled from the headboard.

Neither of us could speak, but I sure as fuck had something to say. This was why I *really* needed a Communications assistant.

But at least I'd said "please."

"Did you bring a purse? I might need to throw up into it."

I looked down at my handbag, then said to Bobbie, "I don't think we're good enough friends for that yet."

"Screw that," she replied with a hiccup and a fist to her chest. "You're the closest thing my brother has ever come to a committed relationship."

What the hell was that supposed to mean? I asked her as much.

"I mean that it takes a strong woman to date Keyser Söze." Bobbie eyed my handbag with a grim kind of covetousness. "As far as I'm concerned, you're almost engaged."

"Don't say that in front of him!" I whipped my head around reflexively, like he could actually hear us as we sat in a coffee shop a mile away from the office.

"Why not? When he does something, he goes all in. You should know that by now."

I did, and it still scared the crap out of me. Every time we made love, it was like learning how to ride a unicycle—wobbly and unforgettable. I had to keep pedaling to retain my balance, but I kept thinking the ground was going to come up to meet my face.

He was strict and passionate and strong and playful, and I was just trying to keep up. By some kind of tacit understanding we'd dialed back the intensity since the night I'd tied him up.

However, I was still recuperating from the game of strip Mario Kart that we'd played the on the weekend.

"You look, uh, good," I said.

She grimaced before taking a sip of something steaming from a cup that definitely wasn't coffee. "Nice way to change the subject. I look fat."

"No you don't!" She really didn't. She glowed. Okay, she glowed like radioactive green slime, but I wasn't going to tell her that.

Bobbie methodically raised and lowered her teabag in her cup, like she was fishing for a cure to her morning sickness. "No, you're right. I don't look fat. I just *feel* fat."

"You're only, what…?"

"Four months. Rumor has it that the puking will stop soon. I've actually lost five pounds." She rolled her eyes. "In the meantime, I am living on this ginger mint tea crap. I miss coffee. I miss sushi. I miss *beer*." Her eyes shone with longing.

"You'll have it again someday, right?"

"Oh yeah. But I never understood some of those 'rules.'" She made air quotes. "Don't pregnant women in Japan eat sushi? Don't French women eat gooey cheese? Bah!"

"Probably. How are you feeling about things in general?"

"Well, I'm still on leave from the lodge. Vacation but

with no pay. I haven't been there long enough, but they're being really understanding." She sat back, sighing. "I'm living with Aaron and we're trying not to kill each other. And I spend a lot of time with my head in the toilet—which, if that idiot doesn't start aiming his dick at a little better, I will drown him in."

My mouth fell open a little.

Bobbie leaned forward again and wrapped her hands around her mug. "And now it's almost Christmas and I'm still trying to decide if having this baby is a good idea."

"Um…"

"I mean, of course I'm having it. But I'm still not sure if I should *keep* it."

Wow. I pretended to look for something in my little handbag, busying myself so I didn't have to look at her. I found a tissue and some lip balm, but no helpful platitudes. What did one say to something like that?

"Uh, have you talked to Aaron about it?"

Bobbie looked like she wanted to sink into the floor. "No. I'm too embarrassed. What if he's just staying with me because I'm pregnant? What if he thinks I'm an unfit mother and wants to take it away from me? What if I lose my job again?"

What if you're an insecure whackadoo with a fuck-hot big brother?

I shook my head. I was being incredibly unfair and judgmental. Maybe I was letting Gage's worries get to me. Then again, he had years of knowledge and experience with her. I had a grand total of six coffee dates to define our relationship.

"I was adopted, you know."

"Really?" Her eyes widened, and I felt like I was under a microscope.

"It doesn't leave a mark, Bobbie."

She flushed and looked down. "Sorry."

Actually, it had left a mark—inside. "That's okay. It kind of sucked, to be honest. But I was in the system for a long time. It's not like I was a cute little baby who went to my forever home from the hospital. My biological father died, and when my mother, uh, went to prison for dealing I went into foster care. I guess there wasn't anybody else to take me."

"Whoa."

"Yeah." That was a succinct way to sum it up. "It wasn't so bad. I stayed under the radar, and most people just did their best. But the kicker is that my birth mother decided to give up her parental rights while she was in."

"What?" She shook her head. "How old were you?"

It was my turn to stare into my latte, uncomfortable with the pity in her eyes. "Uh, I was four when she went in, and I guess about seven when she gave me up."

"So how did you get adopted?"

"One of the families I ended up with asked me to stay." I shook my head at the memory. "They must have been desperate for a moody teenager to hang out with," I joked.

"How old were you then?"

"Fourteen."

"Holy shit."

"Yep."

"And you hate your mother?" Bobbie's forehead creased in worry.

I'd thought about it a lot, but that didn't stop me from

pausing before answering. The sounds of the coffee shop rose and fell around us, the whine of steam building and beans grinding like white noise muffling my inner thoughts.

"No," I said slowly. "I don't hate her. I don't understand *why*. But I don't have any kids, and she went through a lot of shit that I can't imagine. I'm not sure I should judge her." Even I knew it sounded like bullshit.

Bobbie sipped her tea thoughtfully. "But you still do," she finally said.

I slumped a little. "Yeah, I guess I do. I'm sure she had her reasons, for doing what she did, though."

"But were they reasons or excuses?"

"Now you're sounding like your brother." And she was right; I was making excuses for her.

Bobbie stared out the window at the busy street. Her hands tightened around her mug. "I don't want my kid to wonder why I didn't want them."

I felt a telltale prickle in my nose. Sometimes I hated that I was still sensitive about this. My mom—my gotcha mom—was great. They loved me. But sometimes I wondered if they would have loved me more if I'd found them sooner, when I was younger or cuter. It was ridiculous; I knew that.

"What would you say to her if you saw her again?" Bobbie asked me. The question threw me for a loop. For all that I'd been sort of looking for her, it hadn't really occurred to me what I would do or say if I found her.

"Hmmm." How honest should I be? The forced nonchalance in my shrug felt heavy on my shoulders. "Why didn't you want me?" *What did I do wrong?*

Bobbie sipped her tea silently, watching me, but I didn't add anything. Finally, she told me off. "You know that's bullshit, right?"

Another heavy shrug.

"It sounds like the woman who gave birth to you had issues. I doubt they were your fault, any more than my mom's problems are my fault." Self-conscious worry still clouded her expression, though.

"I know."

She leveled a disbelieving look at me. "I'm sure you do. But you shouldn't let your own insecurity ruin your chance for happiness, especially when you didn't have any control over it in the first place."

Then, as if she just heard herself speak, she sat back and smiled at me. Lost in my thoughts, I didn't return it.

❧

"Hi."

Gage looked up at me, surprise relaxing the groove etched between his eyebrows. Despite having two —no wait, three—laptops open on his desk, he focused completely on me. The warmth in his gaze made my heart jump, then dive into my stomach.

"Hey. What are you doing here?"

"I wanted to get something back."

His hand went protectively to the bottom drawer in his desk. Despite the tension vibrating in me, a tight smile escaped me.

He looked so serious guarding my panties. I was pretty sure he'd collected a small stash at his house, too, in the previous few weeks. Soon I would have to repatriate them, or else lose a Saturday afternoon to a lingerie shopping expedition. It might just be easier to just go commando all the time but, well, *ew*. I didn't understand how women did that.

"C'mere."

I tossed my purse on the couch and walked slowly to him, keeping my coat on. When I rounded his desk, I let him pull me into his lap. A shiver raced up my spine as he pressed his lips to my neck.

"You're freezing!"

"My jacket is cold; I'm not. It's below freezing out there, Gage."

He peered out the window. This close to the winter solstice, the sky darkened before quitting time at the office. Not that time ever really mattered to Brian Gage. He didn't quit anything. It was one of the things that weighed on my shoulders on the walk to his office after seeing Bobbie.

The dozen blocks or so between the coffeehouse and his office turned into two dozen as I circled aimlessly, lost in contemplation. It was Thursday afternoon, and with only a couple of weeks until Christmas, people were crowding the sidewalks even at three in the afternoon. I'd almost forgotten about it until Bobbie mentioned it. Unable to decide on anything to give the few people in my life, I usually did all my shopping online at the last minute and paid through the nose for wrapping and rush delivery.

For an hour I'd sidled through the crowds of shoppers in a daze, trying to come up with a way forward where I could have it all. I couldn't think of one. But it wasn't until my nose turned numb that I gathered my courage.

I slid off his knee, avoiding his questioning look. He let out a quiet sigh and reached out to shut two of the laptops. Leaning against his desk, I faced him and the twilight encroaching through the massive window behind him.

"What did you come for?" he asked.

"I want to ask you for my job back—sir," I added.

His eyes lit up at first, then dimmed as he saw that I didn't share his excitement about coming back to work for Apptitude.

"Okay," he said slowly, tilting back in his chair and lacing his fingers over his flat belly. "Why don't you tell me what you're thinking?"

That he was too handsome for his own good, and too determined for mine.

"I can't find a job," I began then paused. "No, wait, that's not quite right. I can find a job, but nothing that makes me feel like I can really do something."

"I know. We talked about this. But Maddie, if you want—"

My hand went up. This was hard enough without his interruptions. "I never thought I'd say this, about anything. It didn't matter to me before. But I regret quitting."

Again, satisfaction transformed his face. *Oh Gage, I'm so sorry.* He'd probably thought he'd finally got me to realize the importance of commitment, and he had. That was the problem.

"If you want to come back, then you know where your desk is. I, uh, never really emptied it."

Oh boy. He wasn't going to take this very well at all.

"Thanks," I said dully. "The thing is, if I come back, then I don't think—well, I think we should take a break."

"I don't get it. The office will be closed for

Christmas in about a week. You want to go on vacation or something?" His bewilderment almost derailed me.

"No." It was time to rip the bandage off my bleeding heart. "I don't think we should see each other anymore. On a personal level," I added, just in case he *really* didn't get it.

"What? Madeline—"

He reached out for me, but I skidded across the edge of his desk to the other side. If he touched me, I might not be able to do this. As it was, the prospect of working on the other side of his office door without sharing lunches or inappropriate groping made me want to cry.

"You said it yourself—I'm not great with commitment. I can't even brush my teeth every night before bed consistently. But this job, this talent you think I have… it means something to me."

"And I don't?" He was hurt. Of course he was hurt. My heart squeezed.

"You *do*. But I've spent my whole life flying by the seat of my pants. I owe it to myself to make something work."

"And that something is this job. Not me."

I turned to the couch, unable to face his disappointment. My arms wrapped around my waist in my wool coat, the buttons in front bunching up under my breasts. Now that I was out of the winter wind, I felt hot and stuffy, almost suffocating inside.

"I'm not saying we can't be friends, or be, uh, close," I tried. "But it's important to me to try to commit to this job." Beyond my own feeling of accomplishment, I needed the financial security.

"And you can't commit to me as well? You can't do both?"

I flinched at the growing disdain in his voice behind me.

"I don't know."

There was the crux of my problem. I've never committed to anything before, much less two things at once. Could I be happy with doing a good job but not doing *him*? Or was the job just an excuse to be around him? If I believed what he said about my skills, and I began to believe in myself, then continuing to date him could cloud my judgment.

And then ultimately would he want to be with me because of the job I did for him, because I was convenient, or for *me*? Or did he only want to give me my job back because of the relationship we'd begun? I was so confused, and I needed to break free a little in order to sort it out in my own head.

I had always told myself that I wouldn't be like my birth mother, and lose myself over a man who might disappear anyhow. My logical brain told me that at this point in my life it was more important to learn how to commit myself to a career instead of a man. My heart wanted to tell my brain to go fuck itself.

"Madeline, please don't do this. You can excel at both; I know you can."

I stared at the couch. Either way I looked at it, I was losing something. I just didn't want to lose myself. For the first time in my life, I wanted to try having a goal.

"But I don't want to 'excel' at being your girlfriend."

"Oh."

My hands twisted together, as though I could wring some kind of clarity out of them. "I'm sorry, I'm not explaining this very well—"

"Fine." He spun in his chair to stare into the darkness. I looked up to see his pained reflection in the window. "You've made it pretty clear that I'm not in charge of you. You want to be on the same level as me, then I can't—I shouldn't stop you from making that decision."

He mumbled something to himself that sounded like "*something something fucking asinine.*"

My throat closed up—not that I knew what to say anyhow.

"I know I can be a bit controlling. But you—your work—is valuable to me, Madeline."

So maybe there it was. He wanted my head instead of my heart. So why did it hurt so much?

He cleared his throat. "I'll back off, but you have to promise me something."

"What?" I moved toward his desk. I ached to touch him, to kiss him and promise him anything and everything. But I'd never been able to keep promises before, so I didn't have a lot of confidence in my ability to do so now. Just trying to make this separation now was taking more strength than I thought it would.

He didn't turn around, instead catching my attention in the reflection in the window. The light in the office was brighter than the lights outside, and the floor to ceiling glass was almost a murky mirror before us. I felt like Alice, wanting to go through it to be with him.

"Promise me you'll tell me if you need anything. *Anything.* I'll be there. Please trust me on that."

His reflection turned hazy as my eyes filled with tears.

"Yes, sir." My voice wobbled on "sir," but it was a term of endearment now—a quiet promise of respect instead of teasing.

"And another thing?"

I nodded, not sure if I could speak anymore without totally losing my composure.

"*Please* look for another job that will appreciate your skills." He scrubbed his hands over his face and let out a frustrated huff. "Because now I really want you to quit again."

He swung around in his chair again, studiously not looking at me while he flipped the laptops open to wake them up. His lips pressed together in a tight line, and I had the horrible feeling that he was doing everything in his power to marshal his self-control.

The silence between us was more taut than the ropes course at the lodge as I picked up my purse off the couch.

"Wait, Madeline." I heard his chair creak a little and a drawer open.

When I turned back to him I saw my panties folded neatly on his desk, as far away from him as his reach could extend. Burning with humiliation, I snatched them up and shoved them in my coat pocket.

"You can start on Monday," he said gruffly, blinking at the screens in front of him.

I hesitated, waiting to see if he'd say anything else. He didn't.

"Yes, sir."

And then I left, closing the door behind me. I only briefly considered using the underwear to wipe away the tears falling down my heated cheeks.

32

GAGE

When Monday rolled around, I could barely speak to her. Although, I was a little out of practice, having not used my voice in a few days. I'd spent the weekend hibernating in my gaming beanbag and working on the January updates on my laptop.

Okay, perhaps I'd spent more than a few hours trying to figure out how to update the biometric software in our most popular app to measure the effect of a broken heart. I was surprised that someone hadn't done it yet, but then I wasn't able to make that breakthrough either.

Christmas was in less than two weeks, and the office was rumbling with discontent now that "Angry Santa" was stalking the halls, yelling at all the elves to crank up production.

Anybody who thought I hadn't seen the disturbing memes being forwarded about me obviously forgot that I was also on the "Reply To All" list.

I tried to focus on what needed to be done before

January first. Although things had been busy for a few weeks, I did my best to get Madeline up to speed—through email. To her credit, she didn't point out that I was being a completely pussy by not talking to her. Her politeness and professionalism threatened to push me over the edge, and my mood grew darker as the days grew shorter.

In approximately two months, we needed to both send out a wide blast and target narrow markets to grab those users who had fallen off the New Year's resolution wagon. *Happit* needed to catch on, big time. Our investors and our fourth quarter relied on those subscribers, and so far my Marketing Director had nothing to show me.

Thankfully Bobbie had headed back to the lodge the day before to catch up on some work there, so there was absolutely no excuse for Aaron to try working from home. I needed him in the office. He came in early every day, but by Thursday afternoon he still hadn't produced the storyboards I needed to see for the February campaign. The clock was ticking, and my patience was already in short supply.

I cleared my throat in front of Madeline's desk to catch her attention. Her eyes widened as she looked up at me, before she blushed and stared at her computer again. No, I hadn't missed the shock and hurt in her expression at the simple fact that I was making an over-ture to her. That brief grunt was the closest I'd gotten to a conversation with her since she asked for her job back, dumping me in the process.

It was close to the end of the day, and several of my minions had already cut out early. I was annoyed and frustrated and pissed off and hungry and horny and everything in the world just sucked right at that moment. I cleared my throat again.

"Madeline?"

She blinked at her screen, the reflected light making her look almost sickly. "Yes, sir?"

My stomach flipped just hearing her say those two words. "I need you to go see if Aaron needs help."

At first she didn't respond, her fingers pausing on her keyboard. Then she replied in a monotone, "You could have emailed me that, sir."

My hands tightened into fists at my sides. I was *trying*, goddammit. "Well, I'm asking now."

"Why?"

"Because you have a knack for this stuff."

"No, why are you asking?"

Now her gaze shifted back up to me. I hadn't known brown eyes like hers could radiate coldness instead of warmth before that moment. Hurt pierced through her veil of well-mannered tolerance, stabbing me in the gut before her expression flattened out again.

"You're asking me in person," she pointed out unnecessarily, making me feel like even a bigger asshole.

"Isn't it about time?"

I definitely wasn't making any new friends this week, and I didn't have so many that I wanted to alienate everyone in the office as well. And the simple truth was that it was killing me to see her every day and not have contact with her. To not help her with her coat. To smell her hair as she passed me in the hall, or watch her pad in her stocking feet to the little kitchen for a cup of coffee.

I wasn't ignorant of the fact that she usually still got me a cup at the same time, only she waited until I was away from my desk before she put it there for me. And yes, the fact that it was cold by the time she snuck it into my office made me a sullen jackass. But she wasn't exactly beating down my door either.

God, we were so fucked up.

All I wanted was to pull her into my arms and tell her that she was smart, beautiful, and she could do anything she put her mind to. But if she didn't know it herself, then me telling her wasn't going to change anything.

And yeah, it was pretty shitty of me to take out my frustration on her—and the rest of the office—but I didn't even have a good excuse.

"Is Aaron okay?" she asked. I envied him the softness with which her mouth said his name.

"I don't know. Bobbie went back to the mountains and his work isn't done. That's all I know."

I raked my hand through my hair for the twentieth time that day. It was probably all sticking up like a troll doll, but I didn't care. I'd abandoned my suit jacket at lunch, and my sleeves were rolled up to my elbows and my collar unbuttoned to the vee of my plain white undershirt.

A month before—hell, maybe even a week before—Madeline would have eyed me with admiring hunger and maybe even felt me up on my office couch. Now her eyes flashed with sympathetic understanding, but that was all.

"Are you mad at her?"

What? "Who?"

"Your sister."

I wasn't following. "For what?"

She lifted an eyebrow as she rose from her chair. "For doing her job?"

"No." I shook my head. "No, of course not. She's a grown-up; she knows what she's doing."

Maddie's surprised smile nearly made me trip over my own two feet as I followed her down the hall. God help me, I wanted to fall into that smile like a freshly made bed, or a bed on which I'd freshly laid her.

We rounded the corner to find Aaron's office door closed. My knock was cursory, my greeting terse. "Aaron, I need those storyboards."

"You're forgetting a word," Maddie murmured behind me.

"Now."

She shoved past me, throwing a reproachful look over her shoulder. "I meant *please*."

Aaron was more rumpled than I was, but I was more shocked at the change in his wardrobe. His pinstriped prep school shirts had been replaced by plaid flannel, and he wore motorcycle boots instead of Italian loafers. He looked a hipster had thrown up on him.

He also looked like he was about to vomit himself.

"I don't have them."

"What the hell, Aaron? I relied on you to get this shit done!" Thank god we didn't have any TV time purchased, but I wanted to get the web ads finalized and some podcast scripts and time placed—before the New Year. I wanted to scream, and I was damn close to it until I felt Madeline's hand land on my arm.

"I know, I know! I've just been so busy…"

Distracted by my sister's unplanned pregnancy was more like it. I snorted, crossing my arms.

"That's not helping, Gage." Maddie's soft voice

eased my hair trigger. "How far behind are you? What do you need?" She cut right to the heart of the matter.

"I sent the brief to the agency."

"Okay, that's good."

"Two days ago."

"That's bad."

My Madeline—the mistress of understatement. I started to say something, but her hand closed over my mouth. Her fingers were cold and a little clammy, like she was nervous or something.

"When did they say they would get stuff back to us?" she asked him, dropping her hand and flexing it a little. Her motions almost distracted me from Aaron's response.

"The twenty-ninth."

Shit. My frustration flared again. "Goddammit, Aaron. There's no excuse—"

"Fuck you, Brian! And fuck your 'no excuses' bull-shit! The world is not black and white, and sometimes shit gets in the way. Did you know that I had to take Bobbie to the hospital three times in the last month to get rehydrated from her puking her guts out? Or that your mother decided to fuck off to Mexico for Thanks-giving and left her dog with us?"

I blinked. "My mother has a dog?"

"Focus, Gage," Maddie sighed, lightly touching my back.

"She's been trying to get a new apartment or figure out a new job and it's not easy for anybody, not that you care!"

"My mother?"

"Bobbie!" he yelled.

An angry black man who had a few inches and fifty

pounds of muscle on me was not something I needed in my face right now. He looked ready to punch me in the throat.

"Get off your high horse for one minute, okay? It must be nice to be perfect and live in your perfect, over-achieving world, but the rest of us—sometimes we fail. Okay? I failed and I'm owning it, and it would be nice if you could help us instead of shitting down our throats all the time."

I stumbled back, and this time Maddie didn't catch me.

"Okay you guys, separate corners."

Aaron whirled around to face the window, his shoulders moving up and down as he breathed heavily. I opened my mouth then shut it. What could I say? He was right. His phone rang on the desk, vibrating an inch across it with Bobbie's face on it. We all ignored it.

Maddie cleared her throat, breaking the near violent tension in the room.

"Let's just try to work together like grown-ups, okay? Gage, this campaign is your baby, so try to take some responsibility and let's get it done. I can help. Aaron, I'm pretty sure you showed me the brief you were working on before I left, right?"

He nodded stiffly, his back still turned to us.

I looked over at her. She was watching me carefully with a strange look on her face. It was knowing but not smug, yet empathetic but definitely not toward me.

Holy shit. I was being infantile and selfish and an overall prick—and I had absolutely no excuses for it. If this was the way I acted with friends who were also co-workers, then it was no wonder that Maddie had backed off from our relationship. I couldn't blame her. In fact, I was damned grateful that she even wanted to work for me again, much less *with* me.

A heavy sigh whooshed out of her as she glanced at the phone buzzing on the desk again. "Okay, let's get this done. Because we *can* do it."

Aaron held up a finger and answered the phone. "Hello?" Frowning at us with a hand gesture that looked like "five minutes" he left the room, leaving Maddie and I alone with each other.

The silence was uncomfortably empty, swollen with unspoken promises and apologies. But I wouldn't let it be for long.

"I'm sor—" I started.

"It's okay, Gage." She walked over to the window where Aaron had been standing, her arms crossed in front of her. I was beginning to think I needed industrial blinds for these windows so everyone didn't become hypnotized standing in front of them.

I shook my head. It really *wasn't* okay. I had no real justification for the way I'd been acting—like a petulant brat whose toy got taken away before he carelessly broke it.

"Madeline, I want to tell you—"

She interrupted me again. "It's *okay*, I said. I don't need to hear any apologies from you."

Her impatient words cut through me, as though what I had to say was so insignificant that she couldn't even be bothered to waste thirty seconds of her life listening to it. *Fuck.* She wasn't even going to let me say sorry.

But when she turned back to me, it was with a gentle smile on her lush lips and no malice in her eyes. She wasn't irritated. She wasn't even angry.

She'd already forgiven me for being an asshole, and probably deep down understood why I was—more than I certainly did. It was downright humbling, and probably exactly what I needed—not that I wanted to admit it. It was just one more example of how I needed help communicating, of how I needed *her*.

Aaron shuffled back into the room, distracted by his thumbs skimming over his phone. When he finally looked up, the strange energy between Maddie and myself gave him pause.

"Uh, everything okay?"

Not even remotely. "Yeah, fine," I grumbled. "Let's get to work."

33

MADDIE

Christmas came and went so quickly, I barely noticed it. My parents kept things pretty simple, as usual, and other than a few phone calls from friends it was a quiet and private day. Despite my parents trying to make the holidays festive for me, after so many years of being disappointed at Christmastime, I usually bypassed all the hoopla.

In my experience, good tidings to all men didn't always include kids in the system. I had one or two case-workers who really tried and went out of their way to make sure I got thoughtful presents, but I stopped asking Santa for stuff pretty early on when he failed to deliver on the whole "family" request.

My fingers itched to call Gage, but I didn't want to interrupt his own family time. Bobbie had sent me a "Merry Christmas" text full of holiday emojis and mentioned that Gage was in the mountains with her and Aaron and both their mothers.

My NYE resolution is to appreciate my family more. So I don't kill them. LOL she wrote. I doubted that she was actually laughing out loud, though I did.

But her text made me think.

In my insecurity about my own birth mother, I had lost sight of the generous gift that my parents had given me—themselves. I spent the day after Christmas wallowing in a pity party, followed by a shame shindig. Then I made a kickass turkey casserole for dinner and apologized to my parents.

The next day my mother and I spent the day hitting sales to get stuff to decorate my room. It wasn't until I got home and unpacked all the bags that I realized I'd subconsciously replicated the colors in Gage's bedroom. By the day after that I couldn't hold off on texting him any longer. I thought about calling him, but was half afraid I would clam up once I heard his voice. In the end, what I came up with was:

Hope you had a good holiday. Any big plans for New Year's?

His response was almost immediate. **About to drive back from lodge. Where are you?**

Home

Can you go to the office?

I blinked at the phone, puzzled. Like Ebenezer Scrooge himself—or maybe Scrooge McDuck—Gage had given everyone the week between Christmas and New Year's off. As far as I knew, nobody was in the office except for a couple of IT people working overtime because they would be working from home anyways.

Is there something you need?

I'll let you know when I arrive.

It looked like I was headed to work, then. I didn't

mind, really. There was only so much online shopping I could avoid sitting around at home.

The brutal truth was that I missed Brian Gage—a lot. I missed the dark slashes of his frowning eyebrows, the lines around his eyes and mouth when he grinned at me, the overwhelmed feeling I got when I was around him.

He made me feel like I was the only person in the world, but at the same time like he needed me more than anything. It was a heady sensation, especially when coupled with his smell, taste and touch.

He'd thrown an improvised Festivus party at the office on the twenty-third, and that was the last time I'd seen him. We took turns raising our glasses in celebration in front of the aluminum pole, and were surprisingly restrained in our airing of grievances.

My personal feat of strength was not attacking him after a glass or two of liberally spiked eggnog. Gage hadn't made it easy—laughing easily and praising everyone for all the hard work they'd done since the mountain retreat a few months before.

When he got down off his high horse, as Aaron put it, and offered to photocopy his own ass for the sake of tradition, I wasn't the only one who was shocked. Susan was quivering with anticipation and there was a lot of cheering from Nikhil and the IT department. *It's always the quiet ones.*

But he looked over at me as I shook my head, silently discouraging him from doing it—and he recanted. His gaze drove into me like, well, an unadorned aluminum pole. He mouthed, "Okay" at me, and I realized that mine was the only opinion that really mattered to him.

I fell in love with him all over again. It seemed to happen daily since I'd gone back to work for him, but it wasn't until after the confrontation with Aaron that the squeezing sensation in my chest felt less painful and more optimistic.

By the time I got to the office, thinking about him had just made me miss him more keenly. I decided to use my laptop in his office, sitting in the big chair behind his desk. When I sat down, I thought I could smell his scent on the chair, but then I realized it was just the leather. Perhaps Gage smelled more like his chair than anything else.

The floor was quiet. Everyone else had been only too happy to stay home for the week. I hadn't bothered turning on the fluorescents overhead, opting instead for the little halogen desk light to cast a sharp circle of light around my computer. I was so busy catching up on some follow-up correspondence that I didn't notice him standing by the open door.

"Jesus Christ!" I jumped. "You scared the shit out of me, Gage." I needed to get him a bell or something; he was always sneaking up on me.

My heart thumped wildly as he walked toward me. I couldn't see the exact blue of his eyes as he approached me in the shadows, but the desk lamp carved the line of his clenching jaw as he rounded the desk to where I sat in his big boss chair. It wasn't until I saw him tracking my movements that I realized I was slightly spinning myself from right to left and back again.

I blushed, stopping myself with my toes. "I'm so sorry. I shouldn't be working in here."

He tilted his head, looking confused. "Why not?"

"It's your office."

"So? It's a comfortable chair. I wasn't here. Go ahead. I trust you."

I looked at him as he began taking his coat off. There wasn't an ounce of expectation in his expression, or a hint of disingenuousness. He meant it. He trusted me, implicitly. Explicitly. What had I done to deserve that trust?

"Why?" I blurted out as he tossed his coat over the corner of the desk.

The zipper clinked and something else in his coat clunked on the glass surface—probably his phone in his pocket. He wore the same faded college hoodie that I'd seen on him in the mountains, and it made him look so much younger and carefree. The sweatshirt I was wearing was from my school as well, but it made me feel older for some reason. We were both teetering, trying to stabilize on the same level in life.

"Why what?" he asked.

"Why do you trust me?"

He hesitated, rubbing his neck. The hem of his hoodie rose to expose the waistband of his jeans. He was actually casual today, not even business casual. "Why do I trust you?" he repeated to himself. "I don't know if I have a good reason."

"Try." Suddenly it was very important to me.

"Because you've been there for me when I didn't even know I needed somebody. Because you've taken my bullshit over and over again and still have a smile on your face. You took my sister's side over mine because it was the right thing to do. You saved Aaron's ass and the resolution campaign, despite being pissed off at me—rightfully, I might add."

I stared at him, my mouth dry.

He leaned over and braced his hands on the armrests of the chair I was sitting in. Because my forearms rested there his fingers wrapped around my wrists. The chair tilted back a little, making him grip a little tighter to prevent it from moving.

"I didn't save—"

"Yes, you did." Now that his head was bent toward me I could see that his eyes were currently the color of the late afternoon sky outside—a blue-gray slate that reminded me of the denim cover on his bed. "And you saved me from myself, which is no small task."

Heat crawled up my face. The way he looked at me made me feel as though the tiny halogen spotlight was centered directly on me. Could he see the pounding of my heart in my throat? My jeans felt tight, my body ripe and pulsing. Every nerve ending was aware of him, like a force field was closing in around us.

"Gage, I—"

"Did you make a New Year's resolution, Madeline?" he interrupted.

I'd once wondered what the difference was between a resolution and a wish. Now, looking into his eyes, I understood.

Only *I* could make a resolution come true.

"Do you want to know what mine is?"

I nodded, not trusting myself to speak. There was no rum-laced eggnog to blame this time around.

"I resolve to make you understand that I love you. I love you, Maddie, and I am not making any excuses for it." He let out a self-deprecating laugh. "So to speak. I want every part of you—your brain, your heart, your soul and your funny bone."

My lips parted as his gaze narrowed on them. I felt

his focus on me like a physical touch, his fingers running across my lower lip and nudging inside. I inhaled deeply, his crisp, masculine scent swimming around my head like a cartoon cloud. Maybe it was all just pheromones. Maybe I didn't really love him. Maybe I was just grateful for the job and the vote of confidence.

Maybe I was full of shit, even in my own head.

"Damn it, Gage." My voice cracked. "How am I supposed to respond to that?"

He knelt to the floor in front of me, his hands rubbing up and down my forearms. "You're the communications expert. You tell me."

Tell him what, exactly? Inside, I knew that the truth was a good place to start. I inhaled then blew out a frustrated burst of air. He closed his eyes as my breath hit his face. And he waited. He didn't push me—just sat before me, ready to accept whatever I said. It was that quiet patience that was my undoing.

"You want me?"

He nodded, his lips pressing together. There was a lump in my throat that wasn't going away anytime soon.

"You forgot something."

His eyes widened in panic, then his lips softened at my wobbly smile. "*Please*."

My attempt to hold in a choked sob resulted in an inelegant hiccup. "Oh god, I love you too."

"I keep telling you people not to call me God," he joked weakly. "I have feet of clay."

I nodded. "They're practically play dough."

"You love me?"

I swallowed hard, biting my lip as my chin jerked up and down.

"Tell me again."

"I love you. I don't know when I didn't." An elastic band inside me snapped, and I hadn't even realized how stretched out it was.

His relieved smile seemed to expand the circle of light around us far beyond the reach of the little desk lamp. He laid his head on my lap, his arms reaching around my waist.

"Can you email me that?"

"Huh?"

"I want a hard copy for the file."

My giggle came out with a sigh attached to it. My hands went to his coal black hair, my fingertips massaging his skull with reverence. I'd missed touching him.

"I'll print it out. I'll text it. I'll Tweet it. I'll change my status on Facebook. I'll send a passenger pigeon if you want."

He raised his head along with one eyebrow. "Let's not get all *Jurassic Park* here—they're extinct for a reason."

I fucking adored him, this closet geek billio—*million-aire*. I'd gone from fearing him and being nervous around him to being aroused and enamored by him.

He was close to being my best friend already, and I trusted him. He was a role model when he wasn't being an asshole, and thankfully he was gracious enough to let me tell him when he was.

"What about my job?" I asked as his hands gripped my hips.

"We have an excellent benefits package." He propped his chin on my thighs.

"I bet." Although I had the feeling we were talking about different kinds of benefits.

"It just so happens that we have an opening in the Marketing department."

I gasped. "Is Aaron leaving?"

"No, but I think he needs some extra support from someone like you."

"And I'm not sleeping with him," I thought out loud. *That just might work.*

Gage growled, tugging me closer until I almost fell off the chair into his lap. "Damn right."

"Okay, okay!" I yelped.

With one arm snaked around my waist and one hand pushing on the bottom castors of the chair, he pulled me onto the floor beside him.

He covered my mouth with his. His body was warm, no trace of coldness from outside lingering on him, but I shivered nonetheless as his hands roamed over me. He traced the line of my collarbone with his fingertips, brushed his knuckles down my spine, and when he slipped under the hem of my shirt I gasped.

God, he could touch me all day and all night long, and I would never complain. How had I gone for even one week without him? How had I gone my whole life without him?

I kissed him feverishly. He sucked my lower lip between his teeth just long enough to make it swollen and his tongue sought entrance. A low moan escaped me, making him groan in reaction. His need was intoxicating, but his kisses made me dizzy. My regret at not replacing my stash of fresh underwear in my desk was overwhelming.

"I need you," I whimpered, a hot blue flame blazing everywhere he touched me. I felt so delicate in his arms that I thought I would see the whorls of his fingerprints imprinted on my skin.

At the same time, he held me with purpose and passion, lifting me up to meet his hungry mouth and hands. He didn't treat me as lower than him, fragile or weak. He used me to brace himself, as though he knew that I was stronger than I appeared. And yeah, I was. But he was part of what gave me that strength—the knowledge that I was valuable to someone. I was worth having, worth keeping.

"Madeline, please." His plea was not for forgiveness or for understanding. It was simply an entreaty for *me*.

And I was only too happy to trade him—my love for his. Tit for tat.

GAGE

EPILOGUE

"This is inexcusable. You can't just *quit*. Try harder."

Maddie popped her head in the doorway, rolling her eyes. "Gage, she's two fucking years old," she chastised me.

I clapped my hands over my niece's ears. "Madeline! She can hear you!"

"She can hear you too. We all can, and you sound ridiculous trying to motivate a toddler."

"Ignore Auntie Maddie, Lily. She's just jealous that she doesn't have a magic toilet."

My girlfriend smirked. "Yes, Lily-bean. He saves all his best technology for you now."

That wasn't entirely true. I'd developed a particularly interesting app that turned Madeline's smartphone into a kind of pocket rocket, and I didn't hear her complaining about *that*. Moaning, yes—but in a good way.

Lily looked up at me with questioning brown eyes, and I dropped my hands from the silky hair around her ears.

"What's going on?" My sister joined Madeline in the doorway to the bathroom, her face flashing into a smile at the sight of her daughter on the floor.

"He's Gaging her."

What? I was a verb now?

"Brian, give it a rest. She'll go when she's ready. Right, baby?"

Lily beamed up at her mother, then proudly peed on the floor where I was kneeling. I wanted to bang my head against the tile, but was afraid of getting urine in my hair.

I'd spent three months creating this program that played peppy music and personal messages when the potty receptacle thing got wet, and the only thing I had to show for it were tears of frustration.

It was tempting to sob into the damn thing just so I could hear "Great job!"

"Great job!" Bobbie said indulgently to the trickle monster beside me. Lily clapped her hands and giggled, then sat on my thigh. *Ew.*

"What the hell do you mean? She just peed on the floor!"

"No, she peed on *you*. That's awesome." She high-fived Madeline.

Maddie nodded in agreement. The two were thick as thieves, which was appropriate since Madeline had stolen my heart nearly three years ago. I gave them a withering look, but they just laughed harder.

"Savages," I muttered.

"Here, I'll clean her up." Bobbie came in and I patted Lily on the head awkwardly before leaving the bathroom with a big wet mark on my pants.

Maddie burst out in giggles again. "You should see the look on your face."

"Marry me."

"I can't, you have pee on you."

It was an ongoing joke—I asked her to marry me, and she came up with a ridiculous excuse. She still teased me about my stuffiness, even though I was a little more understanding now of the difference between excuses and reasons.

It had started about a year before, when I was tired of pinning her down only to the mattress. Or the floor. Or the kitchen counter. Or my desk. I wanted to pin her down permanently, legally.

But the joke was becoming less funny and more awkward. Her rejection was coming slower these days, which meant she was either getting ready to say yes, or getting ready to move out. I was praying it was the former rather than the latter.

Persuading her to move in with me had been easy. All I had to do was give her a book of paint chips. Getting her to marry me was like... eating spaghetti with a whisk while blindfolded.

One of these days I wouldn't accept her lame excuse for refusing my proposal. I leaned in to kiss her, the slight tension in her shoulders easing under my hands.

"I need fresh pants," I announced.

To her credit, she didn't make a dirty joke. "Ask Aaron."

My best friend slash brother-in-law was out back tending the grill with the single-minded determination of, well, me. When I found him, he was trying searing the steak with his eyes.

"A watched steak never grills, man."

"Meat on fire, bro—that's all you need. I was just brainstorming a new slogan."

"Such as?" I handed him one of the two bottles of beer I'd grabbed from the fridge on my way out, taking a drink from the other.

"Come try our poles?"

I spit out my beer. "*What?*"

"You know, ski poles, hiking poles."

"That's *terrible*. Jesus, what happened to you?"

Aaron lifted the steak to look at the underside. "Have you heard of Mommy brain? I think I have Daddy brain."

I snorted. "You've lost your mind."

"Yeah, true dat." His grin stretched into a blinding smile when Bobbie came out the back door with Lily in her arms.

It hadn't always been peaceful for them. Bobbie went back to work at the lodge at four months pregnant, when the ski season really got underway. The manager promised she'd be working strictly indoors, low-key guest services stuff. Aaron drove up on the weekends to be with her, but after two months I took him to a bar on a Tuesday night and got him wasted.

It was Maddie's idea but I wasn't blind. I could see that he was totally exhausted, physically and mentally. He was driving four hours to the mountains on Friday nights, then four hours back on Sundays after dinner.

The boss in me was pissed off that he wasn't committing to his work for Apptitude, but the friend in me knew that something had to give—and it was probably going to be me.

"She says sh'okay, but I think she's scared," Aaron

slurred. "Shit man, *I'm* scared. I don't know nothing 'bout babies."

When we were younger I'd envied Aaron his only child status. Now I saw the downside. He didn't even have any cousins. By the end of the night, I was trying to lug his sauced, six foot five, linebacker ass out to a cab, and formulating a plan to help them out.

In the end I let him stay a week at the lodge, virtually commuting from there, as long as he could be in the city the next week. So he rotated and lived out of a suitcase. But it was good for him, good for Bobbie, and not totally disastrous for the company—thanks to Madeline, who took over a lot of Aaron's work at the office.

They made it through the winter like deliriously happy but busy squirrels, while Maddie and I did our best to hibernate, until Bobbie's water broke a month early. Thankfully the village down the mountain from the lodge had more amenities than just a wood-burning pizza place—it also had a decent hospital. Or so I heard.

Lily Charlotte was small but scrappy, and Maddie told me that she was a beautiful mix of both her parents, with strong fingers and the vocal range to match after she visited one weekend.

She and my mother car-pooled once or twice to go see them, which freaked me out. I was sure they talked about me the entire way, but I didn't have the guts to ask what was said.

But in an immature fit of passive-aggressive avoidance, I didn't go see Bobbie and Aaron or the baby for two months. My mother left messages for me every day. My girlfriend didn't go down on me for six weeks and four days.

It was a fucking nightmare.

But it was my nightmare, and I was waiting for the other shoe to drop. It did when Aaron announced he wasn't coming back.

"What do you mean, you're not coming back? It's a fancy hotel, it's not fucking Mordor!"

I made a mental note at the time—develop an app that allows you to feel some kind of satisfaction in angrily hanging up on somebody with your smartphone. Jabbing a red dot to end the call just didn't have the same effect.

He was serious, however, and later on that evening it was Madeline who had to pour me out of the bar.

Apparently my flighty sister had knocked the manager's socks of that winter, essentially working herself into an assistant GM position—after a few months off of maternity leave, that was. Wanting to keep Bobbie, the GM had offered Aaron a job heading up the resort's marketing and promotions. And they gave them a little chalet-type townhouse on the property, in a cluster where other year-round staff member were also housed.

It was a hard offer for them to turn down. Bobbie was finally happy in a job and doing well, and even with the pay cut Aaron was excited about being with her and living "on the land." I reminded him they weren't pioneers. For god's sake, the lodge's restaurant had a *foie gras* appetizer.

Madeline finally dragged me out there to see the baby when the kid was about three months old. I was less than impressed at having to leave the office for the whole weekend, and more than a little reluctant to even get out of the car.

But while six weeks and four days without a blowjob hurt, I wasn't about to call her bluff on her threat to cut me off entirely. So I grumbled and shuffled behind her to their door, like a recalcitrant thirteen year-old visiting their grandparents.

Bobbie looked tired but strangely content, and Aaron was like a caffeine-powered zombie. Their little chalet reeked of baby shit, despite all the open windows, and some weird plastic smell that Madeline told me came from the diapers. It made sense, since a baby store apparently threw up in there. Cases of diapers were stacked up like towers, and I was frankly surprised that the baby wasn't crated up like the Ark of the Covenant.

I crossed my arms over my chest and watched the three of them act like idiots for this little creature that looked like Baby Luma from Super Mario.

"Lily, this is your Uncle Brain. He might use you to take over the world. Again."

My nose scrunched up. "Really, Pinky?"

"Absolutely."

"I think you lost some brain cells with the placenta."

Yes, I knew what a placenta was, thanks to Madeline, who had delighted in grossing me out by feeding me information through my sister's whole pregnancy. She had considered it some kind of immersion therapy, I think.

Now, out on the back deck with the valley peeking through the tall pine trees, I had to admit that the immersion therapy had worked. Well, I was here anyhow. And I was damp.

"Can I borrow some shorts or something? Your progeny used me as toilet paper."

Aaron glanced down at the big wet spot on my

khakis and gave me a shit-eating grin. I gave him the finger.

"Way ahead of you," Maddie called as she stepped outside with a pair of what looked like black athletic shorts in her hand. "Bobbie let me go through your drawers."

Now it was Aaron's turn to choke on his beer. I took the shorts, grateful to see they had a drawstring at the waist.

I dropped a kiss on her lips. "Marry me."

"I can't, I wanna have a steak first." Madeline stuck her talented tongue out at me before scooping Lily out of Bobbie's arms.

Foiled again.

"Uh oh, Lily-bean! You're getting so big; I don't know if I can hang on. I might drop you!"

Lily squealed at the prospect of her favorite game. My girlfriend held her in her arms, swaying gently and cooing before suddenly dropping into a deep squat. It was like the toddler version of the Drop of Doom.

Bobbie smiled at them while Aaron tried to use X-ray vision on the steaks again. I took the opportunity to go inside and change. I was in my boxer briefs in my sister's bedroom when Maddie waltzed in and dropped Lily on the bed like a pile of giggling laundry.

I couldn't fight my own indulgent smile when Maddie flopped on the bed beside Lily and leaned over to let our niece grab her auburn hair. It was a little harder now that she'd cut it to shoulder length, but I loved that it was still enough to pull her head back with when I was driving into her from behind.

Madeline tilted her head up to me then shielded Lily's eyes, her own wide with alarm. "Gage! Seriously?"

I looked down at the tent in my briefs and shrugged. "I can't control it." It was a naturally occurring phenomenon when I was around her. Like the tides.

"You're kidding, right? *Mister No Excuses*? You control everything."

Lily tittered and covered her own eyes, thinking Maddie was playing hide and seek. *Oh, to be two years old again and have no object permanence.*

The smile on my gorgeous girlfriend's face was faintly stained with sadness as she cuddled her.

She still didn't know what to make of her biological mother's decision to abandon her, and she'd stopped looking for her. Out of sight, out of mind. Her adopted mother was relieved and frankly, so was I. And thankfully therapy was covered by company's health insurance.

"I can't control you," I pointed out, pulling up the borrowed shorts. At least my t-shirt was free of bodily fluids.

"You're not kidding," she mumbled. There was an odd tone in her voice that made me look at her more closely. It wasn't exactly a hardship.

I never got tired of looking at Madeline, even when she had clothes on—such as the simple and easily removable peasant skirt and tank top that she was currently wearing. She was beautiful and sassy and never failed to tell me when I was being an arrogant asshole. She was also smart and funny and, well, up for anything.

A long time ago she'd told me that I made her feel safe, and the pride and pleasure that elicited in me was greater than the day our stock went public.

Her gaze was focused on Lily, who had fallen asleep on the bed. It must have been nap time, or close to it.

Or maybe we'd just worn her out with all the acrobatics and potty training.

Goddamn, I wished that kid would get on board with my magic potty program! She was making me look bad.

The bed bounced a little as I knelt on it and leaned over Lily's little body to capture Madeline's lips in a kiss.

"What was that for?"

"I just love you."

"Weirdo." But she kissed me back, with tongue. *God, I loved her.*

With the collar of my t-shirt clutched in her fist, she led me around the bed. She sat up straight as I stood beside her, her head conveniently close to my crotch.

"Hmmm, these don't stay up very well on you, do they?" she said, plucking at mesh fabric.

"Well, I have to tight—"

My words and thoughts rocked to a halt when she tugged gently on the waistband and the shorts dropped to my ankles.

"Ooops." She smirked up at me. Her hand cupped my semi, making me groan. Oh Jesus, I loved the way she touched me.

I checked on Lily, who had her thumb in her mouth and was probably dreaming about puppies or graham crackers, or whatever two year olds dreamt about.

My hands cradled Maddie's face. "Baby, I can't believe I'm saying this, but this is not the best time for a blowjob." I really hated saying it. I felt a genuine crushing feeling in my chest with the words.

The laugh burst out of her chest so hard that she snorted. She slapped her hand over her mouth, probably partly in embarrassment and partly to avoid waking up

Lily. But in that quiet room, with smells from the grill coming in through the window and my niece snoring on the bed, I felt absolute peace.

I looked her in the eye, done with her excuses. "Marry me."

"I can't, I'm preg——"

I held up my hand to interrupt her, rolling my eyes. "No, this time I won't accept it. I've had enough. 'I can't, I have to wash my hair.' 'I can't, I need to finish this book.' 'I can't, you smell like pee.' That's it. I'm done with the excuses."

Her eyes widened.

"Come on, Madeline." My hands were propped on my hips and the pitch of my voice rose as I mocked her. "'I can't, I'm preg—wait, what did you say?"

"I'm pregnant."

She was smiling, but also gnawing on her lip nervously. I felt like there was a balloon in my chest, slowly filling up and ready to burst. Part of me wanted to puke, and the other part of me wanted to drag her back to our room at the main lodge and fuck her senseless.

We were completely still, encased in carbonite. Her blink was the only movement in the room; Lily's snuffles the only sound. My mouth opened but no sound came out.

"Gage, say something. *Please*." She rose on her knees, her hands wrapped around my forearms. "I know it wasn't planned and I'm not quite sure what happened. Maybe that time you suspended me upside down—"

"With a baby?"

"No, with a very small racehorse. That's why I have to pee like one."

"Excuse me?"

She put her arms around my waist, her voice low. "Poor Gage."

My brain was scrambled. *Baby. Racehorse. Lily. Diapers.* When my brain came back to me—albeit in bits and pieces—I noticed the fear shadowing her eyes. What, did she think I would abandon her? That I'd be angry?

"I'm sorry," I said. Madeline—the queen of effective communication—took it the wrong way, her eyes filling with tears.

"No no *no*! I'm happy, sort of."

She tilted her head back then her breath hitched as I lifted her off the bed to stand her up.

"Sort of?" A sniff escaped her.

"Well, it's kind of a shock. Give me some time to process it."

Her gaze fell to my chest. "Yeah, right. Okay." Her voice sounded as tight and dark as the charcoal briquettes turning to ash outside.

I was fucking this up, royally. I looked over at Lily. She wasn't so bad. A mini-Madeline…? *Hmmm.*

I wrapped myself around Madeline like bubble wrap, until you couldn't fit a coherent thought between us, much less a piece of paper. Squeezed.

"Mmph."

The balloon in my chest popped, my heartbeat floating up to the sky.

"You're going to marry me." *I couldn't wait, and I didn't care how bossy I sounded*

"Because of the itty bitty racehorse?" she asked quietly.

I tilted her chin up to look her in the eyes. "Because I love you so fucking much that my heart aches with it right now. And we need a doll to put in our dollhouse. And I need to perfect that damn potty."

"Are those excuses?" Her eyes narrowed, but the corner of her mouth perked up.

"Madeline, I don't need an excuse to marry you. *You* are the *reason*. And a damn good one at that."

THE END... UNLESS YOU KEEP READING!

"You hanging in there? Are you worried about him?"

I tilted the popcorn bag toward my sister-in-law. "Sure. No problem. I'm great."

"Because I remember when I first left Lily—"

"Bobbie, we're at a movie, not at an all-inclusive resort." Though that sounded wonderful. I shifted in my seat, making sure that my phone didn't slide off my lap.

"Yeah, but—"

I held up my hand, my fingertips greasy from the popcorn. The trailers hadn't even started, and I was already full. In the past year, I had developed the ability to scarf down food quickly, one-handed.

"I'm sure everything's okay," I assured her. "He's an intelligent adult who runs a billion dollar company. I'm sure he can handle a baby."

Our baby. Our son, Jack, now nine months old and crawling... everywhere. Only walls, furniture and stairs could stop him.

It was like I'd given birth to a Roomba.

"It's kind of ridiculous that we're going to a sexy movie with each other, not our husbands," I said.

On the plus side, there were definitely no kids in the theater. On the negative side... there were no kids. I missed Jack, and I'd been gone less than an hour.

"I could have babysat if you guys wanted to go together," Bobbie reminded me.

"Nah. He hates foreign film." This one had subtitles and full-frontal nudity. *Male* nudity. Though, Gage and Aaron both might have been on board if it featured a bunch of bouncing European boobs.

My boobs didn't bounce that way anymore. *I* didn't bounce that way anymore. There was a good chance that I'd fall asleep in this movie. But here I was.

Earlier, Gage had pushed me out the door, saying, "Don't worry, we'll be fine."

Of course, "fine" was a word with a vast spectrum of meaning.

When Jack was born, Gage had taken some time off to be at home with us. He'd said that it was important for us to get some systems in place, to make the transition easier. After a couple of weeks, though, I could see him getting antsy. Even through the haze of sleep deprivation, it quickly became clear that Gage was having more trouble adjusting to parenthood than I was. I just *had to*, there no choice in the matter.

But Gage couldn't breastfeed, and I was having trouble letting go—of anything.

So, after a month I sent him back to work. He seemed almost relieved at getting permission. I was almost relieved at not having him underfoot all the time, like a mopey puppy that wasn't sure what he was being punished for. All that "almost" relief was accompanied by a fair amount of guilt, on both our parts.

And now, I should have been more excited to be out doing something for *me*. Instead, I felt… can you guess? *Ding! Ding! Ding!* Guilty!

There's nothing in the baby manual about guilt going hand-in-hand with becoming a parent. I would have to talk to Gage about that—his tech company was working on a baby app. Naturally.

The lights in the theater went down. Notifications flashed on my phone from Facebook, psyching me out and making me think my husband was texting me with a question or a crisis.

He wasn't.

"*Don't do it.* Don't check in," Bobbie urged in a low voice. "I know you want to. Resist the temptation."

Of course, now that she'd said it, I *really* wanted to. Forget falling asleep. There was a greater probability that I'd make a trip to the ladies' room so I could call home. I sucked down more soda, regretting that I didn't get one the size of my head.

Something pulled in my chest, like an invisible string that ran from the theater to my house.

Bobbie elbowed me over the armrest as a love scene began. "Here we go," she whispered.

The string in me tugged and twanged.

The first thing Gage said to me when I got in the door was, "He's sleeping."

Of course he was. That was a good thing. I wondered

how bad it would be if I woke the baby up, just so I could have the satisfaction of soothing him again.

My handsome, brilliant, successful husband was still wearing a crisp white button-down shirt, which meant there were two possibilities: everything had gone perfectly, or he had changed before I got home.

Was it wrong if I secretly hoped it was the first option?

I stripped off my coat as my husband asked me how the movie was. "Adult."

He smirked. "Oh yeah? How big was he?"

I blushed. "No, I mean it was weird being surrounded by grown-ups again. I'd almost forgotten what it felt like." I looked up the stairs. Maybe I could just…

"He's *fine*." Gage wrapped his hand around mine and pulled me into the living room.

A fire cracked and glowed in the fireplace, displacing the January cold. It said a lot about my state of mind that my first reaction wasn't *"oh, how romantic"* but instead *"oh god, please don't tell me you had a curious, crawling baby by an open fire."*

What was *wrong* with me? I used to fly by the seat of my panties. Now I was obsessed with diapers and couldn't remember what panties I was wearing.

"Have I changed?" I asked Gage.

"What?" He looked me up and down, his gaze still as hot as the fire a few feet away. "How do you mean?"

Resting my forehead against his hard chest, I sighed. "I don't know. I just feel so…"

"Tired? Hungry? Horny?"

"Adult."

His arms tightened around my waist, enveloping me

in his warmth. "That's not such a bad thing, Madeline. Some of the best people I know are adults."

Silently, I considered it. What a stupid funk I was in. Maybe I *was* just tired, hungry, and horny.

Gage put his thumbs under my jaw and tilted my head back. The desire in his eyes made my body begin to throb in response. "You've had some time for you tonight," he said in a husky voice. "Now, how about some time for *us*?"

I blinked, trying to disconnect the Mommy part of me from the Maddie part. Right now I wanted to be just a wife, a saucy sex kitten—or at the very least, consider my breasts to be recreational instead of functional.

With my palms on his chest, I inhaled my husband's scent. Some men smelled like spice or cologne or dust. My man smelled like a freshly ironed cotton shirt, laced with a hint of baby shampoo from bath time.

If I thought Brian Gage was intoxicating before, when he was just my demanding boss, then Brian Gage the billionaire daddy was downright addictive.

I melted against him, like a candle too close to the fireplace. His hands moved over me, pressing and molding me to him. My eyes closed as I reveled in the feeling of his body against mine.

"What did you have in mind?"

"Madeline, I want to do very… adult things to you."

His mouth trailed over my face, his lips landing on mine briefly before moving to my forehead, cheeks, and neck. Back to my parted lips again.

Teasing. Taunting. Tormenting me.

"Oh god." A familiar heat welled up inside me.

"You can call me whatever you want. Just be warned

—I intend to make you lose your voice from screaming my name."

My breath caught in my throat. As long as it didn't wake the baby, I was totally on board with this plan. Although I often craved alone time, I craved Gage more.

I loved him. He loved me. Hell, he adored me, and Jack. But I missed seeing him every day at work. Seeing him at home just wasn't the same. I was always tired and frazzled and covered in strange substances.

Sometimes I just wanted to be the sassy secretary with a tight skirt and the power to decide the future of blowjobs at the office.

I opened my eyes as he leaned back from me. His dark eyebrows drew together in a frown. "Are you okay with that?"

"With what?"

"The screaming my name part." His thumb brushed over my nipple, which tingled in response. I nodded.

Scream? At that moment, as he slid his hand into my yoga pants, I couldn't even whisper. But I did flinch as he palmed my lower belly, which would never be the same after having a baby.

"Don't do that," he said as I stiffened.

His fingers splayed out over the top of my mound, his middle finger dipping into my cleft. "This is the most beautiful part of you. You have no idea…" He trailed off, shaking his head as he explored me. "Knowing that part of me, with part of you, created a new person here —it still blows me away."

My knees felt wobbly. "You blow me away," I murmured. "Every single daaaaay." I finished with a sigh as he found my entrance, already wet and welcoming.

He grunted, covering my mouth with his. We were still getting used to the idea of sharing each other with a little person. Right now, we were selfish and greedy for each other.

Blindly, I felt for the waist of his slacks. The heat and heft of his erection pressed against the back of my shaking hands as I tugged at his button and zipper.

"Wait," he said. *Grrrr.*

He peeled my stretchy pants over my hips, taking my panties down my legs along the way. "Off you go." He pulled my feet free gently, and my mind flashed on him undressing our son. My heart swelled with love.

Then he sat back on his heels with his palms on his thighs, and ogled me. There was no other word for it. He sat there, admiring me, his slacks open and his erection bulging from it while heat from the fire licked the back of my legs.

"Take your shirt off," Gage commanded as he began unbuttoning his own.

I pulled my comfy long-sleeved shirt over my head. The moment I couldn't see him, I felt infinitely more exposed. The air shifted around me. I shivered as he swept his palms up my thighs, his touch affecting me like I was a velvet cushion being rubbed the wrong way.

When I dropped my shirt, I blinked to see him shirtless and at my feet.

"You are so gorgeous," he breathed as he leaned in to taste me.

"Ah!" My hips jerked in response, my body over-sensitized and needy for him. "Lick me. Please."

He did, his broad fingers circling my entrance, then scissoring to widen me as his tongue flicked at my clit.

My nipples pebbled in my beige nursing bra and a familiar ache began in my breasts.

Oh please, not right now. I really want to fuck my husband, not spray him with milk like a goddamn human firehose.

"Does that feel good?" he asked me.

I hummed, a greater sense of urgency coming over me. "More."

He shuffled closer on his knees. With his arms banded around my hips and his hands on my ass, he pulled me to his mouth. The long, lazy trail of his tongue up and down my cleft made me pant and squirm. Pleasure coiled inside me, my climax threatening to be so swift and sharp it felt like I would split open like a ripe peach in his hands.

Just when I began to feel the telltale flutterings deep in my belly, I heard it.

A squawk.

Shit shit shit!

I froze, my hands tightening on Gage's shoulders. He dropped his hands from me and looked up at me.

"What?"

My head whipped from side to side—not in ecstasy, but to scan the room for the baby monitor which surely Gage must have brought down with him. Not that I needed it. Something inside me knew when Jack was turning over in his sleep. Down the hall. Behind closed doors. Whereas Gage seemed to have an uncanny ability to tune him out.

The squawk turned into a staccato whine, which even my husband heard.

"Fuck," he muttered, rising to his feet with some awkwardness.

Yeah, fuck.

The sound began to taper off, just as quickly as it began.

He looked at me, his blue eyes almost navy with arousal. "Wait," he whispered. *There was hope.* We stood there, frozen like animatronic statues from an adult theme park, listening.

My breasts prickled with the threat of my milk letting down. Even though he was eating all sorts of food now, I still nursed him a couple of times a day. He was right on schedule; I was the one who hadn't looked at the time. *Damn it.*

I began to reach for my pants, but Gage grabbed my arm. "Don't. *Move.*" I paused, holding my breath. "Their visual acuity is based on movement," he said.

Eye roll. "Honey, he's not a velociraptor."

Another squawk. Hiccup. Then a full-fledged siren went off upstairs.

36

GAGE

Cock-blocked again.

Madeline disappeared up the stairs with only her bra on. With a sigh and a grimace, I tucked my deflating hard-on back into my pants and zipped up. These things happened. I knew that. Sometimes it drove me crazy that I couldn't control it, but I was rational enough to understand that the baby son came first.

Just once, though, I'd love for my wife to come first, with a spine-bending orgasm of my own following shortly thereafter.

I picked up her clothes, and draped them over my arm while I filled a tall glass of water for her. Then I trudged up the stairs. I could hear Maddie talking to our son, but couldn't catch what she was saying. It only took a few steps down the hall for me to stand in the doorway of Jack's room.

Our house was small, only three bedrooms. We'd turned the guest bedroom into a nursery, which left us with the master and the playroom. I was fine with that. Houseguests irritated me, anyhow.

Maddie called it our little "dollhouse"—not in front of me, of course. Its size surprised some people, considering our wealth, but it had been expensive enough at the time I bought it on my way up the income ladder. We loved the period details and the location in a heritage district, adjacent to downtown, was what made the house valuable in any market.

Actually, to my mind, what made our house so valuable were the two people nestled in a gliding chair in front of me.

As usual, the sight of the two of them together made me smile. The love of my life and the fruit of my loins— and if I ever refer to them as that out loud, just shoot my dick off and put it in my wife's laptop bag.

She smiled at me when I put the water down on a little table beside the chair, then focused her gaze on Jack again. I stood there for a moment, before realizing that they were in their own little world.

As I headed to our bedroom, my phone buzzed in my pocket. I pulled it out and flopped down on the bed, the covers cool against my bare back. It was a text from Aaron.

-Must've been kinky movie. Got a bj when b got home.

I made a face as I raised the phone above me, my thumbs moving quickly.

-Dude, that's my sister.

Ugh. Aaron was my friend before he hooked up with Bobbie, and sometimes the bro speak was TMI. Then I smirked and typed again.

-Can't be that great if you're texting me now.
-So are you. Did YOU get a blowjob?

-I don't kiss and tell.
-Denied!!!!
I frowned. *-Kid*, I explained.
-Word.
Their daughter—my niece—was only a few years older than Jack, still squarely in the "ankle biter" phase of life. Having witnessed some of the joys of living with a toddler, I was in no hurry to have Jack grow up.

Damn, I was tired. Maddie had only been gone for a few hours, but it felt… longer.

I dropped my phone on the bed beside me then draped my forearm over my eyes. When it buzzed again, I fumbled for it in the folds of the comforter. It seemed to take a lot of muscle power to hold it up, move my arm from my face, and blink at it.

-It gets better. I hear.

Great.

"You took my clothes away," Maddie said from the doorway. She didn't sound angry about it.

"I've been known to do that." I propped myself up on my elbows and met her bemused gaze. She'd clipped her nursing bra back up, but was otherwise naked. I wondered why she'd even bothered. "C'mere."

She sat on the edge of the bed beside me, plucked my phone off me and put it on the bedside table. Just her fingertips brushing against my belly regenerated some of my arousal. With one arm I reached out and deftly undid the back clasp of her bra.

"You're still taking my clothes away," she murmured.

"Mmhmm."

She let the straps fall down her arms and it fell to the floor beside the bed. Then she twisted to face me better, her hand smoothing over the front of my slacks. "Seems like turnabout is fair play."

My body rose to meet her touch. "You never play fair."

Her auburn hair swung around her neck as she moved to straddle me. Her sweet-smelling, silky hair. I missed the length of it, missed wrapping it around my fist… but she came home one day with at least six inches lopped off, claiming that Jack kept pulling it.

Well, yeah. I liked pulling on it, too.

Right now her hairstyle wasn't the biggest distraction as she pressed her knees around my hips. Her breasts swayed between us, her nipples large, dark, and still distended from nursing. I never in a million years thought I would find that sexy, but on my wife it was unbelievably erotic.

I fell back onto the pillow with a grunt as she undid my pants again.

"Now, where were we?" she purred.

By the time she removed the rest of my clothes, I was rock hard and aching. I crunched up to pull her to me, but she shook her head and inched back out of reach. "No, it's my turn to make you come."

Grasping the base of my cock in one hand, she lowered her head over my lap and took me into her hot mouth.

"Fuck!" *Always. So. Fucking. Good.*

Her head bobbed up and down, her lips over her teeth and the tip of her tongue tracing a line over me with every pass. I could feel her hot breath on my groin with every dip and take in the incredible sight of her mouth stretched around me each time she rose up again.

"Jesus Christ! You're too good at this."

Not that she was an amateur before, but I'd definitely gotten more—and better—blowjobs since she got pregnant.

There was a point in her pregnancy at which she was nervous about having sex, and then after Jack she was just... I don't know. Wanting to practice? I wasn't about to complain, not with the way she teased the sensitive skin under my balls with one hand and gripped me with the other.

And her mouth... her mouth was unrelenting.

A hiss escaped me as I felt myself swell in her mouth. Suddenly filled with impatience, I pushed myself up to sitting. There was a wet popping noise as she lost suction, but her glare was short-lived as I hauled her across the bed and fell between her spread legs.

"Wait, Gage, what—"

I growled and lunged forward, sinking my dick into her as deep as I could possibly go.

Her little yelp made me think maybe I'd gone *too* deep, and immediately I retreated—a little.

"God, yes!" she hissed, her hands clutching me close.

Fuck, yeah. I drove into her again, grinding against her clit with every thrust. She cried out again, spurring me on. Her body was softer in places than before, and more taut in others. Her chest was slick between us, her pussy hot and clinging.

I wanted to take my time, slowly possess every inch of her instead of this siege—but I was already so near the edge myself that I knew I needed to make every movement count.

With the focus and intensity that had made me a billionaire, I fucked my wife.

Hard.

She panted in my ear, her moans vague and compelling at the same time. I heard "more yes deep full fuck me come" but I don't think she actually said any of those words. My jaw tight and my body ready to explode, I wedged my hand between us to find her clit.

"Oh my *god*!"

"Come now," I ordered her as I tweaked the hard nub above her core, before pressing forward again. "Maddie, you need to come *with me*."

One more thrust and she fell apart.

As soon as I felt her squeezing me I gave myself permission to come. I groaned loudly as my orgasm flooded through me, and I emptied myself into my wife.

"Mother*fuck*," I mumbled as the pulse in my groin finally ebbed.

I collapsed on her, my face burrowing into her neck. The ends of her hair tickled my nose, so I nuzzled her ear to scratch the itch.

"That was amazing." Her voice was low and lazy.

I moved up and down on her chest like a raft on the ocean as her breathing slowed and her hands swept up and down my back. A grunt was the best I could form as a response. I felt absolutely boneless, which meant I was probably smothering her. Indeed, she sucked in a deep breath once I slid off her and lay by her side.

Our breath was the only sound in the room. Vaguely I realized something was off.

Oh.

The baby monitor was downstairs in the kitchen. No blinking blue lights, no hum of white noise and anticipatory crackle of static. Just us, with our skin pressed together. It was so quiet that the swish of Maddie's legs against the covers startled me.

She rolled over to snuggle into me. Her breasts were sticky against my side.

"Did you leak?" I asked.

"Probably a little. Sorry."

I tilted my head to bury my face in her hair. I didn't really care, but now I kind of wanted a shower before falling asleep. If only I could move my legs...

"Can I talk to you about something?" Her voice was quiet.

I held my breath for a moment before exhaling into her hair. "Yeah, I've got an agenda item as well."

Our communication styles had not always meshed well. In fact, I'd originally hired Madeline to be a kind of translator between my self-absorbed cluelessness and the rest of the world. Now, I said "please" when asking venture capitalists for investment. Even in our wedding vows, I promised to love, honor, and cherish her—and keep our lines of communication open and respectful.

It was my great honor later on that night to communicate to her how I planned to respectfully tie her to the giant four-poster bed of the honeymoon suite and fuck her brains out.

Something had been percolating in my mind, which I hadn't brought up. But in the interest of full disclosure and honoring our marriage vows, I felt like I could—no, I *should* say it now.

"Now" was a relative term, however. "You first," I said.

"No, you go."

I shook my head, smiling. "Rock, paper, scissors?"

My elegant, beautiful wife snorted somewhere in the vicinity of my armpit. "Same time," she said. "On three. One, two..."

"I want to have another baby," I confessed.

"I want to go back to work," she rushed out. Her nose collided with my bicep as she jerked her head up. *"Wait, what?"*

37

MADDIE

Crazy man say what? My mouth fell open. Had I heard him wrong?

Judging by the look on his face, I hadn't. The usual intensity of his expression was tempered by a sheepish half-smile.

And it wasn't just a post-orgasmic haze.

I sat up, sitting criss cross applesauce. His gaze narrowed like a laser, right between my legs. Maybe this was a conversation best had wearing something more than a nervous expression.

"I thought you were happy being home," he said as I wriggled the bottom half of my body under the covers. I left my boobs out in the open, in case I needed them for distraction or ammunition of some kind.

"I am. I love being home with Jack. But I miss work. I miss seeing you at the office."

His forehead creased. "You see me here."

"It's not the same."

"Yeah, it's easier to be naked here." He waved at my breasts. *Hmmm. Maybe they were too distracting.*

My eyebrows rose. So did my knees to my chest, under the duvet. "Seriously? We have had naked time at the office, too. In fact, if you were anybody else you'd have a serious sexual harassment lawsuit on your hands."

"If *you* were anyone else my hands wouldn't be involved at all."

"It's just… I got used to having a professional identity. I miss it. I miss being with grown-ups. I miss wearing clothes without Lycra as a major ingredient."

"Look, I get that it's a lot. I told you we could get a nanny—"

Irritation flared in me. "No! I don't need a nanny. It's one baby."

The truth was that most of my resistance to getting a nanny was based on my own irrational emotions. Just because I didn't have much of a mother, didn't mean I couldn't be a kickass one myself. I absolutely planned to be at every Mommy and Me group, teach Jack sign language, have him potty trained by two.

I also planned to have a pet unicorn.

"It's not about *need*, Madeline," he said gently. "It's about you being the best parent you can."

"Are you saying I'm a bad mother?"

His eyes widened with fear—*as they should, asshat!*

"No! Jesus, *no*! You're an amazing mother. Every kid should be so lucky. But sometimes you're just…" He trailed off.

"A bitch?"

He pinched the bridge of his nose. "Now you're just putting words in my mouth to pick a fight."

"*I'm* picking a fight? I want to… fulfill my professional destiny, and you're telling me that we need to get a nanny because I'm an inadequate parent. I'm surprised you'd even want to have another child with me."

My chest tightened to the point where I felt like I couldn't get enough oxygen in. But if I took a deep breath, I was afraid I'd start crying. As it was, my vision was blurry as I moved off the bed. Away from Gage. I started to take the covers with me, but gave up when I almost tripped.

"Stop it. You're being a brat."

He was ten years older than me, and it was times like this that we were both reminded of the gap between us. I didn't want to stand there naked, fighting with him. I crossed my arms over my chest, feeling like I needed to shield myself somehow.

When arguing with Gage, I always needed more arms.

"Now I'm a brat. And an 'amazing mother.' Which is it?"

He glared at me. "Right now, both. I don't believe in corporal punishment for children, but I sure as fuck want to spank *you* right now."

We fell silent, breathing heavily. Angry. Hurt. Waiting for an apology. When none materialized, I pivoted on one heel and stalked into the en suite bathroom. Tears finally spilled down my cheeks. Damn hormones, still making me crazy.

The sound of the water on the tile in the shower seemed extra loud when I turned it on, but at least it drowned out my crying when I got in. My tears were indistinguishable from the stream of hot water. After a moment I realized that I was no longer feeling butt-hurt, but angry crying—angry with myself for crying.

Maybe I was a brat.

But he didn't listen to me! My husband wasn't always good at compromising, but we'd gotten better at active listening. Then again, I jumped right down his throat and I didn't even understand what he was talking ab—

Shit. I hadn't listened to him, *at all.*

I tilted my head back, letting the water soak my hair and slide down my back. My throat ached with the realization that my own kneejerk insecurities fucked up what was, until then, a very nice evening.

The shower door opened. Gage stepped in behind me and wrapped his arms around my waist, his head bent into my neck.

"I'm sorry."

I nodded but said nothing.

"Will you listen to what I have to say?" he asked.

I nodded again.

"I mentioned a nanny because I thought you might be less tired—thereby more happy and relaxed—if you didn't have to do things like laundry. If you could take more naps. Especially with another baby, having the extra pair of hands would be really helpful."

I spun around in the circle of his arms, blinking against the spray. "Okay, where did that come from? You really want another?"

"Well, yeah."

"Right *now*?"

"I'm not getting any younger. The truth is, I loved it when you were pregnant. And I love watching you be a mom. You're so good with him; you don't even know."

"You could have stayed home," I pointed out, then stilled in shock.

Until that moment I hadn't realized that I'd resented him for going back to work so quickly. Apparently he was indispensible at Apptitude, and I wasn't. Part of my desire to go back to work was probably to prove that I was capable at more than one job in my life. At least at work I could hold up an ad or cost-per-click numbers as tangible evidence that I'd done something.

At home, the day was considered a win if the baby was still alive and I hadn't burned down the house. The bar was pretty low.

He stroked my cheekbones. "You don't want another child with me?"

Ouch. The hurt look in his blue eyes got me. *Right. There.*

I lowered my gaze to his chest. "Of course I do. I love you." I never expected Jack to be an only child, but I also didn't expect to start trying again so soon. Then again, we weren't *not* trying. There was really no good reason *not* to have another baby sooner, rather than later. My stomach flipped at the thought of it, but not necessarily in a bad way.

"I love you." He kissed me, the heat from his mouth mixing with the warm water until I felt like we would dissolve down the drain together.

Gage rested his forehead against mine. Were my lips as swollen as his? My eyes as wide and dark? My body flushed and sensitive? He cleared his throat. Then, "How about we compromise?"

It was a concept that Gage still struggled with at times, so the fact that he was suggesting it meant he was serious about this. "How?"

He paused. Pulled away from me. Leaned against the cold tile wall, my hands in his.

He was serious about this.

"We could hire someone part-time to help out around here so you can spend some time at the office. If that's what you really want."

I wasn't sure *what* I wanted anymore, but what he was proposing could give me the space to figure it out.

"If you get pregnant within the next six months, though, then they go to full-time. As long as it's the right person," he added. "But god knows we can afford it anyhow. Really, we owe it to the economy."

Only Brian "No Excuses" Gage could turn negotiation over having a second child into an argument for job creation. But it was hard to argue with.

"What if I'm not pregnant in six months, and want to go back to work full-time myself?" The idea both thrilled and scared me.

His jaw tightened as he considered it. A storm brewed behind his eyes, like he'd never contemplated not getting his way. My husband honestly and sincerely did not expect failure. It wasn't in his vocabulary.

I spread my palms over his chest. "How about this?" I reached up and kissed him gently. "If I'm not pregnant again in six months' time *and* I want to go back to work, then *you* stay at home with Jack until baby number two."

"No nanny?"

My head tilted, my lips twitching as I tried not to smirk. "Part-time, if you want to spend some time at the office," I echoed what he'd outlined moments before. "If that's what you really want."

If he was so gung ho on parenting and thought it

was so easy, then maybe he needed to try a more… immersive experience.

"Deal. No tricks, though."

I made a little X over my left breast. "No tricks." No birth control, no gas-lighting, no interviewing maniacs as housekeepers. "Let the jizz fall where it may."

38

GAGE

At first, I thought Madeline was being a bit picky when she went looking for a part-time nanny slash housekeeper slash marital facilitator. She joined specialty websites, met with local agencies, looked at online ads—both for those needing and providing child care services.

A month went by, and we were no closer to finding some help. I'd asked my mother to come over once a week, so I could have a date night with my wife, but my mom was not a big one for consistency. Or reliability. After she texted at the last minute to bail—for the third week in a row—I gave up.

"I think she filled her grandma quota with Lily," Maddie said, rolling her eyes when she looked at my phone. She didn't seem that surprised, or even disappointed. Frankly, I suspected that she was just as happy staying home for Valentine's Day with Jack. *And me. Couldn't forget about me.*

Was I becoming an afterthought? I wanted to be her forethought. Hell, I wanted to be her *only* thought, but I knew that was impossible.

We had an agreement, though—part-time help, and try for another baby. I was keeping up my end of the bargain. In fact, I was keeping up a lot of things—my dick being one of them and, occasionally, holding up my wife against the wall of the shower.

I was all in. But that was just the way I was.

To my credit, I wasn't counting her cycle days or anything like that. No, that would be creepy. I just made love to my wife every chance I could get—every opportunity, every way. She said I was insatiable.

But after three months, we were no further along. Shark week had just finished—again—and we still had no child care to give Maddie a break.

When I pointed this out to her, she muttered something about needing a different kind of break.

So I booked us a ski weekend at the mountain resort where Bobbie and Aaron worked and lived until a few months ago. Madeline and I had a lot of fond memories of that hotel. The ski season was just ending, with fresh powder and clear blue skies.

Seventy-two hours of grown-up time.

It was going to be fantastic. I was so excited when I told her about it over dinner that my spaghetti swung from my fork. Jack, sitting in his high chair next to us, thought flinging his noodles was a great idea.

Madeline got up to get some paper towel. Looked back at me, puzzled. "You can't ski with an infant, Gage!"

I imagined Jack in his puffball snowsuit, somersaulting down the bunny hill and picking up snow along the way. "I know that, babe. I've arranged for him to go to Bobbie and Aaron's for the weekend."

"You did what?" My wife had gone past confused to horrified.

"They know how to take care of a baby, Maddie."

"But he's never been away from me like that before."

"For a child to form a healthy attachment, they need to understand object permanence."

"You've been reading my bedside books again, haven't you?"

I shrugged. We were talking about a baby with whom playing peekaboo was pointless, as he never expected anyone to actually go away. Sometimes I worried that he was a little *too* secure.

"I don't know…" She looked from me to Jack and back to me again, an agonized look on her face.

Our son began moving his head from side to side as well in mimicry. It looked like a tennis match at the dinner table.

"It will be good for all of us," I said. "We need to have some adult time."

"We have adult time every day, Gage."

"Fucking—"

Madeline gasped and clapped her hands over Jack's ears. "Modeling, Gage!"

I rolled my eyes. He couldn't even say *dada* yet. I didn't think he'd start off his foray into speech by swearing like a sailor. "Fine. *Making love* is not the end all and be all of adult time."

"Can I get that in writing, sir?"

"Smartass. There's also talking," I added, holding up my hand to forestall her comeback, "which doesn't include spaghetti fights."

Her eyebrow lifted. "If I recall correctly, it was a spaghetti dinner that brought us together."

"No, baby. Fate and Human Resources brought us together. The spaghetti dinner at the lodge just made it messier." I reached across the table to hold her hand. "I miss you, Madeline. I miss *us*."

"Oh, hell. You had to pull out the big guns, didn't you?" Her eyes were watery as I lifted her palm to my mouth.

Victory.

❧

I n the end, I got her to agree to thirty-six hours—of which approximately ten would be used up by driving to and from the mountains.

That left twenty-six hours (twenty-four, to be on the safe side) of skiing, sexing, and serious conversations. I was prepared to split the time between all three activities.

"What about sleeping?" Madeline asked, as I told her the schedule and dropped our bags beside the couch.

Damn. I'd forgotten about the sleeping.

She looked around Suite 203 with bemusement. No, we didn't need a two-bedroom suite, but I got it for the sake of nostalgia. This was where we'd first made love. Where I'd first tied her up. Where I'd first made her come.

"Well, we'd better get on with it, then."

It was closing in on ten at night, so skiing was ou —*oh*. My wife had efficiently begun stripping, so apparently serious conversation was not the first item on the agenda.

She finished unbuttoning her plaid flannel shirt, her

black bra peeking through like a shadow. "We should discuss our goals, sir."

Or maybe I was wrong. It did happen occasionally. "What do you mean?"

Maddie strutted over to me and slipped her fingers under the hem of my sweater. She brushed against my belly with her knuckles as she lifted it up and over my head. When she put her hands on my chest, all the blood in my body rushed to my groin.

"Fuck, *yes*. Lower," I urged her.

Her lips curved into a coy smile as she unbuttoned my slacks and teased at the waistband of my boxer briefs. My cock leaped at her nearness, heavy and hard.

"My goal to go back to work."

I tilted my head back and closed my eyes as she wrapped her hot little hand around me. It felt so damn good.

"And, uh, my goal to have another baby," I added— although, at that moment my boys were considering another destination. Her hand wasn't tight enough, wasn't hot enough. I opened my eyes, taking in her flushed cheeks and the way she licked her lips.

Bending over, I kissed her. Open mouth, open heart, open soul. I felt it all the way down to my toes, like it was the first time.

"Suck my cock, Madeline."

"Yes, sir." She dropped to her knees, her shirt still open and jeans still on, and took me in her mouth.

I groaned loudly. "Always so good," I murmured. My wife gave amazing head. She made me feel invincible and human all at the same time, and not just when her lips were circling my cock.

The pressure in my body rose as she tugged down my pants and briefs, her head still bobbing over me.

"Deeper, baby?"

She hummed her assent, making me grow impossibly harder. Slowly, she worked me further into her mouth, her nose nudging its way toward the base of my erection. The softness of the back of her palate met my weeping slit.

"Jesus fuck!" I shouted. Shook my head. *Goals. Our goals.* "SMART goals," I managed to get out. "What you're doing right now is SMART, baby."

I gulped as she nodded slightly. "I love your beautiful mouth, Madeline. You want my cock, don't you? You need it."

Her chin jerked subtly, and then I was all the way there. Her hands were on my ass, pulling me toward her as I thrust gently into her throat.

I looked down at her with amazement. Her eyes watered, her lashes glossy and her lips spread thin around my base. *What a sight.*

"I can't stop, baby." A warning was only fair.

She blinked up at me, unable to smile or speak or do anything, as I grunted through my release and shot ribbons of come down her throat.

Once I'd softened in her mouth a little, she raised her head and backed up a little. I fell out of her mouth with a tender pop.

"Was that good?" She looked up me almost bashfully, like a student trying to please a teacher.

"Good isn't the right word. Fucking out of this world is more accurate," I panted.

My heart still raced from the intense orgasm and the

sight of my wife on her knees before me. If I hadn't just come like a freight train, I might have gotten it up again.

"Smart goals?" she asked.

Brain clunk. Whir. Rewind. Play. "Right." I led her into one of the bedrooms, pulling off her flannel shirt at the same time and dropping it to the floor. "All our goals should be SMART goals, Madeline. You remember—specific, measurable, attainable—"

"Relevant and timely."

Off came her jeans, and my pants. Soon we were naked but for the shadows on our skin from the bedside lamp.

"Right now, my specific goal is to fuck you until you pass out from pleasure," I told her, spreading her naked body out on the bed before me.

Her nipples puckered in the cool air at my words. Moisture gleamed from between her open legs.

"Measurable?" She moaned as I drew my fingers through her wetness.

I tilted my head to the side, considering it. "I think three orgasms should do it."

"Oh god."

"For now." Lifting my hand to my mouth, I tasted her arousal. My cock twitched again in recovery. "That's eminently doable," I reminded her, "and highly relevant to my other main goal."

I kneeled on the bed between her thighs and took one luscious, distended nipple into my mouth. The sweet tang of her milk began to rise, and I laved her gently so as not to be greedy or overwhelming.

My hand went to her core again, my first two fingers finding their way into her snug center. She rippled around me, gasping.

"Oh yes, Gage. Fuck me, please."

"I'm going to put a baby in you, Madeline. That's my goal." The idea of it brought me to full power again, my cock straining to thrust into her. "I love it when you're pregnant, swollen with my seed. It's so fucking sexy," I told her.

My fingers moved within her, curling to find the spongy patch of nerves on the other side of her clit. Her breathing changed yet again, this time almost to a state of keening hyperventilation.

"Oh, shit."

"No, you can't come yet, Maddie. Not until my cock is seated deep inside your pussy, and you can pull all my come deep inside you."

"I can't—oh, *fuck!*" Her walls clamped down on my hand as her hips jerked. "Can't help it!" she gasped, throwing her head back as she came.

My dick ached, but I leaned back and watched her ride out her climax on my hand. She was so beautiful— almost as beautiful as when she came on my cock.

"That wasn't very SMART of you, Madeline."

She opened one eye at me. "Timely for me," she said, running her tongue around her dry lips.

Now I'd just have to start all over again.

"What the hell happened?" Bobbie's laugh didn't ever seem to give her laugh lines, which was unfair on a cosmic level. Especially, I thought, as she'd just been taking care of my child.

How to sum up the past twenty-four hours? We came, we saw, we did not conquer?

I shrugged. "He fell."

"On what run?"

I stared at her for a few seconds before it occurred to me that she assumed Gage's injury was of the skiing kind. "How was Jack?"

"Oh, he's a breeze. No problems whatsoever." She waved her hand, still more interested about the full-leg brace on her brother, my husband.

Whereas, I wanted to know what my son ate, what hours he slept, how many diapers he filled, what activities she did with him...

"The Brain is usually a pretty good skier," she remarked. "I guess it's been a couple of years, but still... it's like riding a bike."

"People fall off of those, too, you know." I caught sight of Jack in Aaron's arms, and shoved my hands out. *Gimme!* I ached to hold my baby.

"Yeah, here she is, little buddy. Calm the eff down."

I frowned at Aaron. Apparently the "little pitchers have big ears" concept was too much for him, as well my husband. Finally, I took Jack in my arms with a satisfied hum.

Yes! I felt like an addict shooting up, only I fiended for the smell of my child's skin and hair. There was a fine line between being a helicopter mom and a pathologically obsessed one, and I feared I brushed up against the line too often. Maybe Gage was right about the nanny thing. If just the idea of it threatened me, then we had a problem.

When I got home, Gage was sulking on the couch.

"This fucking sucks," he said to me as I took off Jack's coat and boots, then mine. I sighed.

"Jesus fucking Christ on a stick, does nobody know how to temper their goddamn language around a baby?"

His mouth fell open.

Oh.

Suddenly I felt bone-tired.

We'd spent pretty much the entire previous night in a small mountain town emergency room and then still had to drive five hours to get home. It could have gone quicker, but Mister Whiny Pants winced in pain whenever the car hit a pebble. As it was, the splint from his groin to his ankle forced him to push the passenger seat back as far as possible and put his foot against the glove compartment.

The doctor had said that without an MRI, there was no way to know how bad the damage to his knee was.

And no matter how much my industrious husband complained his money couldn't just make a machine materialize in the clinic. I had a feeling I'd be driving him to a private sports medicine clinic tomorrow morning.

The irony is that we'd never actually managed to ski.

Brian Gage, wunderkind app developer and technology titan, had wrenched his knee while trying to hold me up and fuck me in a slippery shower.

They never talk about those hazards in sex education classes.

"Dinner?" he asked from his position on the couch.

"Yeah, I'll make some pasta or something."

I plopped Jack down on Gage's lap. Hell, he was just sitting there—he might as well parent or something. Then headed for the kitchen.

Behind me, Gage called out, "A temporary nanny is arriving tomorrow morning at eight, Madeline. No more fucking around!"

"Yeah," I yelled back, "in more ways than one!"

Two weeks later, I was ashamed to admit that it was kind of nice to have someone helping me out. Doing the laundry, cleaning the house, ironing Gage's shirts. I felt guilty taking a nap, but Jeannie insisted that I get some rest.

She'd already figured out that dealing with my husband could be a challenge. Dealing with him when he was a bruised bear was even worse.

So up to bed I went at eleven in the morning for no particularly good reason, and fell into a deep, dreamless sleep. I woke up as Jack was finishing lunch, feeling refreshed for the first time in months.

Jeannie placed a terrific-smelling grilled cheese sandwich and a bowl of soup before me on the kitchen table. I smiled and dug in.

"Thanks. I'm going to take him to my Mommy and Me group, Jeannie. Can you pack up the diaper bag for me?"

"Of course, Missus Maddie."

Twenty minutes later I was out the door with Jack and a designer purse that could rival MacGyver's backpack. I had *everything*, and planned for every contingency —almost obsessively so, since the one day I forgot to restock the diapers in the "diaper bag." Believe me, *that* never. Happened. Again.

The Mommy and Me group was halfway through singing and using sign language for "Wheels on the Bus" when Jack's grizzling turned into a full-fledged teething attack. One hand still on the "bus," I used the other to dig through the bag. When my phone started vibrating with a call from Gage, I had to make a split-second decision which child to put off.

I made the wrong decision.

Fully abandoning the song, I answered the phone with one hand and kept searching for the teething ring with the other.

"Hello?" I whispered. I got some dirty looks from other mothers, but what was I going to do? I had a whimpering baby in the cradle of my legs as I sat crisscross applesauce, and a demanding spouse in my ear.

"Can you take me to the office later?" Gage asked.

"What?"

With his meniscus officially torn, Gage was on

crutches and unable to drive. Despite the fact that he could easily afford and arrange a car and driver on standby, there were times when he used me as his personal Uber.

"I need to go over some stuff in person. There's a limit to telecommuting, Madeline."

"So I'll go for you." Wipes, diaper cream, sweet potato puffs, but no teething ring. My fingers stretched out, searching through all the pockets. The group had moved on to a new song, but Jack was on the verge of a nuclear meltdown.

"No, I need to do it."

"You don't trust me?"

"Of course I do," my husband slash boss said. "But wouldn't you rather be home to put Jack to bed?"

Oh, he was playing dirty, now. *Finally!* I found a teething ring! I shoved it in Jack's face and let him bite and drool to his heart's content.

"Come on, I miss being at the office," I said.

"So do I." He sounded morose.

At least maybe he had some sympathy for how I was feeling, then. The pointed looks from other moms were making me nervous, so I quickly told him when I'd be home and hung up on him.

The group had given up on patty cake or baby massages or whatever the hell we were supposed to be doing to focus their attention on me.

Every single person was staring at me.

I flushed with embarrassment. "I'm sorry, I'm sorry. Husbands…" I trailed off, lifting my hands in apology and bewilderment.

Still, they stared.

One woman's face was bright red. Another woman

couldn't decide what was more distracting—myself or Jack. Her gaze kept going from my face to the mollified baby in my lap. The group leader wore a strangled expression.

"What?"

There was total silence, except for one person trying to stifle a giggle. And a strange buzzing sound. Three people were focused with laser intensity on Jack, which is where the noise was emanating from.

I looked down to my son, who was happily chewing away—on a vibrating, rainbow-colored cock ring.

From what I could tell at a horrified glance, he particularly enjoyed gnawing on the sparkly unicorn horn enhancement for clitoral stimulation.

I just about died. As I frantically tried to figure out how I'd found myself in this situation, I wondered if a person could literally burst into flames. Was this how spontaneous human combustion happened?

The only thing I could think of was that apparently our middle-aged nanny had trouble telling the difference between a teething ring and a clean sex toy that was air-drying on our master bathroom vanity.

"Fuck me," I muttered.

"Looks like someone already did," said a lady on my left.

Where was a hole to open up and swallow you when you needed one?

40

GAGE

"Which one?"

Madeline glared at me over the massive steel and glass desk in my office. "*That's* your first question? *Which* cock ring did our son gum like a toothless old man at Mommy and Me?"

I shrugged, trying not to laugh at her. "The butterfly one, the plain one, the one that lights up, the musical—"

"Unicorn." She slumped further into the visitor chair that sat in front of my desk. "And it just occurred to me that we have too many sex toys, that you would even have to ask that question."

Gasp. "There's no such thing as too many sex toys, Madeline."

I sat back in my executive chair, splinted leg stretched out, and looked over the papers on my desk. For a techie, I was an unusual fan of hard copies. I preferred to have important stuff printed out for me, since I always missed information when I read reports on my laptop screen. Yes, I was responsible for the death of many, many innocent trees, but at least I knew where all the money was.

It made telecommuting awkward at times, though. *Note to self: develop application to improve paperless office.*

My wife's long sigh was swallowed up by the dark surrounding the desk, where only a lamp shone on the reports spread out in front of me. The twinkling lights of the city at night hovered beyond the windows. March was all slush and mud and tantalizing light. It wasn't quite winter, but not yet spring. It was this limbo month, and I felt like I'd been living in purgatory with this goddamn knee injury.

Maddie was trying so hard to keep it all together, and I didn't tell her often enough how much I appreciated everything she was doing. I knew it was hard for her to delegate tasks, even ones for the nanny—who was soon to be banned from our master suite.

I had no problem with shocking women, but I preferred it to be with my wild intellect and scintillating charm, not wayward marital aids.

Not that our sex life needed assistance. But hey, it was fun. And things like cock rings made me feel like a fucking god.

Maddie reached for the first page of the sales report and began reading silently. A couple of years ago it would have been gibberish to her. Then again, not long before that she was graduating from college—right around the time that my company went public with a billion dollar IPO. The differences between us were stark, sometimes.

But I didn't know what I would do without her. I needed her, even before I fell in love with her.

And she'd loved it. Madeline had come into her own

while working for Apptitude, and she missed it. *That's* what she was trying to tell me before, and I wasn't listening hard enough.

She looked up to see me staring at her across the desk. Squinted, as though she couldn't see my expression in the dark—and she probably couldn't.

"What? What is it? Are you hurting?" she asked.

"No, I'm just…" I tilted my head. "Do you want to go to the Austin meeting for me?"

Her eyes widened. "Seriously?"

"Seriously. It would really help me out."

That was a bold-faced lie. I could go myself, but I had an employee who needed a boost in confidence and a wife who was trying to let go of being a mom all the time. It just so happened that they were they same person.

"The doctor told me I shouldn't fly with my knee like this," I reminded her grimly. "They're talking about surgery to fix it." That part was true, at least.

She put the report she'd been reading back on the desk. "Oh god. How long will that you put out of commission?"

"Six to eight weeks."

Her head tilted back in the shadows and she looked up at the ceiling. "Eight weeks," she muttered. "Damn."

"Go to Austin for me."

Her chin came down as she looked at me again. This time I could see a glint of excitement in her eyes. "Are you sure?"

"Yes."

"Are you asking me as your wife or as your Head of Marketing?" She held up a hand. "Sorry, *former* Head of Marketing."

"You're still the Head of Marketing. You're just on family leave. You're lucky to work for a company with such extended health benefits."

"So this is business, not pity?"

I crossed my arms over my chest. "Madeline, you must not think very much of my CEO skills if you think I would send someone to an important meeting on my behalf out of *pity*."

She smiled. "Sorry. When do I leave?"

I practically had to arm-wrestle her into the cab to take her to the airport. If she'd kissed Jack goodbye one more time the boy was going to have a complex.

"Object permanence," I reminded her.

She rolled her eyes. "Okay, okay. I'll just miss you both."

"Naturally. We'll miss you, too."

"You'll be fine with Jeannie there." She looked over my shoulder at the nanny going back in the house with Jack. There was tightness around her eyes, and the cabbie was getting antsy.

I opened the cab door for her, in case she didn't get the hint that she was supposed to *leave*. "She can't replace you, you know."

"I know." But her chin still wobbled.

I didn't think she really did, but that was part of why she was going.

I cupped her cheek, bringing her attention fully to me. "Madeline, you are indispensible in every way—as a wife, as a mother, as a friend, and as an employee. We will all be lost without you, but we will manage. Now please get the hell out of my sight."

"I love you, too."

After she left, I felt like the best husband and the best boss in the world. Damn, I was good.

I was also in trouble.

Jeannie had received a phone call from the hospital that her eldest son had been in a motorcycle crash. I shooed her off, reassuring her that Jack and I would be just fine on our own.

Unfortunately, I was kidding myself. I'd just taken a pain pill, and I noticed I had three crutches and at least two babies on the floor in front of me. My phone beeped. It was a selfie from Madeline in the airline lounge, looking professional and happy, and captioned "Thanks, boss!" Then one of the Jacks started crying.

Shit.

"Suck it up, kiddo. She'll be back soon." He kept crying, and I sighed as I realized it meant more than missing Madeline. "What's the matter, my friend?"

I hobbled over to where he was exploring under the coffee table. With one hand for support on the couch's armrest, I managed to scoop him up in the other arm. *Go me.*

Not done being impressed with myself, I balanced on one foot to try to keep weight off my injured knee. Then I held my son up and chanted gibberish to mimic the beginning of *The Lion King*.

The young prince squealed and squirmed in my hands and I heard a wet, flatulent sound, soon accompanied by a horrific smell that hovered above my head like a cartoon cloud.

"Ugh. We gotta change you, Simba."

From my vantage point in the living room, I was able to see to the stairs leading up to his room and all the diaper supplies. I was also able to see my population of crutches, which had thankfully diminished to only two.

Something was wrong with this equation.

How the fuck was I supposed to get upstairs with a baby on crutches? I mean, on crutches, with a baby? My realistic choices were to abandon the baby, leave the crutches, or let my son sit in a shitty diaper. It was like the old riddle of taking a fox, a goose and a bag of beans across a river—either way, I was sunk.

I could let the kid go free range in the living room while I yanked myself up the stairs to get the changing supplies. But with my luck, something would go terribly, terribly wrong.

If anything happened to Jack, I could kiss goodbye any chance of having a second child. If I wanted to have a girl to call Rosalina (because naming a baby Peach is just stupid), then I had to put my son first.

I was still pondering the problem when I noticed the diaper bag sitting in the front foyer. *Yes!* Free range it would have to be for a moment. I put Jack down on the floor, plucked up my crutches and hobbled to retrieve the bag.

Of course, after that it was a piece of cake. I knew how to change a diaper. Poorly, yes—but I could do it. I even knew what I could feed him. How I planned to do all that while high on codeine and moving around like a one-legged pirate was a different riddle for the ages.

In the end, we camped on the main floor for the next eighteen hours. That was how I discovered that I was older than I thought. As I was getting closer to forty than thirty, sleeping on the floor was *not* good for my aging body.

Then I called my mother. I could have called my sister, but chances were that she would just tattle to Madeline, and I didn't want that.

Finally there was a knock on the door.

"Ah, fuck."

"Nice to see you too, Brain." Bobbie stuck out her tongue at me.

"Mom called you, didn't she?"

"Duh." She swept past me, her gaze scanning the pallet of cushions and throw blankets on the floor and the up-ended diaper bag. "God, it's hot in here."

I'd cranked the heat up and let the baby go mostly naked, since I couldn't make it upstairs easily to get more clothes for him. I'd stripped to an undershirt and my boxer briefs. We must have looked ridiculous.

Jack sat in the middle of the living room, chewing on a silicone pasta server. He was a little disheveled and under-dressed, but otherwise fine.

"Hey buddy!" Bobbie hung her coat on the banister post at the bottom of the stairs and made her way to him. "When's Maddie back?" she asked over her shoulder.

"Tonight."

She stifled a laugh. "You barely made it twenty-four hours?"

"It's not as easy as you and Maddie make it seem."

"*Thank you*, I hate to say I told you so…"

"You just did," I muttered. But she was right, and I was wrong. *We should mark this day on the freaking calendar.* "I could have just hired somebody temporarily, you know."

She rose, with Jack in her arms and her gaze lifting

to the ceiling. "But you didn't, because you wanted to prove that parenting an infant isn't that all that hard. And you want to have another one soon?" She snorted.

"Maddie told you about that."

"Yup."

I needed to talk to my wife about keeping marital confidences… well, confidential.

"Let's get you all cleaned up, here." Bobbie disappeared into the kitchen while I hobbled around looking pathetic and feeling useless and grumpy. Okay, so maybe I'd underestimated how much time, energy, and work taking care of our son took. I owed my wife an apology for that.

By the time Madeline's taxi arrived, the place was spotless, Jack had been bathed and dressed in a nice outfit, and I was slipping into a deep sulk in the couch.

She came in the door with a tired smile on her face —the kind I hadn't seen in a long time—and dropped her carry-on bag at the bottom of the stairs.

"He asleep?"

I nodded, knowing she would want to see him first. Understanding that. Accepting that. Appreciating that.

When she came back downstairs, her smile had broadened and softened, and her blouse was tight over her chest. She swayed over to me where I was stretched out on the couch, and carefully straddled me.

"Hi," she said, dipping down to kiss me.

"Hi."

"You survived."

I blinked at her, unsure if she was faking me out. Had she already laughed with Bobbie about my inept functioning? Or did she really believe in me? Either way, I felt like I didn't deserve her loving, grateful smile—but there was also no way I was going to do anything to risk losing it.

She frowned. "Maybe you don't even need me."

I clutched her hips. "Believe me, we need you."

A beatific smile spread over her face. She kissed me again. Then wriggled on my lap a little. My hands moved from the sides of her luscious ass up her body.

"How... did... it... go?" I asked between kisses.

"Great. Their Legal department is sending over a contract."

"Good girl."

She winced a little as I squeezed her breasts. My hands dropped. She shimmied a little more on my lap. "I missed you, baby."

"We missed you, too." *God, so much.*

Her tongue swept into my mouth, tasting like sugary tea. She nibbled at my lower lip and moaned. "No, I *really* missed you." I felt the heat of her core as she ground against me. Her nipples hardened against the material of her bra and shirt, which gaped between the buttons. "I want you to fuck me, Gage."

My head fell back as she sucked on my neck. "I'm a little tired, babe."

She froze. Rose up. "Seriously?"

41

MADDIE

I didn't want to open my eyes, choosing to focus quietly on being in my husband's arms. They were strong, firm, and warm around me as we spooned.

"Mmmm. Glad you're home," he said huskily.

I sighed my agreement, shifting against him. "Are you still tir—never mind." I giggled, feeling his morning wood against my backside.

His mouth latched onto my bare shoulder, and we luxuriated in the peaceful twilight between waking up and the beginning of the day. I shivered as his tongue made a sensual trail from my shoulder to my neck. Little quivers permeated my skin to all my underlying cells. My response to my husband never failed to amaze me, even after all this time.

He hummed a wordless question, and I tilted my head back against him in response. Behind me, his hands lifted my nightshirt, skimming over my thigh and hip. His palm wound around me to cup my breast, which was full and tender.

"Careful," I warned him.

All he did was flick my nipple with his thumb and I was keening. His hand flew up to gently cover my mouth.

"Don't wake the boy."

I nodded, my heart pounding as his hand trailed down to the spot where I was feeling so much, and yet not enough.

His fingers played with my entrance, spreading my moisture around and just dipping in far enough to tease me. I could feel the heat of his erection rocking against me.

"More," I begged.

With a growl, he shifted behind me to pull down the shorts that he slept in, and pushed me forward onto my stomach. His hand went behind my thigh and pushed my knee up to expose me. It took him only a few seconds to guide himself to my aching center and enter me.

"Ahhh!"

He swore under his breath as I let out a small cry, and we both froze, listening for movement down the hall. On the bedside table, a light flickered on the baby monitor, then it went dark again.

We hadn't realized we'd stopped breathing until we began again. Holding in my breath seemed to make my body more sensitive, and every one of Gage's strokes reverberated through my body.

Making love like this always felt so spontaneous, so randomly naughty. Almost impersonal and impetuous, like we barely knew each other but we just couldn't resist, nor could we wait. It was swift and intense and lazy at the same time.

Our positions didn't allow for massive movements, but I felt every inch of Gage going in and out of me, his cock pinning me to the bed like a wanton woman.

"Love you," I gasped as my climax spiraled.

He grunted the same, his body flexing against my ass, the curve of my back, my elbows and shoulders, the nape of my neck, and all the parts of my body that weren't really supposed to be erogenous zones. They were, though, with him.

His hand went to where we were joined as he felt for my clit. "Are you close?" he panted.

I was always close.

"Please," I said. "I want to come, sir."

And a little rub of his fingers sent me flying.

My orgasm triggered his, as though he was waiting for my body to give him permission. After a taut pause he emptied himself into me, groaning.

"Need to see you properly," he muttered, turning me over so I was flat on my back beneath him.

My first kiss of the morning, and it was *after* a spine-melting orgasm. That was part of what felt so scandalous about making love that way.

We lay there cuddling for as long as we could, silently agreeing not to get up until we had to.

"This was actually a good time of the month," I said while running my hands up and down his arm. The dark hairs on his forearm smoothed out under my fingertips.

He stilled with surprise. "You know, I hadn't even thought of it."

"Really?"

"Really. I just wanted you."

I was pleased by that. "I think we've been forgetting about the fun part of procreating," I said.

He snorted. "Speak for yourself. I've been having fun."

"Yeah, but there's been this expectation in the back of our heads, right? This could be the time. There's pressure."

"Madeline," he said, tilting my chin up to meet his gaze, "I never want you to do anything you don't want to do. Do you feel like I unfairly pressured you into trying for another child?"

I closed my eyes, not wanting to see the disappointment on his face. "A little, maybe?"

He sighed.

"Not much. You were right about getting help, and I did love being pregnant. Getting pregnant again wouldn't be the worst idea in the world."

"But not the best, either." He withdrew from me and lay back on his side of the bed.

"No, I haven't been very fair to you. I resisted getting help with Jack or around the house because of my own stupid pride, when all you wanted was to make my life easier and me happier. I told you that I wanted to go back to work, but then I didn't put any systems in place to make it easier for me to do that."

He nodded, folding his hands behind his head thoughtfully.

I lay my hand on his belly, feeling his muscles tense under my palm. "All you asked for was to *try*."

"Do you think that I asked you to compromise too much or something?"

"No, but I haven't really been respecting your needs and desires enough, either. I'm sorry, Gage."

"You respect my desires just fine," he said gruffly, lacing his hand through mine where it lay on his stomach. "We just need to work on communicating better."

"You've been improving."

"Not enough, apparently."

I rose up and kissed his lips. "You're always enough, sir."

He craned his neck to kiss me deeper. "What did I do to deserve you?" he finally said.

"It must have been something truly devious."

His smirk made my heart sing.

After another few weeks, Gage was given the green light to ditch the brace, but he was still wearing a tensor bandage and going to physio twice a week. His ortho guy had decided that repairing my husband's knee surgically had a poor cost-benefit ratio, and I teased him for not committing fully to ripping his ligament.

"There are no excuses for that kind of half-assed performance, Mister Gage."

"Take your panties off and I'll show you a half-assed performance, Missus Gage."

Giggle. "Yes, sir."

We'd settled into a routine with Jeannie and I was finding the balance between letting her do things I didn't *need* to do, and still doing the things I found meaningful. The reality was that I didn't *need* to do laundry when I could be spending that time on the floor playing with Jack. Maybe in another few years, I could just train him to do it…

In the meantime, I took over packing the diaper bag

before Mommy and Me and found extra time to start doing other things with Jack, like a baby yoga class. Mostly he just sat there pulling stuff out of the diaper bag while I glared at him in downward facing dog, but we were there together.

I also went back to work part-time. After a long discussion one night with Gage, he understood that it was important enough to me that the potential sacrifice of my time at home was worth it.

Happy wife, happy life.

Happy mom, happy dom.

Er, so to speak.

The daffodils and crocuses were shooting out of the ground fairly late that year, buds sprouting like tears on the trees by the time I found out I was pregnant.

I stared at the two pink lines on the test, not completely surprised. In fact, I shouldn't have been that surprised at all. Truth be told, I wasn't quite sure how I felt about it.

Sitting down on the side of the bathtub, I looked down at my bare legs and feet. It was strange to know there would be a time—again—where I couldn't see them. I did the math, and realized that this would be a Christmas baby.

There was a queer feeling in the pit of my stomach, like excitement and dread all at once. It was different from the first time; now I knew what pregnancy and childbirth entailed, from experience. Of course, this could be the worst gestation in the world, and I'd be puking up my guts for the next six months straight… but I couldn't think that way.

No, I was happy about it. Really.

Okay, maybe there was part of me that wondered

"what if" I wasn't pregnant—how would work go? How would balancing things go…? But then those questions would plague me, even with a baby in tow. I'd figure out a way to make it work, and I knew that I had Gage's support in every aspect of it.

Better than that, I had my own back now.

It had taken me a few months to realize that I was a better parent and a better person if I could still work at my job and be a mom and wife. I'd tried so hard to be the perfect employee, then the perfect girlfriend, then the perfect wife and perfect mother, that I forgot to be the perfect *me*. I was so damn lucky that I had the luxury of deciding how much I could work and how much I could stay home.

Sleeping with the boss definitely had its perks.

Speaking of which… Gage was still fast asleep in our bed.

Feeling playful, I made my way downstairs to the kitchen, phone and pregnancy test in hand.

And texted him a picture of it.

Knowing my husband as I did, simply the vibration of his phone woke him up. He always woke up for messages. He claimed it was his job as head of a massively successful app development company, but I suspected he was just addicted to his smartphone.

I heard nothing, then a muffled, "—*the fuck*!"

Pause.

My phone buzzed. **-Where are you?**

I texted back. ***-Follow the trail, genius***

I heard him shift out of bed, the old floor creaking under his weight. "Ah!"

He'd found the panties I'd left in the hallway outside our bedroom.

My sleep pants were draped over the banister on the way downstairs, and he padded along the landing to retrieve them.

"It's not that big of a house," he called out. "There are only so many places you can hide!"

I stifled my comeback, knowing that it would be more fun if he played the game.

On the bottom step I'd put the pregnancy test, pointing toward the back of the house.

"What is this, some kind of spin the bottle thing?" he muttered. "I'll just leave your pee stick here, okay?"

My hand went over my mouth. God, my stomach was aching from holding in my laughter. I wasn't just laughing at him, though. I was tense from anticipation, my body straining from joy and fear and love.

He made his way back toward the kitchen, and found the t-shirt I'd slept in on the dining table.

"You're out of clothes now, Madeline," he sang.

I wrapped my arms around my naked body. Yep, I sure was. But it was a good scavenger hunt.

His eyes widened, then narrowed as he spotted me leaning up against the stone-topped island. "Really?"

Nod.

"I knocked you up?"

Nod.

"Are you okay?"

That was a loaded question. Did he mean physically, emotionally, psychologically, logistically?

Nod. I stretched out my arms, and he moved into them.

He kissed me like I was made out of glass.

"I love you so damn much," he said against my mouth.

"I love you, too. Now *really* kiss me."

His lips curved against mine, and he devoured me. Stole my breath, met my tongue, and all the while his hands wandered over my hips and belly.

Dipped down below.

"You're wet, Maddie."

Nod. "You make me that way," I told him.

He lifted me up onto the island, smiling as I yelped at the cold granite on my ass. I leaned back, propped myself up on my elbows, and waited as he palmed the area below my bellybutton.

"Hi there."

He was talking to the baby, who was about the size of a grape. Maybe a plum. Why was it always fruit analogies with pregnancy, anyhow?

His satisfied smile stretched his lips until I almost couldn't see them, for the blindness of his teeth.

"Hello, baby Mario."

"No."

"Luigi?"

I laughed. "No."

"Zelda."

"No."

"Kirby?"

"Hell to the n—actually, that's not so bad." I tilted my head, considering it.

With large, hot hands he spread my knees and stepped in between them. "Madeline, you're naked on our food preparation surface."

"So I am."

"That means I have to eat you."

"Shucks." I shrugged my shoulders then squealed as he growled and dove down to my damp center.

With one long lick from back to front, finishing at my clit, he brought me back to the place where I felt most secure yet most vulnerable.

In love.

THE END

ABOUT THE AUTHOR

Nikky Kaye is the author of sexy romantic comedies such as *A Model Fiancé* and *A Slip of the Tongue*.

A former college professor, she lives in western Canada, where she is held captive by her young twin boys, a crippling diet cola addiction, and unfinished home projects.

Get Nikky's "Coming Attractions" newsletter for a free book, sneak peeks, reading recommendations and giveaways at **http://subscribepage.com/nikkykaye** or at **http://www.nikkykaye.com**.

facebook.com/officialnikkykayeauthor

twitter.com/readnikkykaye

instagram.com/nikkykayebooks

Made in the USA
Columbia, SC
04 September 2020